I0784441

BROAD STROKES

R. M. VANECKOVA

Printed in the United States of America

Generative AI was NOT used in any portion of this book.

Vaneckova Publishing LLC
vaneckova.publishing@gmail.com
rmvaneckova.com

First Printing, 2026
ISBN 978-1-971733-00-5 (paperback)
ISBN 978-1-971733-01-2(ebook)

Content Warnings

- Death of a parent
- Death of a significant other (semi-graphic)
- Death of loved ones in general
- Suicide
- Blood drinking
- Blood in various beverages
- Depictions of torture
- Organized violence
- Emotional abuse of a child

Table of Contents

For my mom, who has supported me through this entire, crazy journey. One, two, three

1

Masterpiece

Josephine

I never wanted to be a vampire. I still don't. Yet here I am in the local vampire Council building, 75 years after I was turned. A place that has three things that come to my mind: free blood, the day of my death, and having to watch out for Beverly. Currently, the blood is flowing, but unfortunately, so is her mouth. I was just trying to have a nice evening, restock my supply, and talk to one of my best friends about my art as I prepare for my exhibition, and get out of here after a night of good times. The plan was going great until she came over.

"I think that's why I like my current style so much. I can show off elements of myself, even without coming through on the camera." Talking with Michael is easy; he gets it. Not to mention his boyfriend made the device, and like some mad scientist, he got closer to photographing one of us than ever before. Sadly, he hasn't been able to figure out how to photograph *us* yet. Hopefully one day.

"I'm glad it is working out fo-" his words are cut off by the shrill voice of the Council bitch, Beverly.

"I guess I don't see the point in only taking a picture of your clothes. It's not like it's a self-portrait; it's essentially an advertisement." Her tone cuts through the easy conversation, making the edges jagged. Immediately, I whip my head towards Michael, showing him a quick flash of my rage, begging him to help.

"Beverly, fuck off. It takes a soul to appreciate art, and we all know you never had one," he throws an arm around my shoulder protectively and uses his free hand to flip her off.

"All I said is I don't understand why she would do something like that, I mean, what is the point?" Her eyes roll so dramatically that I think one of them might pop right out of her head. If only we could be so lucky.

"The point is that I like it, my patrons like it, and it is the closest our kind has ever gotten to taking a picture of ourselves. The closest we can get to showing ourselves like that. Now, fuck off." My body begins to shake with scarcely contained rage coursing through my veins. My fangs threaten to come out. A quick drink from my glass makes them go back down.

Typically, I never feel the need to defend my work to others; they get it. Particularly the ones here in the Council rec room, except for Beverly, who is thankfully fucking off as requested. I turn to face Michael, "Thank Christopher again for making it for me," I tell him as I grab his hand and spin out from under his arm as he nods his agreement. Christopher made this rendition of the camera a few years ago, but he has never stopped trying to take our pictures in full. He has come farther in the last 30 years than any other vampire in the history of photography and film. "Unfortunately, I have to cut tonight short, I have an exhibition to attend."

"What's the exhibition?"

"Britt texted me about it. Allegedly, I'm going to *love* the exhibition and the artist." I roll my eyes at the thought.

She loves to think I'll meet my happily ever after person. Except, I don't think one exists for me.

"She's playing matchmaker again?" Michael grimaces uneasily. My niece wants me to be happy...to forget my past. It isn't as easy as she thinks it is.

"You know her, she wants to see her Auntie happy. I'll text you about it later," I lean in to kiss him on each cheek before making my way to the bottle filler for a quick top-up on my way out the door.

Leaving the Council building is...difficult. Each of their rooms are perfectly designed for our senses. The lights are dimmed, the rooms are completely soundproofed with no echoing, and it is all perfect. Outside of the Council building? Well, that's the real world, it's loud, it's bright, it's everything constantly. The cars weaving through the traffic alone feel overwhelming, then you add in the streetlamps, the headlights, the honking, and the people on the street. Even their hearts are loud. A quick sip from my bottle calms my nerves. My heels echo as I walk down the sidewalk, trying to tune the world out and think back to my plans. I check my phone,

11:13 pm. I peek at my texts and pull up my conversation with Britt from earlier.

> You absolutely HAVE to come to the exhibition Femininity Unveiled tonight. You're going to LOVE it. Dress hot so I can introduce you to the artist!
>
> Britt

I take a deep sigh and keep walking across town to the event space. Sticking to the side streets makes everything easier. I crave the quiet, and I know that any semblance of peace is ending before my eyes when I make it to the bustling arts district. The vibrant section of the city is always full of life, and life means noise. People are laughing, some drunk from the wine at the exhibitions, others smell like the chemical odor of acrylic paint, or the pungent smell of oils. Others are earthy from the pottery studios, bits of clay staining their clothes. Cars wait on the curbside, some blaring their radios, as they wait for their patrons to hop in. I take my bottle from my purse and swallow some of the cooled blood, its metallic tang drawing out my fangs as it calms me down, the anxieties falling away. My tongue flicks across my fangs, clearing them of the blood, and I swipe on my lipstick. I smile at the packaging as I put it away. I could never give up my standard Victory Red.

My hand wraps around the cool, gold metal handle of the door as I push inside the bustling gallery. I take a deep breath as I try to acclimate to the intensity of the room. The lights are blinding. The people's hushed conversations still pound in my head, and even their blood flowing through their veins makes its presence known. The sharp smell of the paint and wine registers last. Within a few deep breaths, I feel like I can handle moving in the room.

My eyes start to look around, the light less blinding. Britt was right, I was going to love the art. All around me, there are gorgeous paintings on the walls. Each piece depicts women in various states of undress, showing off the softness and beauty in each person. The paintings feel reverential, like a case study on worshiping the magnificence of the female form. Instead of just being erotic, it is intimate, like you are getting to personally know each woman herself in her most vulnerable state. My heels click across the floor as I examine the pieces, lost in the world the artist created so meticulously, I actually tune out the noise. Until a pair of arms wrap around me.

"You made it!" Britt squeals with excitement as she hugs me close. The noise of the world floods back in, my attention being drawn from the soft, sloping frames of the women lining the walls. I focus on my niece; her mother used to say she could be my doppelganger if only her eyes were different. She has my same jet-black hair, pale skin, and hourglass figure. Our eye colors differ, though, my deep, chocolate-brown and her icy blue, and a slightly larger dress size. She is dressed in her business best, a simple black pantsuit with her favorite pink dotting her accessories.

"Yes, well, I figured I would come see the exhibition. And you were right, it is remarkable." I readjust my appearance, fixing my hair and straightening the outfit she rumpled with her attack of affection. "Hot enough?" I gesture to myself, showing off the dress that hugs my curves and my staple shoe: stilettos.

"Perfect," her eyes light up with pure mischief as she grabs my hand and leads me to the other side of the room at a faster pace than any human should be going. If I didn't have supernatural levels of speed, I think I would have been flying behind her like a rag doll. She comes to a halt, racing to make an introduction before I have adjusted to the change of pace. "Excuse me, Gabby? This is Josephine Beauchamp, a friend and client of mine. Josephine, this is my client, Gabby Young. She is the woman behind these masterpieces around you."

I'm sure she keeps talking, but I can't seem to focus on anything other than the woman before me. I think I might be in front of the most beautiful woman to ever live. Her rich, tawny skin is practically glowing, even under the harsh overhead fluorescent lighting. Her brown hair looks streaked with the sun itself where the light reflects off it, her natural curls bouncing as she moves. She is in a flowy gown that reaches to a few inches above her knee, in a pale green to match her striking eyes. It is stunning on her, but she could shine in anything. I think my jaw may have dropped. She is art itself. My world narrows in its focus as she reaches her hand toward me; the rest of the world ceases to exist.

"It is so nice to meet you, Josephine," she brings my hand to her lips to place a light peck. I can feel the warmth from her skin as she pulls back. My cheeks must be equally flushed as hers.

"The pleasure is all mine." I can't drag my eyes away from her. My whole body flushes with warmth. "Are any of your paintings available? They are so beautiful, I can't imagine many are."

"What's your favorite?" Her smile might be the most breathtaking thing I have seen.

"Besides you?" I ask. Her face flushes to a bright crimson, adorable. "The one near the entrance with the view from behind, where a woman's hair is swept up. Where she is still dressed in the silk slip dress. Her head is softly turned."

"I love that one, it shows nothing."

"It shows everything," I respond and Gabby's eyes light up, the look of being understood. The painting features the woman's subtle, soft curves with a gentle expression that whispers promises of what is to come. The palpable anticipation of more is blended with nervousness about what will come next. Like undressing before a new partner for the first time. Potentially like being in love for the first time, baring your soul for them to see.

"It is all yours."

"And what do I owe you?"

"Nothing, if you agree to come over and let me paint you in my studio." Her brow quirks up, as if she needed any more assurance that I wanted to see her again. I can't help but beam at her. She thinks I'm beautiful enough to paint. I hand her my phone with the contacts page pulled up.

"Now that sounds like an amazing evening," she plugs her information in. As I take my phone back, I pull her in close to me, my hand placed on her arm. "And even better company." I keep my voice low, my words just for her. I lean back with a smirk. "I'll text you tonight."

"I hope you do," she smiles with a blush one last time before she turns away, her green gown twirling behind her as she leaves to mingle with other patrons. I thought the part of me that could feel such visceral attraction was broken. I thought it had died. Maybe what it really needed was someone else to resurrect it.

"I knew you would like her!" Britt says, breaking me out of my Gabby-induced haze. Honestly, I forgot she was there. How does this woman calm down the world around me? How can this woman I've just met take the storm of overstimulation and make it a peaceful, sunny day? The sensations flood back in now, though. I take a deep draw of my blood, letting the sensations of the world dull.

"Right twice in one evening, that has to be a record."

"You love me," and she's right. I do. She is my only family left who truly wants to know me. The only one okay with my nature. The rest think I'm evil, a demon, something to be avoided.

"That I do. Now, let's look around a bit more before you call it a night." I loop my arm behind my niece's as we behold the masterpieces on the walls. They all pale in comparison to the artist herself.

2

Memories

Josephine

Opening my apartment door feels like pure relief. Locking the door behind me, I sink to the ground, trying to process everything that happened tonight. The beginning of it felt normal, if not a little infuriating. But that exhibition? Meeting Gabby? That was the highlight of my day. Maybe of my week, or even my year. I haven't felt a genuine spark like that for someone in over a decade. Each and every loss has made it that much rarer; I thought that part of me was broken.

I remember the last time I had feelings for someone. I fell in love with her.

April 2007

The night was colder than usual, and the chill in the air smelled sharp. I was wrapped up in my vintage fur jacket, that my mother had bought me back in the 40s, the one piece of glamour I kept wearing back then. I was experimenting with the styles at the time, taking a step back from the polished look my parents had beaten into me. It didn't last. The low-rise jeans felt uncomfortable; I kept having to fight my hand not to yank them up. The gray vest I had on looked awkward on my frame. But I felt cool. Like I was the *it girl of the night. Until I saw her. Amanda.*

Now she was beautiful. She had on those paper-thin leggings with a long, sparkly shirt on. The sequins must have itched. Each shiny little circle was as blue as her eyes. Her honey blond hair that she straightened flawlessly, was pulled back with a little bump at the front. She was highlighted by bright, colorful lights circling the room. The brilliant colors barely registered; my eyes were trained on her.

The pounding base at the club had me draining an enormous amount of blood, but I was desperate for a night out to have fun. I had never been happier to dance in the discomfort than I was when I was watching her dance.

I remember approaching her at the club that night. My heart was pounding, and thoughts kept whirring through my head. Did she even like women? If she did, would she like me? I wasn't exactly the most fashionable body type for the era. The music was blaring so loud I could hardly stand it; that night the lasers from the DJ booth were overwhelming, and I knew I would beat myself up for the foreseeable future if I didn't at least talk to her.

So, I walked my way over.

"Can I buy you a drink?" I swear my nerves were audible as I yelled out my question, hoping she could hear me over the noise. Her smile though? That locked me in.

"I'd like that." She shouted back, I would have heard her even if she had whispered.

We danced the night away.

I shake my head to clear out the memory. They are always hard; I can feel the pinpricks of tears threatening to fall down my face. When I remember her, I can't help but relive everything again. The excitement. The love. The heartbreak. The emptiness. All of it.

Blood. I need more blood. I force myself to my feet and wipe the tear that had formed in my eye. I snatch one of the bags from my fridge and pour it into a mug, and reheat it quickly. Waiting for it to heat is like waiting for your favorite holiday: it simply never ends. The newly warmed ceramic heats my cool hands. Drinking it feels better yet, like I'm warming myself from the inside out. The sweet, metallic taste calms my nerves again. The salty drops stop threatening to leave, but the undercurrent of sadness stays.

After I drain my drink, I reach for my phone and pull up my contacts, scrolling until I see Michael's name.

"Hey Josie," his voice is cheery on the other end.

"It's Josephine, how are you and Christopher doing?"

"Good, he just made me his famous blood milkshakes and put on Brokeback Mountain for the millionth time. I swear he likes those cowboys more than me." Michael says as Christopher's muffled voice is audible in the background, followed by their laughter.

"I haven't had one of his milkshakes in *forever*." I can almost taste it, the sweet, creamy milkshake flavored with the rich and metallic edge that the thick, red life force provides.

"Now, you don't just call after an exhibition. Spill."

"Britt may have been right. The art was phenomenal."

"And I'm supposed to believe that you called me to tell me the art was good? Josie, I know you better than that." His nickname for me has my eyes rolling. "If it were just about the art, you would have told me when I saw you next. *Spill.*"

"Maybe she was right about the artist, too." My face flushes, and I am beyond thankful in that moment that we can't video chat because he would call it out in a millisecond.

"Does my Josie-"

"It's Josephine."

"Does my *Josephine* have a crush?"

"Can you really call it a crush when you just met?" I wring my hands, the nerves surrounding her are showing up even when I'm home alone.

"Walk me through what happened, and we'll see." His voice takes on a challenging tone, like he knows he is right and is waiting for me to vomit out the evidence. Unfortunately, I think I'm about to prove him right.

"Well, Britt introduced us, and it felt like the world stopped. The sensory overwhelm just stopped. Like the entire world was condensed to only us. You should have seen her. I can still picture her full lips, and I wanted nothing more than to feel them pressed against mine. Is that insane? It feels insane." Images of her in that green gown as she twirled away from me play in my mind on repeat. She is art.

"So a crush."

"Screw you."

"We both know you wouldn't, much to my dismay. We would be a power throuple." Michael's voice takes on a dramatic tone, as if he is thoroughly devastated. We both burst into laughter as I remember meeting him and Christopher for the first time. They *did* try to get me to date them before quickly realizing I am simply for the ladies. Then the laughter dies down, the thoughts of fun moments fleeing from my head.

Silence.

"You're thinking about her, aren't you?" His voice drops, taking on that worried edge.

"Gabby? Of course." I shift around, pouring out another fresh bit of blood. The warm liquid passes through my lips.

"That's not who I meant."

"I may have thought about her when I got home. Feeling a spark for someone else...it feels like a betrayal. The chance of being with someone new is like I'm desecrating the memory of her." The drops start to fall down my face. The worst part of immortality, the part no one tells you about until it happens, is the loss. The never-ending cycle of loss. And how much that hurts. Not just emotionally, but you can *feel* it in every single inch of you. It makes your bones ache, your chest hurt, and you think you could die from it. Sometimes you wish that you would.

"You never know, she may even want to join you?" He tries to sound uplifting, but he can't shake the worried tone.

"But how could I give her this curse? How could I do that to her if I end up caring?"

3

Waiting

Gabby

I hate waiting for a text back from someone new. Or someone in general. Admittedly, I think I just hate waiting. And when that wait is for a 5'5" bombshell in stilettoes...then it is infinitely worse. Fuck she is beautiful. Her small waist with rounded curves and that perfectly fitted dress made her look like she could be a pinup model from the 50s. She has the pale, flawless skin and black, impeccably curled hair to match.

The gods know I'm a sucker for a beautiful woman, but this felt different. You know those moments when reality feels like it has shifted? Like you have entered a brand-new chapter of life? That was tonight. I'm not sure what she is bringing into my life, but I already can't wait to find out.

If she texts me back.

My phone dings from across my apartment, and I essentially parkour over my couch to grab it off my kitchen counter. Only to discover that it was a notification from my latest match-three game. I drop my phone back on my counter with an exaggerated sigh and take a bottle of wine from my fridge, and open it up to take a big swig of it.

I bring it to my couch in the middle of the studio. The entire unit, besides a small bathroom, is in this one room. I was lucky to find a spacious setup, most of which is covered in paints, brushes, and canvases. A few set pieces are shoved into a corner: chaise lounges, chairs, tables, and vases, all piled for some new piece. My bed and wardrobe are tucked into another corner. Near the front door, I have my normal living space, an eclectic set of furniture to make up my living and dining "rooms" and a bare bones kitchen with pine cupboards and a basic countertop across from me. It's simple, but it's home. The first real one I've had.

Halfway through my bottle, my phone finally dings again. Three times.

Hello, beautiful, it's Josephine (From the exhibition)

Sorry, it is a late reply, but do you think next week works?

For the painting?

Unknown

I squeal, a giddy sound I don't know if I have *ever* made before. I quickly add her to my contacts.

No problem! How about Friday?

It's a date. Get some rest

Josephine

Finally. Standing up from my couch makes the world spin around me from all the wine. But I don't care. I decide to go with the feeling and spin around my living space with an excited squeal or two. I feel like I'm a kid again with a new crush. The girl I want to go out with texted me back. Better yet, she wants to come over so I can paint her. I only have to wait a week.

4

Curses

Josephine

I desperately need new lingerie. In less than a week, I'm being painted half-naked by someone I think I might want to go out with. The pressure is as immense as a volcano ready to blow. How do people just...go out with someone and feel ready? Because I'm half tempted to run and hide, even with the excitement of seeing her.

I enjoy my evening mug of blood and wait impatiently for Britt to arrive so we can go shopping. My red nails click on the ceramic as the warm liquid settles in my stomach. The ringing of the doorbell sends a wave of relief through my system.

"Finally," I say as I open the door and set the empty mug down on the table next to the entrance and grab my purse. "You're late, and I have been itching to go for ages."

"I'm only two minutes late!"

"Well, I've been ready for an hour, let's go." I gesture for her to walk as I step through the frame and lock up my place. "I booked us an appointment at Lace and Leather, we have to be on time for it. Did you need anything while we are there?" She huffs out a laugh in response.

"Auntie, we both know I'm not seeing anyone."

"I didn't ask if you were seeing anyone. I asked if you needed anything. You do realize you can look good for yourself, don't you?" She stares down at her hands as we wait for the elevator. I place my hand gently on her shoulder, my face falling as I take in her posture. Her shoulders are bent forward slightly, her eyes looking at the ground instead of at me. "Britt, it is okay to enjoy something just for yourself."

"Okay," her voice comes out shaky. Britt always has her confident, bubbly act going on. But I know my niece and have seen her walls crumble before. Most of her family, of *our* family, hasn't been kind to her. They have always valued perfection, and in their eyes, the number on your tag is part of that. I wish she could see herself through someone else's eyes, someone who knows she is beautiful, maybe then she could recognize it too. Potentially even own it.

"It will be a fun evening out, you're more gorgeous than you realize. Once you see it, those stupid men will too. Sometimes your own confidence makes all the difference. I promise." I give her hand three squeezes, our own little silent "I love you." She returns the gesture, and I throw her a smile, "Besides, do you know what can help with confidence?"

"What?"

"Lingerie. If you feel hot, everyone else will see it too."

The rest of the walk to the shop is filled with idle chit-chat. We talk about her new clients and upcoming exhibitions, and how she booked a gallery space for my photography in a few weeks. I tell her about the advancements Christopher made with my camera. He has been working on creating one that would finally allow for vampires to be photographed. So far, he has gotten close enough that our clothes appear, which has become part of the defining style in my art. Clothes posed as if a real person was in them, but the background shows through wherever the fabric isn't. She mentions trying to increase her standing in the art world, maybe try to land some bigger clients. Unlike my friends and I, she wants the fame and recognition. I just want peace. Unfortunately, she also throws in her consistent bid for immortality.

"Please, Auntie, I would make a great vampire."

"I don't doubt that, but darling, it isn't all fun and games."

"Yes, yes, I know. Louder sounds, brighter lights, a lot of death. But I already only have you; there isn't anyone to lose." She says it like it isn't *painful*. Even on the walk here, I have been sipping on my blood, trying to stop the noise. It is so overwhelming it hurts.

"You have the rest of the family, Britt," I tell her. Her response is only a laugh. "Well, you do, they don't want to deal with the undead, but you are still alive."

"No, they aren't there, I don't *have* them. They think I'm corrupted for talking to you. Like, somehow they can catch vampirism by third-party contact, it's ridiculous." Her tone takes on a touch of frustration, which she never likes to let slip.

"I don't understand what happened there. Your mother never cared, or her mother, or my sister. For fucks sake, I've only ever told our family about it, the boys too. And her." My thoughts dart back to Amanda and her fear when I told her on the rooftop garden that night. The way she backed away. The rejection. The way she-

"What happened is they couldn't wrap their heads around it, they stopped trying to know you and made you the personification of death and all things unnatural."

"I'm sorry they cut you out because of me."

"I'm not. I was the black sheep anyway. Mom never cared; she was always kind. But the rest of them? I was never perfect enough, never thin enough, never removed enough from the things humans aren't meant to know about. Never good enough at keeping their secrets." I clasp her hand in mine to give her another three quick squeezes.

"I would never judge you for any of that, you're more incredible than you, and especially more than they, realize. And I only ask you to keep one secret, and you have."

"I know, thank you. But you could still turn me."

"Not going to happen, I'm not cursing you like that."

"Spending eternity with my only real family isn't a curse."

"Only because you haven't lived it yet." I toss her a sad smile. The curse of losing people again and again is one you can only learn with time. One that never really stops. "Ready to shop?" I arch a brow at her as the building comes into view. It is one of the older buildings in the city, a short, two-story shop between the high rises. The bricks give it a vintage feel, and the ivy brings in the charm.

"Never."

"Well, try and get ready because we are here and it's time to find something that makes us each feel like goddesses on earth."

The next hour and a half is spent getting in and out of various pieces. Britt manages to find two sets she likes well enough. Then there is me, I end up walking away with two bags full of lingerie. Gorgeous corsets, different garters, babydolls, bodysuits, bra and pantie sets. Everything. I love having beautiful lingerie in some of my photography, delicate lace and buttery soft leather adding textural elements that help the pieces pop. And maybe Gabby would enjoy seeing some of them, specifically the babydoll I picked out for her painting of me. One that is the same color green as her gown. The same as her eyes.

Thinking about Friday has me going through a whirlwind of feelings. I'm excited to see her again, and to learn how she sees me. Truthfully, to simply have the opportunity to see myself again. I have pictures from before I was turned, but nothing recent. Sometimes I wonder if I have changed.

But then there are the other feelings. Anxiety. Dread. Fear. What if I get close to her and she slips through my fingers? What if she simply grows old, and I have to mourn another human? Or if she gets scared like Amanda? *Leaves* like her? What if I'm left broken and bedridden from the pain again?

The line between the excitement and the worry has thoroughly blended by now. I am feeling all of it all of the time. It's overwhelming.

5

Beignets and Bangs

Gabby

"So you met a girl?" my best friend Megan asks me at our weekly Sunday brunch, her voice comes out sing-songy.

The brunch spot is beautiful. The restaurant is on a terrace that overlooks the river that cuts through the middle of the town, separating the arts district and the business side of Noxdale. The view from our table shows the lush park around the river. All the chairs are simple and white, with white, shiny tables. Fresh flowers decorate each table, heavy vases keeping them down as the wind gently blows through.

"I may have," I absentmindedly play with my beignet, taking way too long to dip it in the cherry sauce.

"You're about as red as that," she points to my plate, "so I'm thinking it is more than 'may have'. I need the deets." She gestures to keep talking, somehow not spilling a drop of her mimosa despite her dramatic motions. She takes a sip from the flute, narrowing her eyes over the glass until I start to speak.

"She came to my exhibition on Friday." I bite into the beignet, the sweet and tart flavor of the cherries hitting my tongue.

"Go on," another expert motion.

"She was wearing this blue dress with a white grid on it. It hugged her curves so perfectly. She has these full lips with the best cupid's bow. I swear she is like a pinup come to life, but somehow even better? Literally, she didn't have a hair out of place. Even her manicure is perfect. Red stilleto nails, except for two..."

"Oh, so she is *very* into women," her eyebrows waggle. "So did you ask Miss-Perfect-No-Name out?"

"Josephine."

"Did you ask *Josephine* out?" She places her glass down and grabs a bite of her avocado toast, her impatient expression staying firm on her face.

"Sort of?" I shrug.

"How do you sort of ask someone out?"

"Well, I asked her to let me paint her." Another dip into the sauce, averting my eyes from my friend's intense gaze.

"Did she say yes?" My face flushes even brighter. I swear I can feel the heat rising off my cheeks. "I'm taking that as a yes. Hoping to get a little fingerbang action?" I drop the beignet, and my head falls into my hands.

"You're the worst." I groan out. She laughs hard enough that her glossy red hair bounces around her.

"You didn't say no."

“No, I’m not hoping for a ‘little fingerbang action’ when she comes over,” my hands making air quotes to match with my killer eye roll. “I want to talk, learn more about her. Maybe ask her on a real date. A kiss if I’m lucky.”

“So, let me get this straight: you’re seeing a hottie with a body in lingerie or *less,* and you want to kiss her at most?” I swear the bite she takes out of her avocado toast radiates disbelief and disappointment.

“Yes. I want to see what she likes, what makes her laugh and smile. Those kinds of things. You know…what you do when you want to start a relationship.” I have some of my own mimosa, wanting nothing more than to not talk about sex with her right this second in a restaurant full of people.

“Or you could hook up, make sure there is the right kind of chemistry.”

“Or I could get her to say yes to an actual date first. One where I’m not covered in paint.”

“What am I supposed to do with you?” She shakes her head.

"Love me and hope that she says yes."

"I hope she does. You need to get laid. It's been a year."

"A year of working hard." I shove another beignet into my mouth, the tart cherry blending perfectly with the sweet, fried perfection.

"Or one of closing yourself in your studio and leaving me to drag you out so you can see the sun." Her eyebrow arches in challenge. She's not wrong. That whole time was spent holed up in my studio, focused solely on my art. But I made some damn good pieces, and made some damn good money too. So I think my chronic levels of introversion may have been worth it.

"Maybe you're right. But I'm still not jumping into bed with her on Friday." I keep my gaze stern, not wanting to give her room to argue that I should, in fact, get her off immediately.

"At least you learned I'm right." She drains the rest of her mimosa as the waitress approaches so she can request another refill. I lift mine to do the same.

“To new chances at love,” I raise my fresh glass, Megan’s clinking against mine.

“To new sexventures.” We take a sip of our drinks before breaking into laughter at her own twist, still wanting me to put myself out there a little more than my own comfort zone. This will be a good brunch.

6

New Beginnings and Parasitic Cockroaches

Josephine

Hello, beautiful. I'm excited for Friday. Do you think this will work?

I send gabby a picture of the lingerie for the painting, my heart is pounding as I wait for her reply.

Holy shit

It looks incredible, no notes

I'll see you Friday

Gabby

I hold the new lingerie in my hands and appraise it. It really is beautiful. Intricate, light sage green lace on the cups with a dark pink lace trim that almost looks like flowers, delicate. The same green color flows from the cups made from buttery chiffon. All with a matching lace thong, with the same pink trim on the top.

I just hope she loves it.

I shake my head to try and stay on task: getting blood from the Council building and talking to the guys about Britt and her never-ending desire to become a vampire. I put the lingerie away and take a quick once-over of my closet so I can put myself together.

Even in my apartment, I can tell the air has gotten balmy. I keep the look simple, a little black dress and gold jewelry from my mother, and my staple stilettos. I spend time making sure my hair is perfect. My mother used to get dressed all pretty after she fought with my father. When she would get dressed up, I would sit on her bed, and she would always tell me: “No matter how bad you feel on the inside, no one will be able to see it if you make sure you appear put together on the outside.” And right now, I feel like nothing is put together.

Memories of Amanda are resurfacing, Britt wants this curse, the sensations are still too intense, and now I throw in a beautiful artist to pine over. My last touch is my victory red lipstick and a spray of a floral perfume; the soothing notes of lilac and lilies of the valley make their way to my nose. The light scent is relaxing in a world of chaos. I grab my black purse on my way out to make my way over to the Council building.

The night is oddly quiet, even for a Tuesday. It is like the city decided to sleep, like it decided to let me breathe for once. I take a deep breath of the air, letting it fill my lungs with the warm air, as my heels click down the street, and I pick up the pace. When I get there, Christopher is waiting outside on one of the stone benches with casual grace. The streetlamps behind him illuminate his frame in the dark. The neon "BioSang Firm" sign that hangs on the building adds a cast of red over the area. The sign that lets us hide in plain sight.

"Hi there, how's your night?" I ask as I approach, fixing my hair that the speed had mussed up on the way over. He leans in to give me a kiss on each cheek.

"Oh, it is a night. I think Michael is on the hunt for a woman again. I know he wants to find someone to round out our little family, but I think he comes on too..." he pauses like he is trying to find the right words to say, he looks tired. Not the kind you get from a bad night of sleep, just *tired*.

"Horny?"

"Yeah, that's it. Too horny. He wants an actual life with them, but he isn't exactly good at keeping it in his pants. He gives his heart over in a night, but no one else sees that."

"Isn't that how you two met?" I lean against him as we peer into the street.

"That was the 90s."

"It was the AIDS epidemic."

"Like I said, it was the 90s. Besides, we had a super cool vampire friend that kept us around." He nudges me with his elbow.

"And I regret it almost every day," I lean back to face him, trying my best to look serious when the words leave my lips. They are the only people I've ever actually turned. I remember the day I told them I was a vampire, every terrifying and heartfelt moment of it. They were dying. I couldn't take losing my friends; they were some of my first real ones after my human ones kept aging, the first ones I had since I had to leave my human ones behind. They would have seen that I never aged a day. The guys understood me; they understood my art. They still do.

Christopher was a videographer; he loved making little short films. I remember how he would *beg* me to be in them and how I wished I could, but had to keep saying no. He documented a lot about the community during the epidemic; he showed the destruction and the devastation, along with joy and love. I think he still wants to, once he perfects his camera. Until then, he has been trying to figure out the right method, creating new cameras for us both. Michael though? He was all about film, of the erotic variety. I'm 90% sure he has kept all the tapes of the films he was in. I can't say I have cared to watch any of them.

"No, you don't." Christopher stares into my eyes with an expression that shows his sudden lack of jokes.

"Maybe you're right. How could I regret turning the two people who have unconditionally accepted me?"

"How could we not accept an eccentric lesbian who only comes out at night? We always joked that you were some Lovecraftian creature inside a pretty meat suit. We weren't far off." His face lights up with humor, some of his tiredness melting away.

"Oh, screw off," I smile and nudge him with my shoulder.

"Come on, Cthulu, let's get inside and get a glass of the good stuff." His grin could truly light up a room. His arm loops around mine as we enter the sanctuary of the Council. "Fair warning, the wicked witch is here today."

"Why does Beverly always have to be here? I just want a nice night out to calm my brain, and *she* shows up." I don't bother to hide the venom in my voice or the disappointment at her existence from showing on my face.

"First, it's because she is a parasitic cockroach who thrives on the misery of others. Secondly, why does your brain need calming?"

"Gabby. And Amanda. And Britt."

"Are the memories resurfacing again?"

"They are. It's like feeling the start of a connection with someone, or the possibility of one, has brought it all back. But it's different than before. It isn't just the pain of the past. It's the pain of even a chance of it happening again." I feel the weight of the grief in my gut and the anxiety tightening in my chest. Simultaneously, I want someone who can understand it, who can understand what it is like to go through this, and yet I don't want anyone to because it is so soul-crushing.

"What happened wasn't your fault," he says, turning me to face him, keeping his hands on my shoulders.

Looking in my eyes like he needs to be sure his words are registering.

"But I told her and then she-"

"It wasn't your fault. And this Gabby girl won't do that, not if she is the one for you."

"Not everyone has their perfect match like you do." I can only manage an empty look in his direction. Michael and him are adorable together, they just *fit*. Michael, with his goofy nature and sharp temper, and Christopher stays so *even*. I can't imagine many people will ever have the opportunity to experience that kind of love in their lives.

"I know you have one, Josephine. One day you'll find her, and, I don't know, try to get over your fear and turn her. Spend an eternity together." His gaze is still drilling into me.

"I hope you're right and that person is out there, but I don't think I could bring myself to turn someone again."

"I'm always right. Maybe one day you'll realize that goes for turning someone too, that once in a lifetime love changes people." With that, he straightens out, and we continue to walk down the hall to the rec room.

The second the door opens to the rec room, the sound floods in from everyone chatting. Our own little community.

My eyes dart around the room to take in all of the people visiting tonight. Beverly is in a corner with some new turns, already making them roll their eyes; they look ready to snap. Theo, the interrogator for the Council, is talking to the local Council leader. She only goes by her last name, De Medici, as she loves waving around her family's long legacy of ruling. Their words come out in hushed tones, but I can still pick up that they are using the governing language. Secrets upon secrets. They give us an amazing place to connect and keep us fed, but their motives have always leaned towards darkness. The rest of the room is filled with vampires ranging from a few days in age to several centuries, along with the familiars serving in hopes of immortality.

The room itself is simple, art hung on the walls is made by some of us in the local chapter of the Council. Luxurious leather seats and mahogany tables line a few seating areas, games and books line shelves for people to take and use, and a high, black bar sits on one end to serve cocktails and wine mixed with blood. Nothing overly intricate, but enough to serve the local vampire population. The rest of the building is a myriad of rooms, some for the arts, some are apartments and offices, some are cells and torture chambers. Everything they could ever need.

Michael sees us enter and immediately gets up from the leather couch he was sprawled across. He has a wine glass filled with blood and what smells like Cabernet.

"*Finally,* you two got here. I have been waiting *forever*." He leans in to embrace Christopher and then to give me a hug and a kiss per cheek before leading us back over to the couch. He curls up into his boyfriend's arms.

"I had to warn her about the demon in the midst." Christopher glances over at Beverly as he hisses out his reply.

"Now that I can understand," with that, he motions over one of the familiars that circles the room to bring over two more glasses of the wine and blood mix. I've never understood those humans, the ones who want to be one of us so desperately that they sign away their lives to work for us for a *chance* at the curse of immortality. They don't understand everything they will lose for only a morsel of power. Still, I smile and thank them for the drink before raising the liquid to my lips.

"What are we drinking to?" I ask them.

"We are drinking to new beginnings." Michael's smile borders on mischievous.

"What did you do?" Christopher basically groans the words out. They have been trying to find a third for decades now. It takes a toll on him.

"I met a woman for us. She is human, but I think you'll love her." Michael looks positively excited. Hopefully, it goes well this time. He puts on a goofy and aloof front, but he loves too deeply for his own good sometimes. I have been by his side to pick up the pieces time and time again.

"Let's see if it lasts a week before getting too excited." Christopher has picked up those pieces so many times before; we both have. Long nights of drinking wine and sucking down blood milkshakes while watching some cheesy romance movie and going through boxes of tissues. I just want them both to be happy.

"It will last, my love, I promise," Michael says. Christopher rolls his eyes but still leans in to kiss his boyfriend. "Plus, our little Josie might have some updates." His grin is pure mischief.

"It is still Josephine."

"One day you'll give in to the nickname."

"Unlikely. But I do have an update, I think. We have been texting every day. A bit here and there. Mainly about the painting. I'll be picking up the one from her exhibition once it closes, but Friday is the night she is painting me." I try to keep my cheeks from flushing, but I think it creeps on my face while I let out a soft smile.

"What are you wearing?" Christopher asks, his eye for art is perfection. I pull up the picture of the lingerie on my phone and show him. He looks over it carefully while Michael tries peaking over his shoulder like a curious child. Eventually, Christopher sighs and turns the phone so he can see it. "That will be fantastic in a painting. The gauzy look will hide just the right amount to be alluring. She is going to lose her mind seeing you in it."

"That's the goal."

"Damn Josie, you're going to look hot,"

"It's Josephine, but thank you." Out of the corner of my eye, I see Beverly walking over, looking like she is ready to ruin someone's day. "Stake me now. Incoming."

"Josephine, Christopher, Michael." She lifts her chin like she is waiting for a reaction from the three of us, besides our disdain. She clears her throat with a flash of additional rage in her eyes. I think there might be a peek of fang that is quickly quelled by the blood. "Did I overhear you're dating again?"

"Yes." My words are clipped, hoping, praying even, that she gets the clue. She does not.

"Hopefully you don't scare this one to death." Images of Amanda backing away from me and getting closer and closer to the ledge flash in my mind. The pain of her rejection was so strong that it paralyzed me, my ability to move kicking in a second too late. Not even vampire speed could make me go fast enough to save her when she-

"Beverly. I'm going to say this as nicely as I can manage. Fuck off. That is not your place. Maybe you could learn to grow the smallest shred of empathy. Or is that impossible since you seem to have left your humanity behind ages ago?" Michael's words come out fuming as he pulls me out of the memories, from the guilt. His rage always comes out fiery, ready to explode. "That was *not* Josephine's fault. Most of us have experienced love and rejection. Especially after turning into gods damned creatures, literal monsters. Granted, some of us were monsters even when we were human." His glare is so intense, I think it might literally have the power to kill. He is always jovial, until he isn't. His moods flare wildly.

"What? She decided to spill our most sacred secret. Do you really think Miss Scared to Death would have kept the secret had she lived? She jeopardized everyone by thinking with her heart instead of her head." Beverly's face is contorted into a sneer, glaring at us all with nothing but contempt. Christopher puts his arm in front of Michael, whose muscles are tense like he is about to attack. I, on the other hand, am struck with too much guilt to consider retaliating. Did I really almost destroy everything?

"Beverly, listen, you cunt. Almost everyone in this room has told *someone* they are a vampire, including *you*. Whether that person was family, a friend, or someone they love. And the secret still stands. So I'm going to ask you to fuck off and learn a little more of our history and some basic respect for the community around you." Christopher's words come out cold, like all emotion is detached. His rage is always so even, like he couldn't care less if the person before him simply vanished forever. Then there is Michael, who is practically foaming at the mouth like a rabid chihuahua while screaming obscenities at Beverly. All I can feel is guilt and defeat.

I vaguely register her leaving, my head swarming with too many emotions to begin to process the world around me. The sofa dips as the guys sit back down next to me. Their muffled voices call out for some blood, and I feel them tip it against my lips. The world slowly comes back into focus. The sharp tips of my fangs dig into my lip, the metallic blood on my tongue. Then the worried voices come in, some from my friends, the others from onlookers.

"There she is," Christopher coos. Michael fixes my hair for me. "What can we do?"

"Is it really my fault? Did I endanger us all?" My voice comes out flat and monotone; I think my expression is the same. Trying to emote is virtually impossible.

"No. Like he said, we have all told someone. You took as big of a risk as any of us, but people who care tend to keep life and death secrets even if they can't handle being around them." Michael's words come out uncharacteristically gentle.

"And it wasn't your fault she fell either. You tried to save her." Christopher rubs my shoulder affectionately while he talks.

"I was too late."

"But you tried." He acts as if trying is good enough when death is the result. She fell to her death in front of me. I watched her fall. I saw her blood on the pavement below, the streetlamps shining over the glossy red puddle.

“Here, have another sip.” Michael lifts the glass of still-warm blood to my lips, letting it ground me a bit more.

“I think I need to go home.”

“We’ll take you. Love, will you go pack up a box of bags for her? I’m going to run her to her apartment.” Michael nods and walks off to the blood room while Christopher picks me up bride style and runs at full speed to my place. I give him my keys with shaky hands as his boyfriend catches up to us. “Let’s get you settled.” With that, they help me gather my pajamas and bring me mugs of warm blood while we watch various movies from my youth until we fall asleep in my living room.

7

Fame or Fangs?

Josephine

The vibrant rays of the sunset shine through my windows. The small splash of beauty makes me happy I installed the vampire windows nearly 50 years ago, back when they were brand new. I had missed seeing the sun, even if I can never feel it again. Summer had always been my favorite season; the long, warm days were the best for relaxing outside. Now I'm stuck only getting to see it through my window. Christopher and Michael spent the night in my guest room, having reassured me they are only a call away.

Reaching for my bedside table, I grab my bottle of blood for an early evening drink. With every emotional draining, physical exertion, or overstimulation, we need more of it. Newly turned vampires say it's like energy drinks; caffeine doesn't work for vampires, so I can't really say if I agree. Slowly, the blood heals the worst of the pain, but it can't erase it. It can only dull the ache and let me think clearly again. Bring me out of my comatose state.

I rub my temples as I swing my legs over the edge of the bed; the stress is getting to me. Who knew meeting someone, just feeling like there is a chance at love again, could make all the pain come back up. This damn curse. I shake my head to try to clear my thoughts as my feet hit the plush rug. Somehow, I manage to get myself to my closet when all I really want to do is go back to sleep and forget I ever existed. I fix my hair into a presentable ponytail and apply a bit of mascara and my lipstick. Good enough for a day at home.

I walk out of my bedroom to find the guys on my couch drinking some warmed blood.

"Good evening," I tell them as I walk in.

“Hey there, we have a cup on the counter all heated up for you.” I smile my thanks to Michael and head to the counter to pick up the warm ceramic coffee cup. I curl myself up in my favorite chair, glancing at the ray tank in the middle of the living room. Their bodies glide through the water. I wish life felt that peaceful for me, too.

“How are you holding up?” Christopher asks, his brows furrowed with concern.

“As expected. You know, I had wanted to talk to you about something yesterday. Clearly, that didn’t go to plan.” I swiftly try to change the topic, craving a conversation about anything other than my past or my feelings about the entire Gabby and Amanda situation.

“What was that?” Christopher’s voice is tentative. I can almost see him trying to figure out if he should let me get away with it.

“Britt. Once again, she asked me to change her.” I take a gulp of my blood, looking down at the floor.

“I don’t understand why you haven’t yet, to be honest.” Michael shrugs.

"Because it is a curse."

"So you cursed us?" He looks right at me, and I can't meet his gaze.

"Yes. Unknowingly. I had only lost my parents and my brother at that point, and two of them died young. I would have experienced those as a human, too. But I hadn't really lost anyone again and again yet. I thought I was saving you, giving you a choice for something more permanent."

"You did save us," Michael says, always leaning on the being a vampire is a gift side of things. He is wrong.

"I think you're still young."

"What my boyfriend is *trying* to say is we are happy we are still around. Perhaps Britt would enjoy it too." Christopher's hand goes to pat his partner's knee.

"And what if she falls in love? What if they aren't okay with it?" I can feel tears well in my eyes as I see her falling again.

“Then she will figure it out. She could also fall in love with a vampire.” Christopher suggests. Somehow, that might be worse.

“And what if she gets her wish? What if she gets all the recognition for her job that I *know* she wants? The recognition she *deserves*. Fame and fangs don’t go together.”

“If she were turned, she would have to change that,” Christopher says.

“Darling, it is Britt. Her lips are as loose as she is bull-headed.” Michael takes a long draw of his blood, Christopher shrugs, unable to argue against the facts: if she wants something, she will get it.

“I’m not doing it.” I move away from the topic of her career aspirations. I want her to succeed, as long as I am able to be in the background, I want to cheer her on.

“That’s your choice, just think of how she feels.” He puts his hands up with a slight shrug.

“You’re the worst.”

"I'm about to be even worse." Christopher's posture shifts so that he is sitting more upright. "You still need to go on Friday. I understand you want to bail. You have today and tomorrow to prepare yourself, but it is time to stop hiding."

"How did you know I was going to cancel?"

"Because I know you." Christopher cocks a smirk. "And I also know I will be here to push you out the door. You're going. You're going to have a wonderful time. And you're going to look hot."

"I hate you."

"No, you don't. Now, love, will you put something on the TV? I think a relaxing evening is called for."

* * *

It's Friday evening. I have to get ready to go to Gabby's studio. As excited as I was earlier this week, it's like I have a lead ball of pure dread in my stomach. Christopher says I'm trying to grieve before there is anything I could actually grieve. He just doesn't understand, and I'm happy he doesn't. Losing someone you love is painful enough, like a piece of yourself has been ripped out and destroyed. But having them die like that in front of you, *because* of you. That pain is different.

I take a sip of my blood and let out a shaky exhale. I can feel the worry etched in my face. I take another, trying to loosen it up. Nothing. Maybe the makeup and hair will help? I try to steady my shaking hands as I curl my hair, opting for my favorite style from when I was young. It always brings back memories of going to dances in town and going to the soda shops. My makeup is kept simple, wanting to look like myself...just elevated. I may not be ready, but at least I look like I am. I head to my room where the green lingerie lies on the bed. As I slip it on, the luxurious material grazes my skin. Once it's paired with a pair of pink heels in a matching shade to the trim of the lingerie and a white trench coat dress to wear until I arrive at her studio, I think I have the final look. I glance down at myself, feeling a boost of confidence from the armor. A buzz from my phone brings me out of my assessment of my outfit.

I can't wait to see you. I
have our area all set up!

Gabby

Attached to the text, there is a white chaise with a matching, plush faux fur blanket. It looks like a luxe setup.

I send a quick thumbs up in return. I hate how just seeing her name makes both butterflies and pure anxiety flutter up inside of me. Thankfully, Christopher knocks at my door to try and interrupt my thoughts. I take one last big gulp from my cup before going to my door.

“Ready to go?”

“No.”

“Too bad, it’s time. You won’t regret it.” I glare at him as we speed over to her apartment.

8

Divine Femininity

Gabby

Why can't I stop pacing? She is going to be here, she said it herself. Maybe it is because she stopped messaging for a few days? Is she rethinking it? I bite on my lip and try and relax with my tea, no, she can't be. The spark was undeniable. I don't think I have ever felt that way about someone so instantaneously, like there was a genuine connection. She *saw* my art and what I wanted it to convey. I swear time stopped when she smiled. She must have been busy.

9:12 pm. Three minutes to go. It is starting to feel more like three hours, though. Get it together, Gabby. I walk over to my mirror. My curly hair is pulled back into a bun, a few pieces sticking out to frame my face. A deep, rich brown pair of pants flows with the breeze from my vent. The matching crop top clinging to my skin, the AC causing my nipples to peak under it. Is it more dressy than my norm for painting? Yes. Is this a special case? Also yes. At least I hope so.

9:14 pm. The wait is so agonizing it seems like it will never end, until it does. The knock at my door has me racing at breakneck speed to open it.

She is even more beautiful than I remember. Her eyes are wide, the dark brown irises almost bordering on black. Her makeup is simple, clean, and the strong red draws my vision in to her lips. They look plush, perfect to kiss, her cupid's bow strong enough that women would kill for it. Her jaw is sharp but with enough softness to not be harsh, and high cheekbones begging me to paint the light refracting off them. Her hair is left perfectly framing her face with its inky shine. She is a work of art, and I don't want to turn away.

"Hi," my words come out breathless.

"Hello," her voice comes out shaky, too. She wrings her hands while she gazes softly at me. Maybe she is just as nervous.

"Please, come in." I gesture into my studio, and she takes a tentative step in, as if she is nervous putting her foot through the threshold.

"Thank you for having me over," she runs her hands down the front of her coat dress before reaching to fix already perfect hair.

"Thank you for letting me paint you." I lead her over to the chaise I set up for her. "I thought I could have you on your back." I climb onto it so she can see exactly what I want. My head lies against the head of the chaise, turned towards the canvas. One arm is against the back of it. I arch my own back and bend my leg closest to the canvas, keeping the other flat. Letting my other arm fall to the ground. "Kind of like this, keeping a serene and vaguely sultry expression on your face. What do you think?"

"Beautiful." Her eyes have a look of wonder and amazement in them. She stares at me like she is trying to memorize how I look, like I'm beautiful in my impermanence.

"Care to try?" I ask her, and she nods. I try to avert my gaze as she removes her coat and sets her purse down. I climb off the chaise, and she drapes herself down flawlessly, better than I could have ever imagined. "Fucking fantastic. Not just the pose." My cheeks start to burn, hers flush too. "Are you comfortable? Because you're going to be like that for a while."

"I am." I smile and sit behind my canvas. I had prepped it earlier with a layer of paint. I sketch out her body roughly at first. Carefully noting the dips and curves along her body and the way the chiffon drapes behind her. I finish with a basic sketch of the chaise, just enough to remember where to paint it in after she leaves.

I dip my brush into my palette, then. Her face slowly coming to life, stroke after stroke. Painting the light gold flecks in her dark eyes, ones that only pop under the lighting. They have a mix of lust and conflict in them. Her button nose is reminiscent of Marilyn Monroe. Rosy cheeks that are a shade or two darker than when she walked in. I bet she can sense the warmth in them. I wonder if she feels it anywhere else. Fuck I need to get a grip. I finish off her face with those beautiful, bold, red lips, making sure to capture their softness, the roundness. They look like they would leave a flawless mark.

"Tell me about yourself?" I ask her, biting my lip as I concentrate on making her come alive.

"What do you want to know?" Josephine asks, her lips barely move as she keeps herself as still as possible while responding.

"Where are you from?"

"Right here in Noxdale. What about you?" Her questions cause images to flash through my mind of all the different places I've lived, emptiness following each memory.

"Nowhere. My family moved around a lot. I've lived in countless countries and towns, but I can't say I'm *from* anywhere."

"I have hardly left the city. You must have so many stories." She says. I nod and huff a laugh. "You don't seem happy about it."

"It was hard, going places all the time as a kid." The emotional conversation directly contradicts the way my body is responding to seeing her laid out. I simultaneously want to open up my heart and her legs.

I really need to try and control my thoughts. For some reason, my brain wants to run a relay race between capturing her beauty and trying to undress her with my eyes to picturing us curled up on my couch. Close my eyes for a moment, take a long a draw of my water, and turn back to her and the canvas. Time to actually get my head in the game instead of focusing on all the fantasies running around in my head, even hearing the stories of her life can't completely draw me out of the view. I'm a mess. I paint her neck and her arms. They lay gracefully, the light giving them a slight sheen.

Now it is time to really test my resolve. I move on to her chest, it fills with breath slowly, a gentle exhale following. My eyes close in on the fullness of her breasts, too round to be contained in the cups of the baby doll piece. The swell is shown off exactly how I wanted in this position. My brain keeps flashing images into my mind about how soft they would feel. I need a damn lock in my brain to keep the thoughts out while I'm working. I focus on the shading in her breasts, making sure to depict her accurately. I want everyone to be able to witness how stunning she is from head to toe.

"What do you do for fun?" She asks me while I paint the slight rosy blush that has crept up her chest.

"Besides weekly brunch? Honestly, I have put so much into my work, I haven't gone out to have that much fun." Megan has come over for some nights in, but she has a hard time convincing me to go out.

"I get that. I have had my periods of introversion. I mostly go out to spend time with my friends, or to exhibitions before tucking myself away in my apartment. Sometimes a cozy night in is just needed."

"Sometimes a lot of them," I say, she lets out a light giggle before making herself still again. I would love to have a cozy night in with her.

I start to work on her lingerie itself, finishing out the curve of her breasts, covered in delicate lace and trimmings. From the base of the cups is a straight plane, capped off with the smallest bit of roundness at her stomach. The full scope of her hips is hard to see at this angle, but that soft element of her beauty, of that divine femininity, shows in that slight swell. Gorgeous. The chiffon blurs the details, but her figure is still formed below.

Switching to her back, I fill in the flowing chiffon, the arch of her back that is still visible beneath the fabric. As I align my vision closer to her ass, the fabric of the babydoll is bunched up, allowing me to see the lace of her thong and the round globe. An image of me pulling it down with my teeth emerges. I blink it away. Her ass curves into her thigh, shifting the angle up and bringing some more height to the image. Her rounded calf is next, the shape additionally boosted by her heels, contorting her foot into an arch like the one her back is in. I finish up her other leg and clean off my brush. She must be stiff; she's held that pose for hours. I let out a big exhale, the feeling of completion. The background can wait; I can finish it within a day or so, but the centerpiece is complete.

"Did you want to see?"

"Can I?" She beams at me, energy rippling through her expression.

"Hell yes, you can. I'm filling in the background over the next few days, but you're done." I say.

She walks over to me with her heels clicking on my floor. Her jaw drops as she looks at the painting. Her eyes filled with awe, almost as if she hadn't seen herself before. Or at least, she hasn't seen herself like this. It might be some of my best work.

"Wow. It is truly a masterpiece. May I take a picture of it?" She says. My smile widens enough that my cheeks hurt from her praise.

"Of course, it is you after all. And my talent is only part of it. I did have the hottest subject ever." I step closer to her, our eyes meet exactly with her heels on.

"Ever?" Her lips curve up in a smirk.

"Ever. I think even the greatest painters would be jealous."

"And I think you may be one of the greatest painters." And the blush is back with a vengeance. She takes a picture of the canvas before putting her phone down again, where I kept it safe during the painting, and leans against the table with my palette on it. “Seriously, your work is fantastic, Gabby.” She leans back and runs her fingers along her jaw.

“Thank you, I’m hoping to use it for my next exhibition. If that’s okay?”

“Of course it is,” she says with a slight laugh as she turns to face me. There is a wet streak of green along the edge of her jaw as I step closer, reaching my hand out.

“It looks like you got a little paint on you. Let me get it for you.” My voice drops to hushed tones as I brush my fingers against her to clean it off. It’s almost as if our eyes have magnets in them and we can’t look away. I feel myself getting closer to her, needing to kiss her. Needing to have those pillowy lips that I spent ages painting against my own. I lean in, she reciprocates, causing me to give a little prayer to Aphrodite in thanks. Her lips are softer than I could have imagined. I pull back, just a taster to try and quench some of what Megan calls thirsty bitch thoughts. Josephine meets my gaze, and I can’t read her expression. Her eyes are dilated in lust, but everything else screams fear.

Then she runs away. Grabbing her phone and coat and literally running away. Fuck.

9

Long, Lonely Immortal Life

Josephine

Nope. I wasn't ready. I whip out my phone as I run all the way back home to call Christopher. Tears stream down my face, my head hurts, and my lips are swollen.

"How was the painting?" His voice comes out cheerful.

"You were wrong." The words come out garbled through my cries.

"What happened?" His tone immediately shifts

"You. Were. Wrong. It wasn't good. I mean, it was good, but then she kissed me." I try to hold back the sobs so I can speak coherently, but it isn't working.

"Was she a bad kisser?" Confusion is intertwined with every word.

"No." Far from it. Her lips felt like paradise.

"Then why is that a bad thing. You're still attracted to her, right?" He talks cautiously.

"Of course I'm still attracted to her, and that is the problem."

"So this is an anxiety thing. Do you have your blood on you?"

"I just got home, I'm about to heat some up." I rummage through my coat for my keys and open the door as quickly as I can and kick my heels across the room so I can dash to the kitchen to pour a mug of blood and nearly throw it into the microwave. "I can't figure out how to be ready for this. How can I just open myself up again? Could I tell her about myself?"

"That's a lot of questions from one kiss."

"Because *Christopher,* one kiss is how it starts. One fairy-tale kiss that makes you feel like you're floating can be the start of your complete and utter heartbreak." I pace around my kitchen, the low hum of the microwave in the background.

"Or it can be the start of your happily ever after."

"I'm a vampire, not a princess."

"Maybe she is the princess. You give more ice queen vibes anyhow."

I flip off the phone even though he can't see me. At least my crying has slowed down.

"You don't get it."

Gabby's face flashes in my mind, a frozen image of terror as she drops. It makes my chest go tight; it is like that night all over again, but now with Gabby instead.

"You're right, I don't. You have a girl who is indisputably into you, apparently had a mind-blowing moment, and now you're second-guessing the possibility of you ever finding love."

"I may have also run away."

"You *ran* away?" The microwave beeps, and I reach for it and gulp down half of the mug.

"Yeah. Like, grabbed my stuff at breakneck speeds and ran in lingerie all the way home, level ran away." Thankfully, I move too fast for human eyes, because my coat was clutched in my hands as I bolted in lingerie all the way home.

"What the fuck, Josephine. You need to text her back."

"What would I even say?"

"That you're sorry. Or that you're scared and acted completely unhinged."

"I'll stick to the apology."

I'm sorry I ran

Is everything okay? Did I do something wrong?

Gabby

No

Can we talk?

Gabby

I swipe the message away, choosing to ignore it instead.

“There, I said I was sorry.” The glass warms my hands, and I swallow another mouthful.

“Good. Now what are we going to do about this relationship anxiety?”

“Ignore it and live a long, lonely immortal life?” I down the other half of my mug, refill it, and throw it back in the microwave.

“That is objectively the worst option you could pick.”

“I don’t know what to do.” I lean my head into my hands.

“List your fears.” My heart hammers in my chest at his asinine request.

“List them?”

“Yeah, that’s what I said. One at a time.”

“I’m scared she won’t accept me being a vampire.” Surface level, a good fear. A reasonable one.

“So what if she is? That isn’t the end of finding love. Do you realize how many people would legitimately kill to date a vampire?” Upsettingly, I do. Since I don’t live under a rock like he seems to think I do, I have seen the books and shows; people yearn for what they don’t understand.

“But what if she dies from fear?” The image pops into my head again, and I barely hold my hand back from hitting myself in the head to make it go away.

“Well, that cannot be a common occurrence. Once is some of the worst luck you could ever have. What’s that phrase? Lightning doesn’t strike the same spot twice? Maybe just don’t tell her on a rooftop.”

“That’s not funny.”

“I wasn’t trying to be.”

“That was supposed to be romantic. I had lit candles and made us a picnic of her favorite foods.” I say. A memory of Amanda on the rooftop, smiling before I told her the news, resurfaces. She looked so beautiful, so happy. The image warps and shows Gabby there instead. My stomach turns, I feel sick.

“How about a lakeside picnic? Lakes are peaceful.”

“So she could drown herself?”

“You just go to the worst possible case scenario, don’t you?”

“Well, it happened once.” His sigh on the other end is audible.

“Okay, here is the deal. Finish out your night with a metric ton of blood, and tomorrow night, I’m dragging Michael and Britt here, and we are staging a Josephine’s out of her mind intervention. Understood?”

“I don’t need an intervention.” The pain in my chest will go away, I can be alone. I can’t handle more loss.

“We both know that’s a load of bullshit. Do you understand the plan?”

“Yes, Father.” I make sure my eye roll is practically audible.

“Good. Now drink up and get some rest. Good morning.”

“Good morning.”

And with that, my microwave beeps, and I have some more blood. And more after that, too. Eventually, I fall asleep on my couch, still wearing the lingerie from a failed night at dipping my toe back into dating.

10

Spiraling

Gabby

What the fuck just happened? It seemed like it was going well. We didn't talk much; I was too focused on recreating her. Was that the problem? Because I thought the little we *had* talked went well. Was it the kiss? Was it bad? Because I thought it was pretty damn spectacular, her lips were so soft, and she seemed into it. Is she not into me? Did I read it all wrong?

Fuck. And now she isn't even answering my text.

Text Megan. That's what I need to do; she is better at this whole flirting shit.

I need you. I think I fucked up.

What do you mean you think you fucked up?

Megan

Please come over, I'll explain

Begrudgingly, she agrees. Thank the gods she is on her way. How could Josephine just run away? She said sorry, but what happened? What did I do?

Hi, Britt?

Hey girl! How was the painting sesh? Do you think it will be ready for the next exhibition?

Britt

About that, is Josephine okay? She kind of ran out of the studio

Like she bolted

Shit. It isn't you. I can't exactly say more, but she kind of struggles with the ending of her last relationship...it was brutal

Britt

But what does that mean?

Not my story. I'm heading over there tonight, a mutual friend says she's going through it.

Britt

Did I do something wrong?

Not at all. I have to go meet with a potential client. Talk soon?

Britt

I send her a thumbs-up in response. What did she mean by a brutal ending? Was it that bad of a breakup? I have had some bad breakups, but they have never made me *run* from a new partner. The sound of a key entering my door drifts across the space. Megan. She has had a spare since the day I moved in.

"I got out of bed before 10 on a Saturday, so you'd better really need me." Clearly, she has been out all night long, her eyes are dark, and her hair is a complete mess, casually tossed in a bun, along with a pair of athletic shorts and a sports bra.

"I really need you." Tears are pooling in my eyes.

"Finger bang action not go okay?" Her mouth turns down slightly as she walks to the couch.

"No finger banging happened."

"That could be the problem."

"Considering a kiss was too much, I'm going with no." I drop my head into my hands. I feel Megan sit next to me on my couch, wrapping a comforting arm around me.

"In what world is that too much?"

"In the world where she ran away." I just shake my head into my hands.

"Like literally?"

"Oh yeah. Bolted to grab her stuff and ran without a word. She left my apartment without her clothes on, and she was in lingerie. She simply left."

"Holy shit. Why?" She sounds as shocked as I was.

"Look at these," I take out my phone to show her the texts from Josephine and Britt.

"So she had a bad breakup? That isn't a reason to run."

"That's what I'm saying, but it doesn't seem to make a difference. It still happened."

"Sweetie, that isn't on you."

“Feels like it is my fault. I thought things were great. And then that moment, it was nice, short, and sweet. But was it just me?” I feel awful. Should I have asked first?

“Something tells me it was her, too.”

“But she ran Megan.”

“You don’t run from situations that don’t cause fear or pain. If she didn’t like it, she wouldn’t have cared enough to run.” She rubs my shoulder before pulling me close into a hug.

“I guess you’re right. I still hate this.” I wish she would tell me what happened.

“I don’t blame you there. Running away is not cool. So, do you want solutions, to vent, or a distraction?” I lean my head into her as she moves her hand to pet my hair.

“Distraction, please.”

“Then, a distraction you will get. I’m ordering us some greasy diner-style breakfast, and we can do a binge session of that new show?”

“That sounds like exactly the distraction I need. What would I do without you?”

“Probably spiral even more.”

“Probably true.”

11

Blood Bags

Josephine

My friends have been ringing my doorbell for half an hour now. I am in no mood to deal with others. I'm not sure love is worth it right now, not when it leaves you so completely wrecked before it begins. What is the point of adding more emotions, more connection, when it only leads to more pain?

When my father died, I was crushed. But Mother? She was virtually dead too. It took her years to heal, to be herself again. To not be stuck in her shell. I remember when they found the first tumor. He had fallen from the roof of our cabin while setting up our Christmas lights. Mother made him go in for an X-ray to make sure nothing was broken. He had two broken ribs. He also had tumors all over his lungs. Father looked like he felt numb when he told us. Mother cried. I did both.

I had been 16 when that happened. The doctor told us that they could try to cut them out, but it was risky. The first successful procedure to remove them was in 1933, 6 years earlier. Mother and Father wanted to try, grasping at a chance to keep him around. Chemo wasn't around then; it was their only shot.

It didn't work. He died during surgery.

Mother never dated again. I didn't understand why back then, not after it had been years and she seemed better. Now I know why. How can you when it feels like everything is a betrayal? When all you can see is your love dying. When their face becomes your new crush's? How do you date again when the thought of someone else that you may come to love dying paralyzes you with fear?

You don't.

You can't.

Dammit, now they are calling my phone.

"What?" I answer.

"Open up." Christopher has his get in line and listen voice on.

"No. I'm not up to company."

"Josie, it is not an option today. You ran away after kissing someone and fell into a spiral of self-sabotaging depression last night." Michael chimes in, practically groaning out the words like he is already fed up with the conversation.

"Screw off."

"You didn't even correct the nickname. You definitely need to unlock that door."

"Not happening," I say. There are footsteps in the background of the call.

"What did I miss?" Britt's voice filters in.

"She won't open the door." Christopher fills her in on the whole situation.

"Auntie, we are coming in. I'm using my spare." Before I can react to this complete betrayal, she opens the door, and the two men rush to my side, where I'm lying in bed, drinking cold blood straight from the pack with a straw.

"I'm not doing this tonight."

"Not a choice, Josie. Look at you. You're acting like a hungover college student trying to avoid your fucking homework." Michael points at the collection of empty blood bags littering my room.

"Not homework, just people." I tip the bag in his direction before slurping some more down. Christopher yanks the covers off me.

"This whole lying in bed for everything but blood shit? Not happening. You're going to get up. You're going to put on actual clothes. And then we are going to sit down out in your living room and have a chat about what the hell is going on with you." Christopher's eyes are narrowed in on me before he turns to Britt. "I need you to help your aunt put on something other than pajamas. We," he gestures to himself and Michael, "are going to start heating up some blood, hot chocolate for you, and make sure everything is settled."

They are never this efficient, so why do they have to be now? I could very easily nap the night away, but nooooo, they have to have this ridiculous intervention for me.

"Come on, Auntie. It's time to get up. It is nearly 10:30 at night." She tries to hoist me up, but I'm not about to make this easier on her when I don't want to be around people right now. And they are aware of it.

"I already told you that I don't want to do this."

"Noted. Now do it irregardless of what you want. I have already had a frantic text exchange with Gabby, and we are not making this a regular occurrence." She rummages in my closet and throws out a pair of dress pants and a plain shirt. "Put them on."

I lay in bed looking up at the ceiling. I know they are trying to help, but they don't *get* it.

"I'm choosing the single life." It isn't like it is new to me. It is better; there is less pain. Less risk.

"That's what you're calling it? Auntie, you're choosing to hide. To hide your heart and your pain...although you're not doing the best at that second half." Her voice softens with her next words, "Come on, I got you some clothes to wear, put them on so we can talk about it. At least come for the warm blood, it's all coagulated in that pack." She grimaces at the thought of it being chunky.

"Actually, it gets congealed when it heats up. It just tastes better than the cold stuff; it is hard to explain. I think it is a vampire thing."

"*What?* Please tell me that isn't what you got from that?" Disgust coats her face.

"Fine." I finally sit up and suck some more out of the pouch. "I still think this is an awful idea."

"More than aware, Auntie, get dressed, please." I point to the door and watch her exit before I put the clothes on, my hair piled in a top knot. Frankly, I don't have the energy to try and pretend I have it together tonight. Because, I, under no circumstances, have it together.

Every step I take is like I'm wearing iron shoes; the effort of putting one foot in front of the other takes monumental amounts of strength. Somehow, I make it to the living room. It's like I ran a marathon; I'm exhausted.

Everyone is sitting down and looking up at me as I walk. I stare down at my feet, playing with the band on my pants. Sitting on my oversized chair, I place my blanket over my lap and curl up. Christopher hands me a teacup filled to the brim with warm blood, and I take a sip of it. So much better than the cold stuff, it warms me from the inside out.

The light is absolutely blinding. I have my place fitted with the same lights and soundproofing as the Council building. On days like today, when everything feels like too much, it is life-saving.

Even my rays seem out of it. They are swimming in their circles, but it is just *different*. It is almost as if they can feel the tension in the room.

"Can someone please turn that down?" I ask them, Michael nods and gets up to turn down the light until it glows like the sun at dusk.

“All of us are worried about you.” Christopher’s voice is softer than before. His brow is creased in genuine concern.

“I know. I’m not about to stake myself, though.” I roll my eyes.

“That’s good to hear. What happened yesterday?” Exactly what I don’t want to talk about.

“I panicked. I kept seeing Amanda’s death over and over and over.” My head drops to my hands as I try to force the image from my mind. “It wasn’t the normal flashbacks, though.”

“What do you mean?” Britt asks, her hands wrapped around the giant hot chocolate mug, steam rising up with the smell of the rich liquid.

“It was Gabby in place of her. Like every time I saw it, my mind was reminding me of the fact that it could happen to her, too. That I could kill her like that.” Even with that admission, I don’t add in the last part, that I could lose someone like that again.

"Josie, you didn't kill Amanda, and you don't know it will happen with Gabby. Give her a shot." Michael rubs his temple.

"I don't think I can. I think I'm too broken." I take another small draw of the blood, letting the metallic tang keep my tears at bay.

"You're not broken. Scared and acting irrationally because of it? 100%. But not broken. You had been texting her nonstop for almost a week. People broken by love don't feel those butterflies anymore." Christopher has me crying with his words. He grabs the tissues and hands them to me.

"I feel it."

"I know. But what can we do to help you get through this?" Britt comes over to my side as she speaks, gripping my hand with one, two, three squeezes. I return the gesture.

"Here is my thought. It is a simple enough plan, I think. One, we cry and talk it all out tonight. Work out those fears, those hopes, the real nitty-gritty. Two, tomorrow night we go out for a drink and a movie. Just pretend to be normal. Three, we plan for how you can realistically overcome this shit. And four, you simply go out there and try to talk to her again. Four days. Four steps. A brand new attempt at getting out of this slump. " Christopher always manages to come in with rationality. It can be so damn infuriating that he *knows* what to do when all I *want* to do is lock myself away for a lifetime.

"I'll try. But I think I am too broken for it."

"And that's what the feeling night is for Josie, for your little pity party moment." Michael, on the other hand...not so cool, calm, and collected.

"Oh, and one additional thing, you're talking with De Medici about this grief thing on day three." Christopher averts his eyes; he is well aware of our history, certainly enough to anticipate my reaction.

"You have got to be kidding me." I can't believe he would do that to me.

"Sorry, I already made you an appointment. Love you though."

"I think I hate you."

12

Slashers and Charcuterie

Josephine

I haven't been out to the movies in forever. As the years have gone by I've become more introverted. I think grief does that to people, this feeling like you can't enjoy things when the other person is no longer there. I was always like that for at least a few months, sometimes a couple of years, for other losses.

Those losses didn't contain this undercurrent of guilt; I feel like I shouldn't enjoy *anything*. Not to mention the regret over what I did to Gabby. I wish I could tell her *why*. I can't, though. So I will sit in my guilt.

I take a drink of some of the blood from my bottle as I wait for the others outside the theater. Apparently, they got tickets to some gory slasher film. I think all vampires secretly like them. There is something primal about watching a hunt. The elders talk about the old days, back when we didn't have blood banks, and we actually hunted. Stalking our prey at night, or posing as a lover only to suck them dry. There are whispers that Jack the Ripper may have been a particularly brutal vampire, one in blood lust. De Medici herself loves to brag about her kills; she would keep a finger bone from each one. She was especially cruel. She would make her servants wait on her, to the detriment of their own health. When she got tired of them, she would kill them, drain them dry, and wear their fingers when her house was empty of other courtesans, just to make their fear so intense it never faded. I, however, am glad we have blood bags. I don't want to hunt people.

From the corner of my eye I see Britt approaching, dressed comfortably for the evening, leggings and a hoodie in her signature pink, her blue eyes shining through the dark.

"How are you holding up, Auntie?" She asks me as she approaches, her tote bag bulging at the sides.

“As expected. Bringing some snacks?”

“Even a few for you, if you want any?” Contrary to popular belief, vampires *can* eat, we just don’t tend to because our digestive tract changes. We can only process the blood, so it doesn’t exactly digest. Decently uncomfortable, but worth it for the occasional bite of comfort food.

“Did you bring-”

“Yes, I brought sandwich cookies,” she smiles and holds up a package of the cookies, chocolate with frosting. *Comfort*. On special occasions my family would buy them when I was a kid. Back then they came in red boxes. I loved getting them. Mother still made the best treats, but something was exciting about these because we got them so rarely in our household. The smile that erupts from my face stretches wide enough that my cheeks begin to hurt.

“You’re the best. Hand one over.” I stick my hand out to her and she drops it right into my waiting palm. I shove the whole thing in my mouth at once. “I haven’t had one in a year, I think.”

“You should treat yourself more.”

“Are those cookies?” Michael asks excitedly, reaching into Britt’s bag to snatch one. “So good, who doesn’t love them?” His mouth is full as he excitedly talks, the brown color of the cookie over his teeth.

“Gross. Chew first, then talk.” My nose scrunches up at him, and he wiggles his eyebrows in response.

“Alright, you cookie fiends, let’s head inside and grab some slushies and a seat.” Christopher wraps his arm around Michael and gestures me and Britt forward. “Ladies first.”

The inside of the theater is overwhelmingly loud, people are going from corridor to corridor in search of their room, kids shrieking in excitement at whatever movie was released last, with their tired mothers chasing after them, people waiting impatiently in line, and a handful of people arguing with the ticket sellers. Absolute uncontrolled chaos. My water bottle is in my hands immediately. Britt reaches for my hand to give me three squeezes as we enter.

I hate how loud places get. Humans tend to be noisier than vampires because their ears just don’t work as well. The historical prey to our highly specified predator. It is why we can hear their hearts pounding, their blood in their veins. I simply hate it. I'm far from a hunter, so why do their instincts have to plague me?

"I am going to go get the tickets, go order us some cherry slushies. Whatever flavor you want, Britt." Christopher disappears in the sea of chaos as the three of us make our way to the food counter.

"Three cherry and one blue raspberry slushies, please," Britt orders at the counter, holding out her card to tap it. The overworked teen nods in response and fills up the cups as she pays. This has clearly been a trying day because he looks ready to cry, or scream, maybe both. Moments before we came up to the stand, I saw someone dump an entire soda and popcorn all over the floor in front of him, accidentally, I'm sure, but that would be enough to ruin anyone's day. "Thank you," Britt's sing-songy voice comes out as the slushies are handed over. Michael grabs two, and Britt and I take our own. We are walking towards the hallway for our movie when Christopher appears again.

"I brought vials for the slushies," he says with a wink as we all begin to walk to the room. It is relatively packed, but our area is only four seats on the edge of the aisle and in the back. Further from the lights and the noise, perfect. After we all settle in, Christopher hands out the vials. I dump two in my slushy and stir it up. The blood disappears into the bright red frozen treat. I take a sip of it and relish in the sweetness with a hint of metal the cool liquid brings. It is delicious. As the ads start playing, I reach into Britt's bag to steal out my cookies, swatting away Michael's hand anytime he reaches for another.

* * *

"That was amazing!" Britt squeals out. "That one guy was so hot." She reaches into her bag for some paper to fan herself with.

"Ugh, I know, right? That one brunette with the juicy ass?" Michael says while Christopher nods with a smirk.

"No, not him. The masked guy." She swats Michael with the paper.

"We literally never saw his face. How is he hot? Especially when Mr. Whole-ass-bakery was there?"

“We didn’t have to see his face. Hot body plus hot mask equals hot man. It’s simple math, really.”

“Well, I, for one, found none of the guys attractive. But the blonde woman? The one who got her stomach ripped open by the therizinosaurus claw fossil? Now she was enticing.” I jump into the conversation, men have never been attractive to me. But a beautiful woman? Hell yes.

“I would have loved to get prehistoric with her,” Michael quips in response.

“Babe, you’re disgusting.” Christopher’s face contorts in a playful display of disgust. How he can merge the two, I cannot say, but I think it might be magic.

“And you still love me,” the guys lean in to give each other a soft kiss.

“On that note, I think we need some drinks. To the wine bar!” I lift my finished slushy in the air as we walk to the door. On the way out, I throw it in the trash.

“The wine bar?” Britt’s voice comes out in a whine.

“Yes, the lights are low, and it is quiet. Plus, they have cheese, and you love cheese.” I place my hand on her shoulder. If she were going to pick a place, it would be a pub or a brewery.

“Who doesn’t love cheese? You all have to have some too; I am not going to be the only person in our group enjoying it.” Cheese convinces every human.

“If you go there, we will all have some of the cheese,” Christopher reassures her as we walk the 4 blocks to the bar.

It is incredible, the lighting is soft and low, and the music is a low enough hum that it is tolerable. We each got a flight of wine, 6 half glasses of different wines, and a charcuterie board to share. We all have a night filled with laughter and talking, and for the first time in days, I genuinely forget about everything happening. Until she walks in.

13
Let's Talk

Gabby

"Okay, okay. We can go out for some drinks. Just keep it lowkey, *please*." I stare in Megan's direction while I lie on my couch, attempting to toss blueberries into my mouth. Hopefully, she will actually go for something simple for maybe the first time.

"Fine. It is boring, but fine. Let's take your heartbroken little ass for lowkey boring ass drinks." Her eye rolls are iconically over dramatic.

"What about that wine bar by the theater?" I ask as I start to pick up all the fallen blueberries.

"Ugh, you meant *that* level of boring?"

"Yeah, like have a nice, quiet drink."

"You owe me."

"First round will be on me," I say. Her face lights up like a damn Christmas tree at that.

"Deal. Now, let's pick you out an outfit because you cannot wear yoga pants and a tank to a wine bar." She says, I let out a groan and sit up, running my berries to the fridge before following her to my wardrobe.

"What are you trying to put me in?" I ask as she is rummaging through my wardrobe like she is on the hunt for some treasure or something. Suddenly, she holds out a dress I basically never wear: a long-sleeved maxi with a fairly deep V-neck, a big slit. It's cobalt blue and white with a patchwork of different patterns.

"This. It would be perfect. You can pair it with those sandals your parents sent you. The ones from Greece." She holds it up to her body.

"Fine, but it shows how little my tits are."

"Plenty of people like itty bitty titties." She thrusts the garment in my direction. "Get dressed."

"Yes, mother." I grab it from her and snatch up my shoes on the way to the small bathroom. I quickly change, slipping the clothing on and the sandals. After a touch of makeup, I decide to let my curls down for the night, only clipping back one section of my hair with a silver clip my parents had picked up in some country or another. "Megan, can you bring me my matching belt and that one necklace, with the long tail down the front. Oh, and the bangles!" my call echoes across the studio.

"Here bitch," she says as she opens the door and hands me the pieces. "Let me help you with that." I lift my hair, and she clips it in place. It is a choker with a long sapphire in a baguette cut. From the bottom of the sapphire, a silver chain covered in small clear crystals hangs down into my non-existent cleavage. I slide on the bangles and fasten the belt up before turning to my friend.

"So, what do we think?" I do a little spin.

"Hot. Now let's go have boring grown-up drinks at the wine bar."

* * *

The wine bar is cozy inside. Nice, warm lighting, mellow music weaving through the background. Warm-toned wood makes up the floors and furniture, sleek, dark green walls, and gold accents make up the rest of the space. There is only one problem with it: the girl who ran from my studio is there with her friends, looking at me like a deer in headlights.

"One second, Meg," I hold up my finger to her, not looking or waiting for a response, and I cross the wooden floors to her. She takes tentative steps in my direction. "You never returned my texts."

"I'm sorry." Josephine reaches for my hand, but I take a step back.

"Why didn't you?" I don't bother trying to conceal the hurt on my face.

"Is it a cop out if I just say trauma? Having interest in someone again is harder than I thought. I panicked." She wrings her hands.

“What do you mean?” I ask. What kind of trauma makes someone run away?

“Can we talk? I’ll tell you about it, but I don’t really want to go into all of that around all these people. Truthfully, I don’t know if I could.” She swallows, even without a glass in her hand.

“Deal.”

“Does my place work? I can’t tonight,” she gestures to her friends, “and tomorrow I have a meeting. But Tuesday night?”

“Tuesday it is.” I nod, keeping my face composed, but I just want to scream in that moment. She *ran* away. She left me right after *that*. I turn without another word or another glance back. When I do, I see Megan is smiling at the guys at Josephine’s table, weird. Once I reach Megan, I look her dead in the eyes, knowing she will love what I say next. “You win, somewhere slightly less chill. What about a distillery?”

“I thought you said less chill?”

“Come on, let’s go have a cocktail and a big pretzel instead. The place is only a few blocks away.”

“*Fine.* Let’s go to the distillery.” The door closes behind us, and she immediately changes the tone. “Want to tell me what happened?”

“She apologized for not answering my texts.”

“*And?*” She gestures for me to continue.

“And she offered to explain her reaction on Tuesday, at her place.”

“Did you say yes?” Megan loops her arm with mine as we walk.

“I did. She said she ran because of some sort of trauma, but she is willing to explain it in private.” I shake my head, unsure of what she means by all of that.

“Fair enough.”

“I’m just mad, you know?”

“Understandable. How about tomorrow we go to my gym. They have some punching bags we can hit,” She removes her arm from mine and pretends to swing a punch before resuming her grip back like it was before.

"I could go for that."

"Set a reminder to take Gabs to the gym," she commands her phone, the electronic voice repeating her command. "There, all set. I'll text you the time tomorrow, and we can go throw some punches. Remember, closed-toed shoes."

"Thank you. Now, let's go for that drink."

14

Hit It

Gabby

Thankfully, I made Megan stick to our 3 drink maximum for last night, or my head would be in too much pain to go to the gym today. Sometimes it is hard to let out those emotions, like they are so bottled up inside, so people see me as easy-going and sweet. Inside, it doesn't feel that way. There is a lot of anger there. For my parents for toting us around all the damn time.

Traveling was nice, but when traveling is your daily life, and you have no basecamp, no place to have roots, it isn't so fun anymore. I'm angry at them for that. Anger at them for continuing to travel, barely calling or texting, and seeing me even less. Typically, it is just the occasional little trinket from some country or another with a little card that says "Thinking of you" with their names signed.

Right now, that's eclipsed by the pain and rage over being left like that, of her disappearing.

As a child, I used to run away a lot; the anger and the hurt overwhelmed me. When that mask couldn't stay up anymore, I would leave. Never when things seemed good. I guess that is what bothers me the most about her running. It was a happy moment, I thought so at least.

I can't go over there feeling like this. I need to get the emotions out of my body so I can handle tomorrow. I don't like showing those harsh feelings. I just want to be the person people feel comfortable with. The one who is kind and easy to talk to. Not the one who is ready to snap.

I really need to hit something. Something bigger than the mini punching bag Megan already gave me.

I check my phone again. Megan said she is coming over here at 4 pm, and we can go out for a quick bite to eat after. Twenty minutes until she gets here. I dress comfortably, choosing freedom of movement over any of my more flowy pieces. My hair gets thrown back into a ponytail, and I slip on my sneakers. My leg is shaking like crazy while I wait. I need to work out that nervous tension already. Hit some shit, stuff our faces with some diner food, and try to sleep so I can go have an uncomfortable as fuck conversation tomorrow.

A quick trip to the kitchen has me grabbing a snack, some beef jerky. I think you're supposed to have protein for a workout anyway, or something like that. After it has been obtained, I head back to the couch to relax until she arrives. The knock at the door couldn't come quickly enough. I jump out of my seat, toss the jerky in my backpack, and race over to the door.

"I have been waiting forever, Meg," I say as soon as I fling the door open.

"Excited?" Her mouth quirks up in amusement.

"Yes. I yearn for the gym." I say. Her laugh comes through, making me burst into laughter with her. "Sorry, I just could use the release before tomorrow."

"Let me know if you need to go again after."

"Always." I very well might.

The gym is across the city, so we hop into the ride share and chat the whole way there.

"I may be seeing someone," Megan says coyly.

"And what's their name?" I gently prod.

"We aren't exactly telling people yet. I'm genuinely giving this a shot, and I just want to make sure it is all going to work out first."

"Anything you *can* tell me?" I leaning in her direction with my chin resting on my fist.

"They are both really sweet guys. That's the important thing. So far I've only slept with one, but holy shit, Gabs, it is mindblowing." She grabs onto my forearm.

"Hold up, both?"

"Get with the times, a little polyamory never hurt anyone." Her hand waves me off flippantly.

"No judgment, just surprised. But I'm glad the sex is blowing your mind." She has never been the type to settle into a relationship, and to be committed to more than one person? Shocking.

"I was surprised too, but it is really nice. It is still new, but we have a really nice dynamic going on. And I've seriously never had sex so good. If I could put it into words, I would, but the best I have is life-altering with orgasms that I think could send you into another dimension." I take a peek into the rearview mirror, and the poor driver's face is as red as a tomato.

"Fuck I could use something like that, it has been a while." Well, truthfully, it's been over a year.

"Looking to end your dry streak?" Her expertly manicured brow raises.

"I'm hoping to."

"Maybe things will go *really* well tomorrow, and you can have that wish." After she finishes her sentence, she sticks out her tongue and flicks it rapidly.

"We'll see if I forgive her. If I do, I need to make sure she won't run again either." I think my tension and worry comes out, even when I try to hide it, because her next words soften.

"You're going to her place, so the running part should be handled." She shrugs.

"I need to make sure she doesn't say 'Get the fuck out' after I kiss her...or worse after I sleep with her. Can you imagine?" I think I would die from the embarrassment and shame.

"It will go better than you think, I promise."

"We made it to your destination, ladies," the driver's uncomfortable voice cuts through our conversation. He is obviously ready to be done with us. I can't exactly blame him.

"Thank you," we say basically in unison and climb out of the car. He speeds away far more rapidly than normal. Oops.

* * *

"That felt fantastic," I tell her as we finish up our workout.

“I know, right? It feels so damn powerful.” Megan gives me a quick side hug, and we gather up our stuff. “To the diner!” She raises her fist in the air. We head out into the warm summer day and walk our way over to the nearest one to get our hands on some cheese fries and burgers.

The diner is full of people having a quick dinner before heading home. The chatter in the background provides a constant hum of energy. We sit down with a heaping portion of fries covered in melty cheese sauce, our burgers piled high with tomatoes, onions, lettuce, pickles, and a melted layer of cheddar. We enjoy some creamy milkshakes in glass cups as we talk about what tomorrow might bring.

“I’m not sure what to think yet. I want an explanation, but that shit hurt.” I say, popping a fry into my mouth.

“And you still kind of like her.” She points out.

“Hence the hurting.”

Megan takes a long sip of her milkshake. “I’ve never seen you hung up on some girl who did you dirty. You drop them and move on, or just stay single in your little bubble, and *still* would never give them another shot. Shit, you wouldn't even mention them again."

"She just seems so different. I can't place my finger on it, but I've never met anyone quite like her. I can't help but want to know her more, and I feel stupid for wanting it when she ran." I take a bite of the juicy burger, taking the moment of reprieve it gives me from talking.

"What if she has a legit reason? Either way, it was bitchy."

"You're way too passive about all of this."

"I can understand trauma, I guess. Sometimes it makes you do crazy things. Hear her out and see if it makes it less painful." She plays with one of her fries before popping it in her mouth.

"Are you encouraging forgiveness? You have cut people off for way less than I have," I pause with my burger halfway to my mouth, arching a brow.

"Like I said, trauma. It does weird shit to your brain." She shrugs, like she knows more but won't tell me. I bite into the burger to stop myself from digging further quite yet. She always tells me things in her own time.

I slurp the remainder of my milkshake, thinking about what Josephine could say. If Megan Miss. Kick-them-to-the-curb-if-they-look-at-you-wrong thinks she could be redeemed, then maybe she can be. I think I want to hit something again. I'll settle for painting.

15

The Vampire Boom

Josephine

I cannot believe that Christopher and Michael would set me up to have to talk with De Medici. They *know* our history there. And she is supposedly going to help me? With grief? She has caused it. Suffering is her only art, and she is a master at it.

The one thing I *do* know I'm doing is dressing to kill. I'm not letting that monster find a single chink in my armor. I keep my hair perfectly straight tonight, flat-ironing it to smooth perfection. A simple little black dress that fits my frame impeccably is already on, the sheath cut with a high neck that's classy enough for her not to critique it, without looking docile either. My makeup has been kept simple: a basic red lip and winged liner. Faux silver jewelry adorns my neck and ears. My necklace is a collar-style with a variety of beads creating a netting; the outer edge is made up of points shaped like small dagger blades. The earrings are dangles with the same dagger points. I add on a few of my fake silver rings. The last touch is my black stilettos and a black clutch with metallic details. I only pack a small amount of blood, knowing it will be flowing within her office.

I don't bother walking at a casual, human pace to the Council building. Why delay my inevitable misery when I can just get it over with? The lights of the city whir past me, all of the sounds coming in and out rapidly. It's exhausting. Needing a break from the chaos, I pause to take a sip from my bottle halfway through, the level of light tunneling around me, the sounds warped by speed, sending me waves of overwhelm. The warm blood makes everything go calm for a second, like taking deep breaths does when you're alive.

I think I always had sensory issues, but having everything amped up like this made them next level. As a human, I would always seek out quiet corners and low lighting. Panic would set in whenever it was *too much*. Nothing compared to my first time outside as a vampire. I dropped to my knees and screamed from the pain. I pick up my pace once again to hurry over to the quiet of the Council, a place that will feel less like a sanctuary this time. As I make my way to De Medici's door, Beverly is rounding the corner, of course.

"De Medici's Office? What kind of trouble did you get yourself into this time?" Her eyes shoot daggers at me while she snarls. I swear her fangs are more elongated than they should be.

"You know this interesting bit of information I learned recently?" I step closer to her, ready to recite the gossip I heard on my way to the office door, the familiars had been whispering in the hall. "Some vampire, named Meverly, Peverly, or was it Deverly, has been put on Council probation for telling a human so loudly that onlookers saw." Beverly's face pales. "Rumor has it the Council had to turn every last witness to keep them from spilling. Oh, and I remembered the name, *Beverly*. Who is endangering the species now?" I walk right past her gaping expression of shock, a slight peak of her fangs poking past her thin lips, and ring the bell.

"Enter." De Medici's icy voice comes through the speaker on the outside of her door. The heavy oak door pushes open to reveal the person I've grown to hate. "Josephine, lovely to see you again." Her voice comes out sickly sweet, like she is forcing an unnatural tone out.

"De Medici." I keep my tone level, trying not to make the encounter any worse than it will already be.

"Take a seat," she gestures to one of the hard chairs in front of her. She loves the power dynamic of sitting in a large, plush chair while anyone opposing her sits on a hard, metal one. Attempting to sit comfortably is an impossible challenge, yet I try. "I heard you're having trouble with *grief*. I said I would try to help, but I'm not really sure I can. I never formed those pesky bonds with humans." Her face contorts, and she waves a hand like she is shooing away a fly.

"Didn't you marry one?"

"You can tell you're young yet. It was the 1600s, I was human, and I didn't have a choice in it. I never *cared* about my husband. Besides, I killed him." Her expression makes it look like it should be obvious to me that she would never care. Maybe it should have been knowing how she is.

"You killed him?" This was new information. Her grin grows wickedly.

"Faulty heart. I made him run around the palace day in and out until it finally gave out on him enough that he died. A long game of delicious torture." De Medici's smile makes me more uneasy than her words. It would never be allowed now. If you kill a human, you're considered to be at the point of no return for blood lust; your life is the cost.

"Your family, either?" I ask, trying to change the subject from her cruelty towards her husband. Her laughter sounds like it is pure ice, not a trace of warmth in it.

"No, I had a duty to them, a legacy to protect. They never raised me; we didn't have little story hours. I had loyalty, not care. What you need to learn to survive in this existence is to simply not care. Not about humans. You could blink your eyes, and they could have lived their entire lives. You're meant for permanence. You need allegiance to your own kind, alliances." She leans forward and acts like she is giving sound advice. I understand family loyalty; I would do anything for Britt. But is there even a point in relationships if they are only for power?

"I'm not like you." My statement makes her eyes roll as she leans back in her chair, as if she is saying something as casual as the weather.

"Well aware. You were one of my mistakes as a sire." She lifts a flawlessly manicured hand and picks the dirt out from under her nails.

"I never asked to be turned."

"We needed numbers. As I said, we are built for permanence, for power. I don't live my life by letting the weak control me. I survive by keeping our race strong. And *you* were a pretty young human, just what we needed. If only you had the same strength in your heart." She takes one of those nails and lifts my chin with it. I want to crawl out of my skin.

"It is against Council rules to turn without consent now." She removes her hand.

"*Now*. Only because you weak little worms couldn't handle the *gift* that *I* gave *you*." After WWII, the vampire population had been depleted from the fighting, as many of our kind had apparently joined a secret branch of fighters. From 1945-1955, countless people were turned against their will. Once the Council realized its mistakes, it outlawed forced conversions. Well, unless it saves a human's life or they have to turn them to maintain our secrecy. For those of us who were turned at that time, immortality is no gift.

1950

I was walking back to my brand new penthouse, my Mother bought for me with the best photography studio you could get at the time, the same one I have today. The theater had just let out, and I was high on the new-play buzz and maybe a few glasses of fine wine. I was giddy as I walked home. I was dressed in my favorite evening gown, I was looking my best.

As I was passing the park a few blocks from my apartment, I felt someone seize me. Their icy hands were gripping tightly into my flesh. Terror filled my veins, and I tried to scream, but there was a hand clasped firmly over my mouth, so only muffled noises came out. Their hand was quickly replaced by someone else's, a metallic tang touched my tongue, and I thrashed my head trying to escape. No matter how hard I tried, I couldn't stop the blood trickling down my throat.

"Hold her still." It was the first time I heard De Medici's voice; it came out as a cold command. Not annoyance, but an order as if this were an everyday occurrence for them, and not the most terrifying moment of my life. The other man, the interrogator Theo, held me tighter. I couldn't move a muscle. His hand came up to replace hers. My eyes were wide with fright, but no matter how hard I tried to move away, I couldn't. Even when I tried to thrash around wildly, it made no difference. I know now that I never stood a chance; they were inhumanely strong. That's when I felt her fangs enter my neck. I had never been more scared, my entire body trembled, my hands clenched into fists, and I'm sure I would have had crescents along my palms if I hadn't been wearing gloves. My head got lighter and lighter, my body unclenched, and I felt myself go limp in his arms, all while she drained me dry. Suddenly, everything went black.

Waking up was worse. So, so much worse.

"What happened?" My voice still came out in a transatlantic accent; my mother had set me up with lessons for years to master it perfectly. She made her way over to me, the ice queen herself.

"I gave you a gift. Eternal life." That was the moment my life changed. Later, I learned why they did that to me. There was no going back to our human lives. We were changed. I was changed.

"So your answer to grief is to what? Not care?" I attempt to casually lean back in my chair.

"It would do you well. Get yourself a familiar, keep them desperate for your power. If you did that, you could rise in our ranks too. Think of the control you could have." Her smile is wicked, like she thinks she may have an opportunity to coach another evil protege. I don't want control. I want a life where I can be happy. She took that.

"Hard pass." I stand up quickly and walk to the door when she speeds in front of me, barring the door with her arm.

"You were not excused."

"Then excuse me," I tell her. She practically growls in response.

"One day, you should learn a little gratitude. I am the reason you're young and beautiful forever." She uses her free hand to point to her chest.

"You're the reason I experience so much grief." I push her arm aside and exit the room; her enraged noises follow me out. I simply throw a few more blood packs in my purse and head home to try and wrap my head around what I have to reveal tomorrow, and what I can keep to myself a little longer.

16

Pinky Promise

Gabby

I spent all night painting out my feelings. The portrait I did of Josephine serving as my reference for a variety of poses. Seeing her face in different expressions, from angry to apprehensive, to the pure look of fear on her face when she ran, to the one of guilt when she apologized. I couldn't stop. I haven't been that productive in a while. I found my muse, but the feelings right now are so mixed. It's as if the gods sculpted her themselves, but she still *hurt* me. I just hope the reasoning means *something*, that it isn't some second-rate excuse or a shitty pattern of hers.

I ended up sleeping until the evening when I had to get dressed to leave for whatever this night would become. I throw on a long dress and a belt, my curls sitting nicely today. With a final look in the mirror, I walk out the door, taking a ride share across the city to her building. I arrive in front of a historic-looking building, not as tall as the modern skyscrapers but tall nonetheless. Her text said she is in apartment 40A, so I count the rows of windows, stopping at 40. Penthouse. Something tells me this will be very different than my studio.

The lobby is grand, the ceilings are high, and chandeliers hang from the moulded ceiling. The walls are simple, with one having a large fireplace unlit due to the heat; it is surrounded by plush furniture. The building attendant is at a desk on the opposite side of the fireplace. I make my way over to him, trying not to gawk at the room around me too much. It's beautiful here, even in the lobby.

"Hello, Miss, how can I help you?"His weathered face shows he has probably been here for a long time.

"I'm Gabby Young. I'm here to see Josephine Beauchamp." I swallow the nerves I have about what will come now, especially after last time.

"I'll ring up to her, one moment." He turns to a panel and presses the button 40A. "Miss Beauchamp, I have a Miss Young here to see you." The pause takes an eternity. Will she reject my visit? Did she change her mind about wanting to talk? "Yes, Miss, one moment. I'll send her up." He turns back to me with a smile, "Our elevator attendant, Marcus, will help you. Have a good night."

"Thank you. Have a good night." When I make my way into the spacious elevator, the attendant and I make idle chit chat, but my heart is pounding out of my chest in anticipation. I twiddle my thumbs around, anxious to get to the top floor. It takes forever. Once I exit, I step into a hallway with only three doors, hers and the stairwell. I approach the door and give it a hard knock, hoping the sound carries to wherever she is. Every second feels like a minute as I wait for her to answer.

When the door opens, my jaw nearly drops. She is always so beautiful. She is dressed casually, a pair of tan linen shorts and a basic red halter top tucking into the high waist of the shorts. Her hair is uncurled and pulled back into a sleek ponytail; a couple of pieces of her hair frame her face. She has on her red lip that she never goes without, and subtle makeup. She leaves her feet bare.

"I'm glad you made it. Come on in." She moves to the side as I enter her enormous apartment. "You can leave your shoes on the rack." The rack in question is empty, clearly meant for visitors. But the rest of the room is full. Her furniture and wall colors are basic, all white. The little touches around the room give it life. There is a deep, blood red rug on the floor that is surrounded by her plush sofa, love seat, and chairs that have matching pillows and blankets placed precisely. A few glass tables are placed by the furniture, with a large glass table in the center with an aquarium in the middle. The aquarium has gorgeous rays in it. Against one wall, there is a red brick fireplace with a flat screen TV mounted above it. Little antique trinkets line the mantle. The walls are covered in art, various paintings and photographs add interest to the walls. There is a wall with a large opening in it that looks into a kitchen in shades of blue. A swinging door sits on one side of the opening in a rich mahogany color.

“Thank you for being willing to talk after...that.” I shift on my feet.

“You were right, you deserve to hear why. Are you comfortable talking out here?” She gestures to her living room.

“Of course, your home is beautiful.” It really is; every detail is intentional. She has her style down to a science.

“Not as beautiful as you,” she sends a playful wink in my direction, and I can’t help but feel butterflies rise in my chest. I don’t know what to think about it all things considered. “Can I get you anything to drink?”

“Do you have any herbal teas? Or hot chocolate?”

“Only the hot chocolate, but I can buy some teas for next time.” She pauses, like she just recognized what she said. “I mean, if you want to again.” She throws an awkward smile my way and goes to the kitchen. From the living room, I get lost in looking at her as she grabs out a blue pot and pours in cream, adds in pieces of chocolate, a bit of sugar, and some vanilla, and heats it on the stovetop. She grabs out two mugs and pours the hot cocoa into each before going to her fridge and reaching for the whipped cream, adding a big pile to each of our mugs. I take the warm mug from her and immediately go to try it; it is ridiculously rich. It might be the best hot chocolate I have ever had.

"Thank you." I lick the cream off my lips.

"Of course, sit anywhere you like." She places herself on one end of her sofa, and I choose the other. Seeing where I am, she turns so her knees are bent, and her feet are off the edge of the sofa, her back is to the armrest. I move similarly, having my knees bent upright and leaning them against the back of the couch. The silence stretches for a moment, like neither of us knows exactly what to say.

"What happened that night?" I decide to break the silence.

"I got scared. Can I tell you a story? To help explain it?" She places her mug down and plays with her hands. I think it might be an anxious tic of hers.

"Please do."

"Years ago now I had this girlfriend, Amanda. I loved her more than I know how to express. Her blue eyes were like the ocean come to life. Silky smooth blonde hair, too. She looked like an angel." Her face takes on this nostalgic quality. I can't help but wonder if she still loves her, and that is the problem. My chest tightens in response to my own fears. "We used to go on these midnight picnics in the park, and lots of movie dates. Clubbing too, I was a bit of a partier for a short time. One day, we were up on the rooftop at her place. That night, I had planned out a romantic night of stargazing, champagne, and her favorite treats. I was ready to tell her something huge, something personal." Josephine falters, searching for her words. Her face drops as she continues. "A medical condition of sorts. My thoughts were racing that night. I just wanted her to be happy, to open her heart a little tiny bit more to me." Her voice starts to break, a tear forming in one of her eyes. The drop slowly begins to fall down her cheek as she continues. "She didn't take it well. She looked at me like I was suddenly terrible, evil. I was frozen in my rejection." The tears are flowing down continuously now, her eyes turning faintly red and her lips growing fuller. "She started backing away from me. She backed into the ledge. I snapped back into reality a moment too late. I couldn't save her in time. She fell all 15 floors. I lost her, this woman I couldn't imagine life without." Josephine wipes away her teardrops with a tissue from the table behind her. “I haven’t exactly gone out since. I guess—I guess I’ve been afraid that someone else would act the same. That I would open my heart up and they would leave, or die. Dying in general, I can’t imagine going through it again.

“I’ve lost a lot of people, truthfully. But only one love. Family and friends have died over the years. Each loss feels like a stab right into my heart. I think I fear loss of the people I love in general, if I’m being honest. That one, though, that one broke me.” She takes a long sip of her hot chocolate before tipping her head back, like she is trying to make the salty drops go back into her head. “I’m sorry I ran. I shouldn’t have done that; it was cruel. In that moment, though, all I could see was your face falling. I was afraid to lose someone I don’t even have yet, afraid that you’d become terrified of me.” I move closer to her and hold the hand that isn’t around her cocoa.

“Thank you for telling me that. Honestly, I think I would have done the same. I used to run a lot as a kid, when things got too overwhelming. How do you feel now?”

"Just as scared," she laughs through her tears, "but I think I would be missing out if I didn't try this with you. If you want to try with me? I mean, if I didn't ruin it."

"As long as you don't run away again." Grief is one thing I have never had to navigate. I can't comprehend her pain, having to actually *watch* someone die in front of her like that.

"I won't, I promise."

"Pinky promise?" I lift my hand off hers and hold my little finger out with a raise of my brows.

"Pinky promise." She links her finger in mine, giving it a little shake.

"Great, because now if you break it, I get to cut off your pinky." I smile at her, and hers comes back in return, like I'm seeing the sun for the first time. "You're so beautiful. You look like you could have been on the silver screen, all golden age of Hollywood style."

"My sister actually used to want to be an actress. We looked a lot alike. Imagine me, but with blue eyes and chocolate colored hair. She used to do a lot of little plays in town."

"Why did she stop?"

"She died. Surgery complications."

"I'm so sorry you lost her. Isn't that rare?" I ask, she nods in return.

"It is. We were the best of friends." Her expression takes on a quality I can't quite figure out, like there is something more to explain, one day I hope she tells me what. I reach my hand back to hers to give it a little squeeze. "What about your family, what are they like?"

"Flaky. They describe it as 'going where the wind takes them,' but I'd describe it as a fear of settling in. I never had a solid home growing up, and they still don't have one. I never got to have a normal sense of community, so I moved to the city when I was 18 to try and do this whole art thing. I tried school, and then dropped out after a year. I think I've done alright, though, at least now." It was a whole ordeal moving here. I had earned a bit of money selling art wherever we went and had saved every penny I could until I had enough to pay rent here in Noxdale. It was the biggest adventure in my life, and the one I wanted more than anything.

"You've done phenomenally. Your paintings are something special. It caught my eye right away." She strokes her thumb on my hand.

"And it wasn't just the tits?" My words have her laughing brightly again.

"No, not just the tits, it was their expressions and body positioning. You captured their emotions. It was vulnerable. Reverential of their form too."

"Thank you," I can feel the heat in my cheeks. I break eye contact and peer into my hot chocolate as I take a sip. "This is delicious, by the way."

"I'm glad you like it. My mother was from Paris; she came here as a little girl, and my father came over as a child, too. My grandmere taught her this recipe; she taught it to me. It reminds me of cozy nights at home when my parents would read to us during those cold winter evenings." That nostalgic smile of hers comes back; it's adorable. We sit in silence that is somehow comfortable as we drink. I finish off my hot chocolate about the same time as she does. “Here, let me take those to the kitchen.” She stands up with more fluidity than I think I ever could as she grabs my glass.

“I can help you with them.” I stand up from the plush sofa to my feet to follow.

“You’re my guest,” she calls over her shoulder as she walks through her swinging door. I follow to stand outside the opening in her wall. “Would you mind if I photographed you?” She asks over her shoulder as she rinses out the mugs.

“I would love to. What kind of images are you hoping to take? Britt sent me your artist page. You don’t have a lot of portraits.” I think back to her pictures, they are incredibly unique. Focused on clothing and the human form, but without the body in them. I can’t begin to figure out how she takes them; they look magical and unique. They are uniquely her.

“I used to do more of them, I guess my style has evolved into what it is now, mostly.” She shrugs as she cleans the pot out as well.

"It's mind-bending. Maybe one day you can show me how you do it?" She takes a long pause, freezing like time stopped. Suddenly, her face snaps back to an easy-going expression.

"One day. But for now, I guess I just want to capture your beauty. I have a photography studio down the hall, we can have fun with it."

"Let's do it."

17

Cameras and Communication

Josephine

I open the door to my studio with Gabby close behind me. She wears a subtle perfume that smells herbaceous, minty with a hint of rosemary, with an underlying current of a subtle spice like pink peppercorns. Practically good enough to eat, and certainly not with my fangs. When she came in tonight, her heart was racing; she was nervous. Since then, I've been able to get her cheeks to flush and her gorgeous laugh to come out, her heart rate having slowed to a relaxed beat. After I lead her into the studio, I drag out the backdrop that has been in my head. The curved, emerald green backdrop will bring out her eyes exactly how I want. I smile to myself as I set it up in the room. From the storage area, I bring out a white netted hammock on a stand that I can edit out so it looks like she could be between trees instead.

"Maybe I'm crazy, but I think you'd look phenomenal in this. You're always so relaxed and calm. Serene. Plus, it's simple so you stand out, just like you should." I flash her a quick smile, and she blushes again. The sight is addictive. I turn away to set up the photography umbrellas before I kiss her right then and there. Once those are set up, I turn back towards her. She is walking around my studio, looking at every little detail. "To start—" she startles and jumps a little, "Sorry, I didn't mean to scare you. I was going to say, to start with, how about you sit in the middle of the hammock, cross your legs, and then lie back so your head is resting by the top of it." She follows my instructions and gets into place. "Stunning, put your far arm behind you, bent right under your head. Yes, exactly. Now bend your closest arm and rest your hand on your stomach. Gorgeous." I begin snapping pictures of her. She is the most beautiful woman I have ever seen. Simply stunning.

"What should I do with my face?"

"Whatever you want. You'll be beautiful no matter what. You can smile, blush, daydream, or think about sad times. Or all of them." She gives a slight nod, and from there she tries out different expressions. I could tell the moment she tried to think of more, she bit her plump lip and looked up. It broke me; I fully stopped thinking like a rational person when she did that. I want it to be my teeth biting into her lip. I may have even audibly gasped when I saw it.

Over the course of the photoshoot, I help guide her into different positions, some with her lying in ways that had my mind racing to far more provocative moments, some where she was sitting and making direct eye contact that I felt in my soul, and others where she was looking off into space. Every angle of her body is gorgeous, flat planes with delicate curves, a beautiful contrast to my own. I only wish I could photograph us together to see how we complement each other.

The thing that got me the most in her pictures is her face. Tanned skin surrounded by light brown curls that are almost golden where the light reflects off them. Vibrant green eyes that display each emotion plainly. Even the ones she tries to hide, flashes of her anger and anxiety earlier in the evening, then her sadness when I told my story, and the brightness in them when she is happy. She has the lightest smattering of freckles on her face as well, the bridge of her strong nose and cheek dotted with the dark brown dots. Plump lips that have begged me to kiss them again. Every single piece of her is a masterpiece. I don't understand how I could be so lucky to have one chance with her, let alone a second one.

"I think we have enough. You must be exhausted." I tell her as I set my camera down in its case. Her laugh sounds like music.

"I'm basically a night owl. I think I sleep better when the sun is out." She stands up and takes a long stretch. I can't look away. How is she so beautiful?

"Honestly, I'm the exact same way. Would you want to talk longer? Maybe I can get us a drink?" My own heart rate picks up. I hope she says yes. Hopefully, she wants to stay time and time again.

"I'd like that," her face flushes that beautiful color again, her heart rate picking up.

I flash her my own grin. "What would you like? We can have it back in the living room?"

"How about I order in some food for us?" Shit, I forgot she is probably starving by now. I won't forget again.

"You're my guest; it is my treat." I pull up the delivery app I use when Britt comes to the house. "What are you in the mood for?"

"Chinese?"

"Sounds great," I hand her my phone with a place pulled up that has good reviews. "Add whatever you want. I can pour us some wine while we wait?"

"Ooo, my favorite place! And wine sounds great." She grabs my phone and plugs in a few options. I order one or two things that sound like they would be good. I don't think I have had Chinese in over a decade. When I decide to indulge in a meal, I generally go for my comfort items like the ones Mother used to make, or sandwich cookies, but I'm happy to try it for her. I tip the driver and submit the order for delivery at my door before looping my arm around Gabby's and walking to the living room.

"I'll grab a bottle from the cellar, white or red?"

"Red sounds amazing, thank you." I give her a quick smile and turn to head to my wine cellar that sits right next to my pantry. Needing nourishment myself, I yank one of the bags out of their hiding place for the evening in the cellar and down it, letting my fangs sink back into my gums before heading back out with some Chianti.

Vampires may not be able to process caffeine, but we can get drunk if we have enough. Wine is the overall favorite, it makes it easier to disguise a blood and alcohol mix. I walk back to the living room with a bottle opener, the Chianti, and two glasses.

"Hopefully you like it. I had it imported from Italy last year." I set down our glasses, she chose to sit on the loveseat, so I sit next to her. I open the wine and pour out a glass for each of us. Lifting mine, I look at her and say, "Let's make a toast to new beginnings and happy days ahead of us."

“To new beginnings and happy days,” She clinks hers against mine, and we each tip our glasses back. Her eyes never leave mine, and I feel like I could be entranced by them and be under her spell.

“Can I ask you something?” I lean forward, an elbow on my knee.

“Anything.” She nods.

“What do you need from me if we are making this a relationship?” I try not let my worry seep through, but I’m scared. What if she says she doesn’t want one with me?

“Communication. I know some things will take longer to open up about. I’m assuming the condition from your story is one of them. Understably, by the way. But I want to be able to talk about what we feel, no lying.”

“I agree. I hate lies; they can ruin a special thing, and I think we have a shot at being special.” Her face flushes again. I could get used to that view. “Also, I appreciate your understanding of my condition; it isn’t easy to open up about.” Technically *not* a lie. It *is* a condition; how else could one begin to describe the curse of immortality? It might be the only way.

“I get it. I have my own wounds I don’t let other people see very often.” She pauses and lets more of the wine slip past her plump lips. “I also need dates.”

“I can do that, are you free Friday?” I can do dates *well.*

“No, I have another weekend for my exhibition at the Dimont Center. What about Thursday?” For a moment, I thought my heart stopped beating when she said no, the rhythm starting again when she chose to reschedule.

“The Dimont Center, that’s wonderful! They barely accept anyone to do exhibitions.” It’s known for only being open one weekend every quarter; only 4 artists a year have the opportunity to showcase there. Most of the time, it is a rental space for meetings and a collaborative workspace, but their exhibitions are always the best of the best. I remember when I had my own there. My cousin owned the place when it was first opened. There were so many evenings that I spent in the center, giggling over a glass of wine with Margot. I haven’t been in ages. Britt must be thrilled; she has been begging me to apply to have another exhibition there, it would make her career skyrocket.

"I'm really excited about it. Will you come?" She tries to dull the hope in her expression. Nothing could keep me away, not now.

"Of course, I'll be there both nights. I'll plan something for Thursday to celebrate." I reach for her hand to give it a quick squeeze, and she returns it. I can feel the ache in my cheeks from smiling with her so much tonight.

"What should I wear?"

"Something comfortable, I have an idea in the works." I give her a sly smile.

"Do I get a clue?" She leans forward.

"No." I lean closer to her as well, our noses almost touching. The air around us is electric, like my hairs could be standing straight out. The room around us fades away, and I can only focus on those green eyes that always seem to call to me.

"What about for a kiss?" My lip raises a tad at the side as I cup my free hand along her jaw and press my lips gently to hers. Just a gentle peck before pulling back, my thumb rubbing against her jaw, and dropping my hand. I think I could have kissed her all night, and it wouldn't be enough.

"I'm not running this time." I lean forward again to place my lips against her cheek, right next to her ear. "Our date will offer a glimpse into another world," I whisper before fully pulling back and taking a sip of my wine with an amused expression on my face. Gabby's mouth is slightly parted in confusion.

"Well, what the fuck does that mean?" She eventually asks. I immediately burst into laughter. I wasn't sure what her response would be, but I hadn't guessed that.

"That's for you to figure out in two days when I take you."

Her face contorts into the most adorable expression while she thinks about what it could be, her lip between her teeth again. The only thing that draws me away from looking at her and all her beauty is the doorbell ringing. I rise up to answer it and retrieve the food and lay out all the little boxes on my coffee table.

“It smells amazing,” her eyes widen in a ravenous stare, and she examines the table to figure out what to eat first. She grabs some orange chicken and a set of chopsticks, and I tentatively take what I think they call a ragoon. She moans as she takes her first bite, and I completely forgot what I was doing for a moment. “It’s so good,” another moan of delight leaves her lips. I can hardly taste the food, I’m so distracted by her. I’d deal with the discomfort of processing human food every day if it meant I got to hear those noises. I shake my head and try to focus on the meal, it is creamy and crunchy all at once. It is pretty good. “I was meaning to ask, what is with the tank table?”

“I love rays. Fish in general, to be honest. But these are Potamotrygon Henlei, polka dot stingrays. They are nocturnal, kind of like us. See the fish in there, and the mussels?” I ask. Gabby nods, looking carefully at my pets. “That’s what they eat, they like to hunt their own prey, it keeps them happy. I do give them some frozen squids as treats, though. Next time you come over, we can take the top off the table, and you can give them one, if you like.”

“I’d like that. Can I pet them, like you can at some of those aquarium tank thingys?” Her expression is giddy, like mine was when I got to pet my first ray.

“No, sadly, their stings are venomous. They are calm overall, but I want you safe.” Unlike the ones at the aquarium, mine aren’t as docile. That addictive flush comes back to warm up her cheeks.

“Well, either way, I’m very excited to feed them a squid next time.” Her words make me smile more than I could have imagined. My rays aren’t your typical pet, but I absolutely adore them.

“I can’t wait,” I toss a wink her way. “Tonight, though, I just want to get to know you better.”

“What do you want to know?” She curls her legs underneath her.

“Everything there is.” I try another bite of the food in front of us, it really is delicious.

“That’s a lot of things.” She says as she bites off the end of an eggroll, looking ridiculously adorable even when she eats.

"What got you into art?"

"That is one thing I liked about traveling, seeing the art from different places. I always thought that one day I would be like them, either the artists lining city streets to sell their goods or maybe have it in a museum if I was lucky. My parents got me a travel set of paints and an easel when I was 6. I never stopped using them; it is one thing I absolutely needed to bring with me to every new place. It was my constant, basically the only one I had." Her face drops; it sounds like she would have been lonely. I wish I could relate, but my problems are the exact opposite, too many connections that end in a way my own never will. Both would be devastating.

"That sounds like it was hard."

"It was. It is why I like giving myself stability now, not moving around much, only a trip here and there to see my parents. But the best thing about those trips is that I come home at the end of them to my own bed, with my own things, in my own neighborhood, with my own friends nearby. Oddly enough, the stability feels more like freedom than going wherever the wind carries you."

“I can only imagine, coming home would feel grounding.”

“It really does, but what got you into photography?”

“That would be my father. He got me a camera when I turned 10. It was a nice one for the time; I still have it tucked away. It was a little luxury; there was a big recession going on, so it felt like the best kind of luxury. I would take pictures of absolutely everyone in my life, the people around town, too. I documented everything I could. I went through so much film I think I nearly gave my father a heart attack. The passion for it never really went away.” I can’t help but laugh when I think of my father when he saw my film costs, he was in shock at how much I could use and develop.

“Do you still have them?”

“I do, I keep the photo album locked away for those days I feel nostalgic. Sometime I’ll have to bring it out for you. One I took was of Mrs. MacHuley. She was this woman who had worked by cleaning houses back then; my childhood best friend’s family was one of her clients. I would try to sneak pictures of her. I thought she was incredibly pretty. Except, she didn't think it was so charming. I think she felt it was some sort of joke, this spoiled rich girl photographing someone doing their job. But I thought the light captured her well. Anyways, in that picture of her, she had lifted up the broom she was using and glared at me. I stopped after that, but she really was pretty." I remember my Mother and Father talking to me that night about how it was rude. It was so new to have your own camera, particularly for a child my age, that it had never crossed my mind.

There is always this sense of lightness when talking about my childhood. Life was good for me back then, especially before the depression. My father owned an oil company, so we never suffered too greatly, but it was still a shock for us all. I remember him reading the paper on the day the stock market had crashed. In that moment, our whole household knew that life had changed. We sat in complete silence while he read. The world shifted in such a cataclysmic way.

My mother had grown up poor. She was working at a shop when she met my father, and he was taken with her immediately. The crash affected her terribly; she wanted to make sure her old community was cared for. We would bring food to the neighborhoods and gave them out once a week. She would cry those nights. The rest of the time, both of them plastered on happy faces and tried to hide it from us. Our family had enough that we could still purchase new clothes, we could always eat, and I could still take my pictures. But we were never hidden from the suffering around us. How could you be when it was so prevalent? I still try to keep my mother's work alive, in my own way. While I can't exactly go out during the day to bring meals, I can give to charities that do. I always put it in her name, for a dead woman, she has a lot of donations.

"Was she your first crush?" Gabby's brows waggle.

"I think she was, before I really knew what that was. My first actual crush was Tiffany Feldmann. She had this deep brown hair, plump lips that were kind of short lengthwise, she looked like she had an almost cartoonish mouth. She was cute. Of course, I never told her, she liked boys, and I was supposed to, but I got so nervous anytime I saw her."

"Mine was this girl, Liza Whitaker. We were in the Pacific Northwest for a while, and she was the concessions girl at a movie theater. I was probably 11 or 12 at the time, and she was, I think, 17. I had the biggest crush on her. I was always going to the movies so I could talk to her. She was a blonde with completely straightened hair that she probably had burnt to a crisp with a flat iron, brown eyes, and one of those faces that could kill. I think she went on some modeling show a few months later when she turned 18. I was devastated. It wouldn't have mattered, though, not really. A week later, we left. My mom and dad only gave me a day's notice, and we flew out to Japan for a few months."

We spend several more hours just talking, laughing, and curling up on the couch before she has to go. I can't remember feeling this at ease, feeling this human, in a really long time.

"Are you sure you can get home safely?" We are standing by the door, faces inches apart. Looking up into her eyes is electrifying, even after hours of holding her gaze.

"I called a ride share, I'll be safe."

"Text me when you are home."

"I will." She leans down to me and gives me one more soft peck on my lips. I'm tempted to draw her closer then and there, to not let her out of my grasp. But I don't. "Goodnight," she tells me as she opens my front door.

"Goodnight, beautiful." The door clicks behind her, and I stand at my doorway, touching my lips where the feeling of her kiss still lingers.

18

Date Night

Josephine

The entire next night has me feeling like I'm on cloud nine. I called in a favor for my date with Gabby tomorrow; the entire evening is planned out, and I just hope she likes it. I think she will be surprised, and hopefully in the best way. I edit a good chunk of the pictures I took of her, my least favorite part of the process. Somehow I'm supposed to figure out favorites, which seems impossible when she looks like that.

The peace can never last for long, though. As I'm getting ready to curl up into bed, my doorbell rings. I make my way to the peephole, my silk nightgown brushing against my thighs. Britt is standing there. I open the door, and she rushes in.

"Hi Auntie, I have the best news." Her smile is so wide that my own cheeks hurt looking at her; she is basically bouncing.

"Hi," I can't hold back my yawn. "What is it?"

"Sorry for waking you up, it is just so important." She flops down on my couch, practically vibrating with excitement.

"What is the news, Britt?"

"You know your exhibition coming up?"

"Yes, of course. I have my shooting dates planned out now, actually. What about it?"

"Well, this interviewer contacted me. He has this massive art podcast called Unframed: The Stories Behind Art. He wants to talk to me about your work, you know...since you're all secretive and all. People have apparently been requesting one about you for ages. He said I have the inside scoop, and I would be a great interview for one of the episodes. Auntie, they get like a million views a video! Isn't it cool?" Her smile is so genuine, and my stomach drops.

"You can't take that interview." I feel sick to my stomach; the entire idea could bring everything down. Her smile breaks, she pauses, and looks at me, confused and dejected.

"But, it would be amazing for both of us." Britt sits upright, her spine gone rigid.

"One wrong detail on a podcast with that many people and I'm screwed. Every last vampire is screwed. Britt, it doesn't even have to be a big thing that slips; people on the internet can find information on anyone from a tiny detail." I can't believe I have to say it out loud. The stress already has me needing more blood before bed.

"Please, Auntie—"

"No. That's final. You may be my agent, but it is my safety at stake here. Word of mouth only. I don't attend the exhibition. And my pseudonym changes every 10 years. That is how we do it. That is what is safe."

“I—” The hurt registers across her face. It makes my chest ache to hurt her, but it is too big of a risk.

“I’m sorry. I get how much it would mean to you, but I can’t risk it.” I place my hand on her shoulder, giving her three squeezes.

“I understand, Auntie.” Britt stands and walks back to the door, her shoulders slumped in resignation.

“Thank you.”

“I’ll leave you to sleep.” She walks out the door before I can respond.

I shut off my lights and close the blackout blinds. But I can’t sleep. My head is whirring. The conversation felt too easy, and unfortunately, I can’t shake this dread that has started to coil itself around in my gut. It takes hours before I fall asleep.

* * *

My alarm blares while the sun is still out. Thank you, modern vampire science, for windows that block the sun. I open my blinds and stretch in their light. I only wish the warm rays could touch my skin. I am exhausted. It’s almost as if my legs are hardly moving and I'm on autopilot as I plod over to the kitchen to warm myself up the biggest mug of blood that I can. I drain it while standing in my kitchen and refill it just as quickly. I take the drink to my living room and watch an episode of my favorite new crime drama. By the end of the episode, I am full of energy, the blood coursing through my body.

I take my time getting ready, basic makeup, and a romper to deal with the oppressive heat of the day. I keep my hair down with the sides pinned back, having spent longer than I'd like to admit on curling it until the curls were loose. A far cry from the beauty of her naturally bouncy locks. I wish I could see myself in the mirror, feel the confidence I used to when I did. Instead, I simply have to trust that I look good and hope that she agrees.

I glance at the clock. I still have an hour before I meet her. I feel like I should be doing something, some other little touch to make tonight even better. But I have no idea what I could pick. So, I run through my checklist again.

Dinner scheduled?

Check.

A rush fee put in for tonight to be set up?

Check.

Flowers waiting for her downstairs?

Check.

Music picked out?

Check.

Ride share scheduled?

Check.

There is nothing left to do except wait. Not exactly my strong suit. The moment the clock strikes five minutes prior to our pickup time, I race down the stairs, retrieve the flowers, a large bouquet of peonies, from the building operator, and rush to her building. I fix my hair briefly while I wait for her to come to the door.

"Hi," Gabby's smile is bright. The second she notices her bouquet, it widens more. "Those are beautiful, Josephine. Come inside while I put them in some water." I step inside and close the door behind us, the fragrant smell of the flowers still hitting my nose as she carries them away. She is wearing a simple outfit that is impossibly beautiful on her, a vintage flowy skirt and a cropped shirt on her look like they could be designer. She hurries over to the other side of her small studio and grabs a vase from her top cabinet, even with her height, it is like an obstacle course to get up there. With my 4-inch stilettos, we are the same height; she must be 5'9". And the damn cabinets are still built too high. She fills up her vase with some cool water and puts them in before scurrying back to me. "I'm sorry that took a while. I swear this place was built for an NBA player or something. I basically do parkour every time I need something from up there." Her smile makes my face flush. I let out an easy laugh as I imagine her jumping around her kitchen.

"It is absolutely alright. I have a car downstairs waiting for us." I bend my elbow to stick my arm out for her. She takes it, and I lead her downstairs and help her climb into the car. It is taking every ounce of effort from me not to press her against me already. I watch her as she peers out the window, trying to figure out what her surprise is. As she tries to figure it out, her face contorts in the most adorable way, she bites on her plump lower lip, and her brows form a crease; her little nose is scrunched up too. When we pull into the parking lot, her jaw drops.

"The *aquarium*? Josephine, it closed hours ago." She gently taps my arm with the back of her hand.

"I know some people. Come on, my little owl, it's ours for the night." I slide out of the car and offer her my hand. She grabs it on her way out as we make our way into the building.

19

Another World

Gabby

A fucking aquarium date, at ten pm, *three whole hours* after it closed. I wasn't sure what to expect, but it sure as shit wasn't this. There is someone waiting for us at the door, Josephine says it's her friend, and she locks it behind us. The entire building is quiet, a stark change from its normal chaos of children running up to the tanks and the chatter of patrons. Josephine's heels click on the floor as we walk in.

“Let me know when y’all are done. I’m gonna take a nap over on in the office ‘till then,” her deep southern accent comes out.

“Thank you, Shelby,” Josephine tells her. “Come on, let’s go check it out.”

Hand in hand, we walk through the exhibits. Some of them are quiet, barely any activity in them, while different animals rest, only moving slowly. It is beautiful, though. There are fairy lights placed across the aquarium, allowing for a dim glow to illuminate the paths instead of the typical fluorescent overhead ones. We keep relative silence outside of her telling me about different animals, it’s peaceful. I don’t think either of us feels the need to fill in those gaps. At least, I know that I don’t, I’m just happy to be with her.

“Did you know some sharks are nocturnal? People think they never sleep, but that’s not quite true.” She tells me as we approach the shark tunnel. “They have one kind here, the nurse shark. Most of the tank will be pretty dull this time of night, but that one will still be moving.” Sure enough, a bottom-dwelling, brown shark is swimming across the tank.

“It’s beautiful.” The active movement makes it stand out compared to the slight motions of the other sharks.

“Not as beautiful as you,” Josephine says. I can feel my cheeks heating. She seems like she is about to lean in and kiss me. I draw in a breath, hoping she does. Instead, she takes a quick bite of her lip and turns away to tell me more about the various fish and other creatures swimming around us. She tells me to close my eyes right before we head into a dark tunnel.

“What’s down there?” I ask, trying to sneak a peek around her form.

“The biggest surprise of the night. Come on, close your eyes, and I’ll walk you down there.” She says. I flash an expression of curiosity and mild annoyance that she won’t tell me what the surprise is. I’ve never been the biggest fan of surprises. Still, I comply, she loops her arm in mine, and we take slow steps down the tunnel until she tells me to open my eyes. When I do, I see the most beautiful setup. The room is filled with tall, cylindrical tanks with various jellyfish that look like they are glowing under the water. All across the room, fairy lights are placed carefully to create a cozy, dimly lit environment. In the middle of the room, there is a table set up for two, fake candles are in the center, and plates set around them piled with sushi. “I promise it was brought out here five minutes ago; it’s fresh.” She looks nervous, so I hold her hand and brush her cheek with my lips. Somehow, she makes it even better; she clicks a button and music starts pouring out, slow romantic songs making the entire thing feel infinitely more intimate. It has to be the most thought someone has ever put into a date for me. I felt lucky when my ex-girlfriend booked a reservation.

“It is perfect, thank you. " Her smile glows brighter than the jellyfish. She pulls out my chair before sitting in her own. The sushi spread is delicious, a tasty note that fades in the background. All of my focus is on her, talking and laughing about life and the exhibition tomorrow. She told me about her frustrations with our mutual agent, how she wants to be unknown, and is worried about the interview Britt mentioned. “I’m sure it will be fine.”

“I’m not so sure. She never just drops something like that. Not that easily. I’m scared she’ll do it anyway.” She plays with her hands and places her chopsticks down for now.

"She is a good agent, it will be fine. I am going to check out your exhibition, though." Her cheeks flush so damn red, I wish I could have that color bottled.

"I hope you like it." I think her blush gets deeper.

"Well, my next exhibition, which I just booked a new one for this winter, has a lot of your paintings in it already. I think you might be my muse." I say. Josephine has been all I have wanted to paint lately, the image of her seared into my brain, compelling me to paint her again and again.

"Your muse?" Her chin barely drops, and she looked legitimately surprised. I don't see how. I think she would be anyone's inspiration.

"Well, look at you, at that figure. Who *wouldn't* want a painting of you on their walls?" She dips her sushi in some soy sauce and quickly takes a bite, her slight smile showing through even that. The song on the speaker changes, a new slow love song coming through. She gracefully gets up from her chair and offers me her hand.

"Would you like to dance with me?" I nod, my own blush creeping across my face. I give her my hand, and she takes me over to an opening in the room. We settle into a rhythym and she places her arms around my neck, mine are draped across her waist. I can't let go of her eyes, they look so deep I could fall in.

As I lean in closer to her, her pupils dilate, and I feel her warm breath against me. I pull my lip into my mouth, dropping it at the moment she gives in, and our lips meet. I can't stop kissing her, we forget the dancing and the music becomes the backdrop to our embrace. She moves to hold my head closer to hers, my tongue passing across the seam of her mouth, the taste of her lipstick coming through with the saltiness of the soy sauce barely creeping past her plump lips. Josephine's teeth tug gently at my lip, and I can't help the needy moan that leaves my own. I make myself step away before I drop to my knees and eat her out in this very room.

"Your kisses are addictive," I murmur, my lips tracing the shell of her ear.

"Good, because I don't want to stop kissing you. Every time I see you, it's as if there are magnets pulling us together." She leans in to give me one more light peck before leading me back to our table. The rest of the night finishes beautifully. We finish up at the aquarium, and afterwards she sits in the car with me to take me home. One kiss later, and I'm left floating on a cloud thinking about the night. A whole ass aquarium date at night. Who does that? And why do I feel like a teenager again?Feelings are weird.

20

Muse

Josephine

Tonight is the last night of her exhibition at the Dimont Center. Going to the building is always bittersweet. My cousin's family runs it, but they never stayed close enough to pass down my secret. It is like a reunion that only I know is happening. My cousin Edmund and his wife Margot opened it up 5 years after I was turned. They have kept it in the family ever since; their grandchild, Patrick, owns it now. Margot loved the arts. I was their very first artist to be on exhibition. She had begged her husband to let her have an art exhibition one weekend every quarter. Edmund agreed; he always adored her. He would look at her like she was the most precious thing in existence.

Back then, the building was an events center, not the communal workplace it is now. I think they changed that within the last few years, but they still keep her tradition alive. Thankfully, I would have been devastated if my friend's passion was lost to time like she was. We were such close friends. I didn't leave my bed for a month after she died. She had the simple diagnosis of old age. Edmund never cared for me as much after I had been turned; he certainly didn't trust me around their kids. I never got to know them, so with Margot, that part of my family died as well.

It takes a few deep breaths and a chug from my bottle to get through the door. It is like I can still feel and see her along the walls from that night.

1955

I was wearing my pink silk evening gown, which I had just bought for the event. It hugged my curves, with elegant draping around my hips. I wanted to look perfect for the black tie event, but back then, my identity as the artist was already hidden. I couldn't appear in pictures, so no one could realize they were photographing the artist. They all assumed I was a man irregardless. Margot looked stunning; she had a beautiful gown made with black silk and wore her diamonds proudly. We drank champagne all night, and I even nibbled on some of the cheese. The beautiful crystal chandelier sprayed rainbow slivers of light across my photographs, giving them an extra little glow. I was drawn to the shimmers.

Margot and I had found a bench to sit on, talking about everything under the sun and the moon. From how I was handling the turn to how well the center had come together. She was one of my best friends. She had even wanted to turn after she had her children, but Edmund refused. He thought the turning was evil, that it implanted a shard of true horrors into you.

I remember getting so drunk that it made me wobbly, a hard feat for the undead. My sister had come halfway through the night, and she hardly got to look at the pictures before taking me home. Margot didn't understand why the transition was so hard for me. How could she have? She was lucky; she hadn't been taken from the street and changed. Yet she wanted that taste of eternity.

Still, she was proud of me. Every last picture sold. In the decades that followed, I had an exhibition every year or so. Until Margot died. My sister went to all of my exhibitions, big or small. Until she died, too.

As I enter the building, it is clear how much it has changed over the years. The chandelier is gone. The walls have lost their gilded touches. It is more box-like and sterile now, the grayification of the modern world. The charm that was so painstakingly crafted is like a distant memory now. Even the smell is different, I can still picture the tobacco the men smoked mingling with the florals from the various perfumes. That's when I found my signature, lilacs, lilies of the valley, and a bit of vanilla.

One thing stayed the same. A photograph of Edmund and Margot by the entrance, they looked young and happy. It was from that night, my first exhibition here. I took it before anyone else showed up. She said it was her favorite picture of herself, a smile stretches across my face, my heart warm with nostalgia. I'm glad it is still there. Suddenly, a pair of arms wrap around me, and a kiss is pressed to my temple.

"Hey there, I'm glad you could make it." I turn towards Gabby, and she is stunning. The event is black tie, as always. She is in a deep green gown with a V-neck that goes down to her stomach. Simply stunning. "Where did you get that dress? It is beautiful. It looks antique," she runs her fingers along the pink silk fabric, a gown I had to wear again for nostalgia's sake.

"It is, it is from 1955. It has stayed in my family since then." Not *technically* a lie. I am my own family afterall. "You are incredible." I lean in to give her a quick peck on the lips. That adorable flush comes back; I think my life's purpose may be to make her blush now.

"It is the same art from the show we met at." She changes the topic, looking around at her pieces on the walls. "Did you know the first artist here was a photographer like you? Apparently, he took that picture," her delicate hand points to the very picture I took of my cousins. The old rumor that my art was from a man continues. Why they never assumed a woman could do it always infuriated me; at least that element of misogyny is better now.

"I did, if you go back our family trees meet up." I hate these partial lies and half-truths, but I want her to know those parts of me, to not have it be all so surface-level. Give her those little nuggets of myself.

"That's so cool, I guess it is a family skill," she nudges me while her warm smile lights me up inside. Then she takes my hand to walk me around the room.

"Looks like you two made up," Britt comes over carrying three glasses of champagne that look like they are about to topple all over someone. Probably herself.

"We did, and you *know* that. We had the whole group chat texting about it." I take two of the glasses from her before a spill of epic proportions happens, handing one to Gabby.

"The group chat? Anyone want to fill me in??" Gabby asks, good natured chidding in her tone.

"My friends and me. Britt, Christopher, and Michael. You'll meet those two dumbasses at some point."

"I'm absolutely telling them you said that." With that, Britt is pulling out her phone.

“No, no, no, no. They will *kill* me.” I reach for her arm, gripping her wrist while I frantically shake my head.

“No, they won’t. Michael will just tease you for all eternity, and Christopher will act like the know-it-all he already is.”

“So, virtually death, but never-ending.” I sigh dramatically and lean my head into Gabby’s shoulder, causing her to laugh. “I promise, they are next level. I remember when they got together, and the sheer amount of personality in the room was overwhelming.”

“I believe you,” her lips seal her statement with a peck on my cheek.

“They grow on you,” Britt adds in

“Like a fungus. I do love them dearly, though, fungus qualities and all. They are practically brothers to me, and Britt, if you text them anything, it had better be that last comment.” I wag a finger in her direction.

“Oh, it is all going to them.” I give her an are you kidding me look as she dramatically hits send. My phone promptly dings.

“Look at what you did! Michael said ‘Josie,’ which is already bad; he knows I hate that. ‘Josie, are we siblings now? You little amanita death cap you. A dumbass wouldn’t know that.’ with a winky face. Then Christopher said, ‘You saved yourself with the brothers comment, but I promise to bring my A game in trivia night to kick your ass into next week.’ Do you see what you did?” Britt is dying of laughter, and Gabby is giggling too. Traitors, both of them.

“I want to go to trivia night!” Gabby says between the music of her laugh.

“We have it once a month. It does tend to be chaotic, though.”

“And I want to go.” Her smile is so bright, how could I ever say no to her? I just need to figure out how to hide our supernatural inclinations.

“We run ours a little differently than most of them.”

“How so?”

“Okay, so, everyone comes with their own set of questions to ask, highest total score wins. It is like 20 questions per person, so with you, we would be up to 100 total, best score out of 80. It is *so* fun, we will have a blast with you there." Britt breaks into her entire spiel, going through all of the rules of trivia night.

"Well, it is decided, I'm coming, and I'm going to bring some seriously cool facts." Gabby reaches for my hand again and gives it a squeeze. "If you'll excuse us, though, I want to walk around the exhibition with my *girlfriend*." My heart flutters in my chest.

"Girlfriend?" I ask once we move away from Britt.

"If that's okay with you?" She quickly faces me, a hint of worry creeping across her face.

"More than okay. Especially since I have the most beautiful woman on my arm, *and* she is my girlfriend, *and* she is an incredibly talented artist." Her cheeks darken again. I think it is the best, most beautiful color I've ever seen, besides her eyes.

"I did add one extra painting," we take a few steps forward, and Gabby gestures to a new painting, the one she did of me in the green lingerie with the title *Muse*. "Do you like it?"

“I don’t think I have ever looked better.” All I can do is give her hand a squeeze and look at the art she created of me. Yet she is still the most gorgeous piece in the room.

21

Secrets

Josephine

I really don't want to go back to the Council today. Not after my last visit. But I'm low on blood, and the guys will be there. I think I need a little friend time. I have had my last few weeks wrapped up in Gabby. I love it. But I also love time with those two, and I have been severely lacking that. They keep me grounded, I think. Having friends who are in my position, who will never die, it is a sense of normalcy and level of consistency I haven't found elsewhere. Just them and my art.

I quickly throw on some clothes, for once I'm not feeling the need to have my armour on. I feel good. It has been a long time since I have felt like this. I'm happy I agreed to actually try. I practically have to gush about her, and I can't wait to do exactly that. My basic sundress, heels, and signature red lipstick are all I need. I do bring a large bag to hold the blood bags when I come home, though. I race my way to the Council building. Pushing through the doors is like submerging yourself in calm after the chaos of the world. The rec room is filled with other vampires tonight. Laughter and chatting come from every direction. Suddenly, I notice a hand waving at me from across the room.

"Hello, you two," I give each of my friends a kiss on the cheek and a quick hug.

"You have gone MIA on us, Josie," Michael says, already hitting me with the damn nickname.

"The name is Josephine, and you know it. And sorry about that. I think I've been wrapped up in that new relationship high. She called me her girlfriend at her exhibition the other week," my smile stretched across my face, I can feel myself beaming. I have hardly seen the guys since then, only once or twice for photo shoots. "Besides, you haven't exactly been around a lot with whoever this woman is." They had canceled our last game night because they were wrapped up in her.

"That's so exciting," Christopher's body relaxes in relief that I didn't fuck it up again. Understandably, after the whole running incident. He also conveniently forgets to mention his own relationship. So secretive.

"It really is. I am kind of thinking about telling her." I shift my weight around and play with my hands

"That's huge." Christopher's eyes go wide in surprise.

"More than huge, Josie, that's serious. You must really like her."

"It's Josephine. I don't like lying to her. I trust her too. And I think I might also be falling for her, is that crazy? I just need to think of the right moment, the right way to tell her." I take a seat next to them, calling over a familiar to bring me a wine and blood mix. I need something to do with my hands.

"I mean, you're both artists." Michael shrugs like he is saying something that should be obvious.

"Soooo?"

"Soooo, why don't you go to an art class for something *besides* painting and photography. Pottery or candle making, something artsy. Tell her after."

"That's actually a really good idea." I run through the different art-based businesses in town. Jewelry, candle-making shops, paint your own pottery, wood carving, mosaics, and glass blowing. If there is an art form, Noxdale probably has a class about it.

"I do have some of them." He rolls his eyes. I lean over to give him a hug, even with his dramatics, he returns it.

"We have a friend who runs a candle workshop. Want me to set something up for next weekend? She is out of town right now, so it can't really be sooner than that." Christopher grabs out his phone, already knowing I'll agree.

"You're the best. Let me know when and I'll get everything else planned." I pull him in for a hug as well. I have the best friends.

"No problem."

"There was a bit of an incident while you were in your little love bubble." Michael's voice sounds tense; he generally hides his pain under humor, so hearing the difference in his speech is concerning.

"Is everything alright?" Unease paints my own voice.

"Maybe? It's Britt."

"What now?" I love her dearly, but she has certainly perfected her own brand of chaos, and I don't think I can handle more of it at the moment.

"She mentioned she has an interview about you, and that we aren't supposed to tell you. Which absolutely means you told her not to, and we definitely have to tell you." Michael looks like he is bracing for impact. I down the blood in my hand and raise it for another.

"I don't want my identity to be known. When we talked, I explicitly said to her that this could ruin everything." My hands drop to my head. What am I supposed to do? "When is this apparently happening?"

"Right before your exhibition." Christopher is seething, his cold brand of rage coiling just beneath the surface. "I knew you had told her no. But hearing it confirmed, it only makes it worse."

"I knew she dropped it too quickly." I hate that my gut was right. I should be able to *trust* her with this. Like I have with everything else.

"Why the long face? Aren't you having fun with your little human pet?" The shrill voice of the she-demon known as Beverly meddles in the conversation.

"Go back to the hole you crawled out of." Michael's arms cross his chest defensively, clearly not in the mood for her shit either.

"Beverly. You know, I did hear a rumor when I was coming in, perhaps you can tell me if it's true or not. One of the people you revealed the secret to, one of them that was turned, is being held in custody? Apparently, Theo has had to be *rough* on him." Her rage isn't veiled at all; she doesn't attempt to. No matter how much shit she spews, she can never handle any of it being thrown her way. Fangs peak from behind her lips, her eyes are almost red with anger, but one shot of blood and they are back to normal.

"That's right," Christopher chimes in. "Didn't he threaten to tell our secret? Even being a vampire himself? Seems like he is willing to put every last one of us in danger. Maybe we look upset because we have to deal with the stress of your inadequacies." If looks could kill, his would, like an icicle stabbed through the jugular. Brutal and cold. She walks away from us in a huff, evidently, the rumor was true. If it were false, she would have loved nothing more than to gloat and tell us exactly why we were wrong. I turn to glance at Theo across the room and try to tune into his words, curious about the situation.

"He has been on a continuous cycle. Have you ever skinned a vampire alive? It regrows by the time you've finished a section. I've had to switch to a silver blade to make it stick for a while. That bitch Beverly has stuck me with a massive problem. Two actually. De Medici is breathing down my neck to do *more*. I thought I was being cruel, she told me to stick needles in his-" I shake my head, quickly averting my attention elsewhere. The torture talk never sat right with me. Disturbingly, it is a part of the Council's strategy for handling any security risks. And Theo is good at his job. Too good.

The Council has laws, from major to minor. Each are created by the different levels of it, from local to regional, to national, to global. De Medici controls the Regional Council; she controls this entire section of the country, but her Council building itself is the main victim of her iron fist. The biggest rules come down to who you can tell: family, the most serious of relationships, or the people you want to turn. The other major ones are no killing humans, no turning without consent unless it saves a life or protects the secret, no feeding from humans without consent, and no killing each other unless it is to save yourself or save the secret. Any breach of the rules can result in any number of punishments; it all depends on what the Council wants to do with you. It could be torture, imprisonment, execution, or, if you're lucky, a warning. Warnings are few and far between.

Beverly has to be in hot water with the Council. Especially if her fledgling vamp is trying to spill. I can only imagine the disarray the world would fall into if they knew about us. There would be fear, potentially death. It can be a big burden to bear knowing the actual world isn't what humans think it is. That some of the things they read about in their scary "fictional" books are real. That we live among them every single day. Except we don't say boo. Or "I vant to suck your blood." So many stereotypes.

22

Falling

Gabby

Next weekend I have something planned for us, I'll text you the address

Josephine

I can't wait!

Every time she has planned a date, it has been incredible. The aquarium, a date on the pier to go on the Ferris wheel and play games until our arms were full with prizes, carriage rides through the park with snow cones, picnics under the stars up on an overlook, and art exhibitions across the city. She keeps it interesting, and I keep lapping it up. In the moments we are away from each other we have been diving into our next collections. More and more paintings of her pile up in my studio. She has posed for a few of them on nights when we don't go out. Whenever I finish her face we start talking about life, art, and the world around us. Others I have made from memory, and the other paintings strewn about. It has felt like I'm living in a fantasy.

What kind of food do you
want next weekend?

Josephine

Every time she asks, I swear she writes down all of my favorite foods and places; she always makes sure to stop *somewhere* I like. Whether she asks about a new place or takes me to my favorites, she remembers my Chinese order even, she had it for us to eat on one of our picnics. Every single thing I ordered. Even my favorite flower, peonies, she gives them to me on every date. She dotes on me. I paint her tiny little trinkets, making her a variety of small paintings with the extra money I have. Her smile is massive whenever she gets one. She essentially has a gallery wall started of my paintings. Each of them our own brand of remembering.

Whatever you want. We always get my favorites.

Because I'm taking you out. Now what are you thinking of?

Josephine

Greek?

Sounds good little owl, I'll make the reservation.

Josephine

I can't wait to see what it will be this time

Unfortunately, I will actually have to wait; she at most gives me an address to meet at, and it's seldom where we are going, or maybe a cryptic clue. Otherwise, the only info she tells me is the date, the time, and the dress code. I think I kind of love the surprise. It is a weird feeling, enjoying surprises. They normally have my anxiety on high, some bullshit I'm sure comes from my parents surprising me with a new country to live in, with little to no warning. But I *know* Josephine will only have good surprises for me. She makes sure every date is something that will make me smile. It feels good. Apparently, she has to talk to Britt today, but I don't want to be alone when I could be with her. So I call up Megan.

Hey girl, wanna come over
while I paint?

Yeah, be there in an hour.
Just leaving the bfs' house

Megan

I still need deets btw

I have some, I promise

Megan

See you soon for those deets, let yourself in. I'll be painting

Bet

Megan

I sit down at my canvas. I'm filling in the background of the painting she posed for two days ago. She had chiffon draped over her, that's all. It went from one shoulder and ended up only covering her breasts and between her legs in a sheer covering of black fabric. She was standing in the studio, looking like a statue. One of her hands is gripped around a raised wine glass filled with a deep red wine, the other is hanging gracefully at her side. She is looking off in the distance, not quite a profile but not straight forward either. Every inch of her is perfection. The background has already been sketched out with hardwood floors, and an orangey-red wall with a sparkling chandelier, and matching crystal vases on simple tables in the background. I matched her lipstick shade for the wall, wanting to bring in her iconic color. I don't think I've ever seen her without it. It is just *her*. And I think I might be falling for her.

Too soon.

Right?

It has to be; it would be insane to feel that way already, it's only been a few weeks. Either way, I can't stop thinking about her. Or painting her. Or talking to her. I can't envision my life without her either. I want her in *every* sense of the word. I want to know every part of her. Every single piece of her that makes her soul light up, that gives her life. Bit by bit, I think I'm getting to see that part of her.

The door opens and draws me out of my fantasies, all while my brush continues its meditative strokes while I paint the wall. Shading the edges and creating the shadows across it. Her lips matching exactly with the background.

"That looks hot," Megan says as she drags a chair up next to mine. "I'd kill for those tits."

“Oh, please, you have a great body.” I may have more feelings than I know what to do with for Josephine, but no one can tell me that my friend isn’t hot, too. Normally, I think she recognizes it too, but who doesn’t have doubts every now and again? Especially growing up in the era of skinny women still being called fat, if you weren’t their definition of perfect, you were shamed

“Yeah, but not *that* kind of body. I’m all pear-shaped. My booty is fire, but it feels unbalanced.”

“You don’t look unbalanced. I’m a stick.” I pick the nicer insult I have had thrown my way. I’ve been called a skeleton, skin and bones, or any number of insults for being thin. People seem to want to put women down for their bodies, no matter how those bodies look. That’s why I like my art, a variety of shapes, sizes, abilities, ethnicities, just showing their beauty as a whole.

“Please, you look like a model. You’re rocking that whole runway vibe.”

“Maybe we need to agree that we are both hot, we just aren’t our own type.”

"Maybe you're right." Megan grabs a snack from her purse and starts crunching on a pretzel. I pick up my brush again and focus on creating the shadows that will appear when I paint the crystal vases over the backdrop. Finishing those up, I move on to paint the light that would refract through them, mostly bright highlights but with a hint of a rainbow edge to them. I want the painting to look as magical as she does. "So, you wanted deets?"

"Desperately. I *need* them." I bite my lip as I focus on making sure the highlights are flawless.

"Let's just say that trivia night in four weeks has an extra person." Her expression is pure mischief. I whip my head in her direction as she smiles cheekily.

"*What*?"

"Well, remember how the last one with your girl got canceled because the guys were busy?" She leans forward, still keeping her cheeky grin on her face.

"Yeah, I was disappointed." I was looking forward to it. Who wouldn't want to meet their girlfriend's friends *and* kick their asses at their own game?

"It was busy because they were railing me." Her eyebrows wiggle as she smiles, clearly happy with those two.

"Wait, so these mysterious guys you've been seeing are my girlfriend's best friends?" And neither of us knew? They must have kept the details locked down.

"Wild, isn't it? When I found out, I thought it was a small fucking world too. But, either way, next time we have trivia night I'm kicking all of your asses." She tosses a pretzel into her mouth and leans back, prematurely triumphant. I flip my middle finger up at her.

"Bring it on, me and Josephine are going to bring the heat."

"You're on bitch." We hold an intense stare for a few seconds before we both break into laughter. The laughter doesn't subside until our bellies are aching and we have tears to wipe from our eyes. I turn back to my painting and keep up the paint strokes, making the wall come to life little by little, all while trying not to start giggling again. "Have you painted anyone besides her lately?"

“No. I can’t think of anyone I would rather paint if I’m being honest. I think I’m kind of falling in love.” Admitting it out loud has me freezing, my paintbrush pressed on the canvas mid-stroke.

“It is about damn time. Are you going to tell her?”

“Maybe on our date next week, she is planning something special. I have had this feeling that she wants to tell me something. I kind of think she might be planning to do that, too. What about you and your boy toys?”

“You know me, I’m not saying it first.” Megan shrugs and glances off to the side.

“So you want them to tell you.”

“Well, obviously. We have been dating for as long as you have.” She crunches another pretzel.

“True. How is it going by the way?”

“Really well. The guys are amazing. It has been *slow* for me, though. I mean, not the sex, that part is fucking fantastic. Emotionally, though.” Hearing my best friend talk about being in love, even if she won’t say the words, is like I've been dropped in a parallel universe. *And* too slow emotionally? They must mean the world to her.

"What do you mean?"

"They are kind of guarded. They still give me a lot of care and attention, but they have these walls up. I'm not even officially their girlfriend, even though we spend most nights together. It is frustrating. It is like I'm always there and with them, but not fully *with* them yet."

"That whole group is guarded."

"Unfortunately, I think you're right. And it's some bullshit."

"I'll drink to that."

"I'll grab the vodka." Shit. Apparently, we are literally drinking to that. I clean up my paints while she pours us each a double shot to start off the debauchery.

23

Revelations

Josephine

Time to talk to my niece. Again. I show up at her apartment a few blocks from my own and try to steel my nerves and cool my temper all at once.

"Hey, Auntie," she beams at me, clearly not knowing her little game has been revealed.

"We need to talk. Now." I shove her to the side, not needing an invitation as I'd been there before. I point to her chair and say, "Sit your ass down now. You have some things to explain." At my words, recognition flashes across her face

"Auntie, it really isn't a big deal. It will help both of us out."

"It could lead to people being killed, Brittany. Killed. It could have vampires getting staked, and it could have you land your ass in the interrogation cells. Do you even comprehend that? Having this damn interview could *end* your *life*. It isn't just a career move. It is potential death and torture for who knows how many individuals." I can't control my rage at this point. I can feel my fangs protruding, a sign that my rage has gotten too high. I take a swig of my blood to help stop the boiling of my own. Once a vampire loses full control, they can go into blood lust. No one wants that. Not everyone can be brought back from it either. My fangs sink back in, but I am still shaking. "I am trying to protect you."

"Auntie, I-"

"No. Brittany, this is not up for discussion. You *cannot* have this interview. Cancel it now."

"I'm not canceling it, Auntie. This could propel my career. I love you and representing you, but I also want clients I can show off. Ones that can make it big. I want *more.*"

"I want more for you, too, just not like this. So I suggest you change your mind, for everyone's sake." My fangs are threatening to pop out again, and I tip my bottle back again, trying to calm down enough.

"I'm not going to reveal your secret." She appears offended that I would think she could reveal it. If only it were that simple.

"You better hope you don't. No one can protect you if you do. No one would be able to protect any of us." I storm towards the door, turning around at the last moment. "Unless it is canceled, don't bother showing up at my place. I can't afford to let a threat in." With that, I leave the apartment and slam the door, ignoring the streams of tears down her face. She can't expect more. She won't get any better treatment if she ends up in Theo's grasp. I chug the rest of my bottle to try and ease the temper that has been rising in my veins. I yank out my phone as I race to a little bar near Gabby's house, it rings one, two, three-

"Hey, muse," her sweet voice comes through the phone.

"Can you meet me at Greg's? I need to be around someone that makes me happy. I need to be around you." I try to hide the pained sound in my voice, but I can't. The sky begins to rumble, and rain starts coming down in sheets, and I'm drenched to the bone with only a block to go. I decide to slow down and enjoy the feeling of being caught in the storm when everything feels like it could fall apart. My life. My relationship once I tell Gabby *what* I really am, the career I love so much. It's all on the brink of ruin.

"Of course I can. Are you okay?"

"No," the word comes out in laughs. I just can't stop laughing. The clothes feel too wet and sticky against my skin. The smell of the rain providing a soothing undercurrent to the thoughts in my head, and a pathetic attempt at concealing the smell of piss and cheap beer from the bar. "I feel like life is falling to pieces and I'm not sure what to do."

"I'll be right there. I can hear the rain. Head inside before you get sick, and I'll be there. I just have to call a car over here for Megan." The water from my eyes starts to blend in with the drops hitting my face with more force than I thought they could. "It is going to be okay."

"Okay." I hang up and start to take slow steps to the building. Greg's is a shitty bar, people like to drink until they are so wasted that their equally drunk friends have to try and carry them out while they also stumble. It isn't the best place. But right now, I don't want to be in a perfect, happy place; I can't fake it enough. I reach the bar with its once nice wood falling to pieces and take a seat on the ripped bar stool, placing my purse on one next to me, making sure I can keep one hand on it. I remember when it was new a few decades ago. Back then, it had been considered a nice spot to grab a cocktail with friends, not the debauchery it is known for now.

"Tequila," I say. I don't know how I would begin to force myself to make a more complicated order or bring out any typical niceties this time.

“Starting a tab?” He looks somewhat bored as he dries a glass with his towel. Like he sees people’s lives falling apart every day. A quick glance around tells me he really might.

“Yeah.” He nods and pours me out a shot, and I down it before he can get the salt and lime out. “Another one, please.” There, a bit nicer.

“You want a few right away?” I nod, and he takes out two more glasses and fills them up. I take each one down the line, trying to have enough in my system to feel it.

“Looks like you’re drinking enough for a whole party,” Gabby’s voice floats my way, and she leans in to give me a kiss; her own breath smells like vodka. “How are you holding up?” I move my bag for her, and she sits down next to me and takes my hand.

“Well, I’ve been here for only a few minutes, and I’ve had four shots.” Her eyes go wide, and she nods.

“Pour me one too. In all honesty, I had a double back home. I was trying to paint, but I think Megan wanted to get drunk.”

“She’s on my tab.” The bartender nods and pours her a shot. Gabby waits for the salt and lime before taking it and giving her head a little shake at the end.

“I love tequila, but I’m not sure it loves me. This one has some kick back.”

“It is really bad tequila. Another round for us, please.” And he does. She takes her one, and I take my three.

“We are good for now.” She has the bartender leave, and I look at her to protest. The alcohol hasn’t affected me yet. It takes significantly more to impact a vampire than it does a human. “Sweetie, I think 7 shots in 10 minutes is more than enough. What happened?”

“Britt.”

“She kept the interview?”

“And she is going to cause people to be seriously hurt because of it.” The tears start again, and I wish I could stop them.

“Why would they be hurt?” I try to think of how to tell her without directly saying the words out loud.

"Something about me, something I want to tell you about after our date next week. Some people just don't understand when someone is different. They get angry, they get *violent*."

"You can tell me whenever you want, you know that, right?"

"I do. I—it is personal, and I want the night to be perfect, something meaningful. And maybe I'm worried you will react badly. Like Amanda." I shift my gaze downwards, trying not to let the insecurity be so plainly visible in public, but I can't help it; it shows anyway.

"So it's about that. Both the thing you want to tell me and this Britt thing?"

"Yes." I play with the strap of my purse, nervous to tell her. Nervous to not tell her.

"I'm not going to run away." She grabs my arm and gazes at me with affection, affection I'm not sure I deserve, having kept this part of myself to myself. "You can tell me."

"Not here, I can't." Her mouth turns in a lopsided half smile.

"I understand. Just know I love you," her eyes widen in surprise, not the confession she intended to make. My own heart skips a beat, suddenly bringing out a smile I didn't think I could have tonight.

"I love you too." I lean in and press my lips to hers softly. When I lean back, we are both smiling. She loves me.

"Let's get you home so we can talk, yeah?" She waves the bartender over, and we close the tab.

As we start to gather our things to leave, a man walks over to the bar. His breath smells like cheap beer and cigarettes. He is short in stature, balding, and has an unnaturally orange spray tan. His entire energy gives slimey douche bag as he stares us up and down, staring far too long at our bodies. What a creep.

"Hey, ladies," he tries to look like he has some level of game. He does not, in fact, have game. "My name's Ric, with a 'C', who might you be?" Gabby and I catch each other's gaze and break out laughing.

"Ric with a C? What kind of douchey ass nickname is that? Was Dick already taken?" Gabby's comment only makes me laugh harder.

"Seriously, who goes by that?" I look my love in her eyes before turning back to the douche in question. "Were you trying to sound cool? Had to be so different you lost the K? Do we really look like the kind of women who would be impressed by that?"

"You bitches don't know what you're missing." He taps his hands to his chest like he is some big, bad, tough guy. I could topple him with my finger, even before I turned.

"What? Three inches and three seconds? We'll be fine. Come on, babe, let's go to your place." Gabby grabs my hand, and we walk out of there, leaving him to sputter his rage at the bar. The bartender even barks a laugh as we exit. I'm assuming this isn't the first time Ric with a C has gotten told off. We quickly take a ride share to my place.

* * *

"The rain is really coming down," Gabby says as she gets a blanket to wrap me up once I change. Her worry visible in her dotting. On the ride over, she said a few times that she was worried I would get sick. I couldn't tell her yet that I *can't,* sickness doesn't work the same for my kind.

"It is. Can you believe that creep?"

"The way he was staring at your boobs. I wanted to punch him in his smug face." We laugh and scootch closer to each other, the tone suddenly shifting to something more serious. "You can trust me."

"I do." I mean it more than I ever thought I could. I trust her, I'm just scared.

"Then please tell me, I can lift off some of that weight."

"I love you," I say as I curl into her shoulder.

"I love you too." She rubs my back as I take a deep breath.

"I'm not exactly human." The fear coursing through my veins as I confess to her, I think my heart stops beating. The fear of rejection is one powerful thing, and I hate it.

"What do you mean? You look human to me." She gives me a playful pinch.

"I'm a vampire." I pull back and stare into her eyes. She gives a little laugh, like it is a joke, before her face falls.

"Oh, you're serious."

"Follow me," I gulp down my nerves and take her hand and lead her to my wine cellar. She hesitantly follows behind. One thing I've never let her go in is the small fridge in there, where I started storing my blood bags when she came over more and more. I open the door so she can see my stash of them.

"Is that blood?" She sounds shocked. I nod and grab one out and take a sip while it is still cold, so my fangs pop out, and I open my mouth to let her see. Her eyes widen, her shock on full display, and she reaches a hand to me. "Can I touch them?" I nod again, and she touches them and tries to carefully pull on them, like I managed to slide on a prosthetic. As the effect of the blood fades, my fangs sink back to normal, and she jumps back. "Holy shit, you're a vampire." I only nod once more, unsure of what to say at first. We simply stand there.

“Please don’t be scared. I wouldn’t hurt you, I love you, I just want you to know me.”

“I need time to think. Time to process.” She says, I gulp again and nod. She takes a step back, and my mind flashes back to the rooftop all those years ago.

“I get it. Learning we exist is kind of a shock.” I try to stay still, but I want to reach out to her and bring her to me, to comfort her.

“Understatement of the year. I’m going to go home and think. I’ll text, okay?” She takes another step back.

“Okay, I love you, Gabby.” I need her to know that I *love* her.

“I love you too,” and she turns to hurry from my apartment. I wish I could get rid of the sinking feeling that she may never come back, and I could have lost the best thing to ever happen to me because I told her the truth.

24

Research and Running

Gabby

Holy shit. My girlfriend is a vampire. I can scarcely think the entire ride home, or I think too much. Everything feels like a blur to the point that I can't even tell which. My girlfriend is a fucking *vampire*. She isn't even alive. She has *fangs*. She drinks literal blood.

I try to rack my brain to think of any signs I missed. The most glaring one is that we have never gone out during the day. I mean, I'm a night owl, but holy shit, that's a different level. She doesn't have any social media. No pictures of herself. She never talks about specific years in her past. The antiques I've seen scattered throughout her home, I assumed they were ones she had bought or heirlooms, not things she has always owned. I try to remember if I have ever seen her in a mirror, and I can't. I feel like I only know a fraction of her.

I think I still love her. But I know that I don't *know* her anymore.

I pull up my laptop and start researching vampires. Some of the things don't make sense in regards to her. Some sources say they are evil or demons. That isn't her. She is sweet; she *hates* death. They talk about drinking blood and killing people. I can't *picture* her taking someone's life. They can't appear in pictures and mirrors. I still rack my brain for any moment in front of a mirror, but I don't think I would have paid attention to that. Super speed and super strength were mentioned, too. If that's real, I kind of want to see her do that. Is it all real? Fake? Will silver actually burn her? No, it can't. She wears silver jewelry sometimes. Maybe it's not actually silver?

I think my brain is melting.

I wish I could call Megan about this, but I can't. She is already worried about Britt spreading her secret. I can't be the same. Especially knowing *what* that secret is.

Shit. She wants to do an interview about Josephine. And she *knows*. I need to talk to her.

"Hey, how's it going?"

"Josephine told me," I tell her. Britt's gasp is audible through the call. "Before you ask, I'm still processing. But please, please don't do that interview. I know you want to help, but she is terrified. *Please*."

"Gabby, I'm glad my aunt told you. And honestly, after tonight, I have been thinking about canceling it. I'm just not sure. It would boost my career so much, but you get it. Either way, I wouldn't share the fact that she is a vampire."

"Your aunt?" More and more revelations show that I don't know my girlfriend as well as I thought. The feeling is cataclysmic.

"Shit, she didn't tell you that?"

"We didn't exactly make it past the fangs bit. I needed to process, I ran."

"Well, um, she's actually my great, great aunt. Her sister was my great-grandma." I didn't even consider the fact that they were related. But I feel stupid not recognizing it. They have the same straight, black hair and pale complexion. Their faces have similar features. Even their figures are similar, both have an hourglass shape, just a different size. They look so similar, and I never noticed.

"Good to know. Please, Britt, cancel it and talk to her."

"I've got this." Then the line disconnects.

Suddenly, I remember Josephine telling me she is related to the Dimonts. I go back to the laptop and search for Dimont on some genealogy website. Edmund and Margot Dimont opened the center originally. I click on his expanded family tree first, and there I see her name: Josephine Beauchamp. Edmund's cousin. Her mother and his father were siblings. Elizabeth Dimont married Henri Beauchamp in 1919. They had five children. Only three survived to adulthood. Mary was born in 1921 and died in 2004. Josephine in 1923. And their brother Louis in 1927.

There is a photograph someone found of her. It is dated to 1947. She was 24 in it. It's the face of the woman I have fallen for. I click on her profile to learn more. She had gotten a high school diploma, no college education. She appeared in a few newspapers for her photography and her family's business ventures.

There was an article with an artist J. L. Beauchamp, but saying the artist chose not to attend, an artist the article assumed was a man. Something tells me that's not entirely accurate, the picture from the center flashing in my mind. The last piece of information on her that is listed was her brother's obituary from 1952. She was listed as part of his remaining family, that he died in the war. Her father was already dead by that point, too. She really has lost almost everyone in her life.

Then I ran away too.

I'm still processing. Just reminding you I love you, I'm not running.

The guilt of running, of being afraid like her last partner was, eats at me. I made her feel just as rejected.

I love you too. Whenever you want to talk I am always here for you.

Josephine

I debate texting her back. I wonder if I'll ever be able to handle it. But for now, I choose to put my phone down and dive into more research.

25

Shut Down

Josephine

Receiving her text sends a wave of calm through me. The tequila is still coursing through my veins, making the entire world feel off, mainly because I drank more once she left. In one night, I almost went into blood lust over one of my closest friends and last member of my family, got tequila drunk, told my girlfriend I love her, told her I was a vampire, and then watched her walk out the door. It's like I have been whiplashed and that the entire world has shifted in one night, and I'm not sure what to do.

2007

I remember the days after she fell. I did nothing. I laid in bed crying until no more tears came out. Michael and Christopher brought me blood. They were there for me through every second. It was all a blur. I didn't change. Or shower. Or talk. I laid there comatose. I was basically a corpse that, for some reason, couldn't die no matter how much I begged for it.

Every death I've experienced has shut me down. The depression would strike, and I could hardly do anything. But that was the first death where it felt like it was my *fault. The guilt was undeniable, inescapable, and overwhelming. I couldn't cope at all. The entire time the world felt like nothing, yet oppressively too much. Like I was wholly in darkness, and the light was never going to be coming again.*

It feels pretty bleak right now, too. I heat some blood with some hot cocoa, my mother's recipe with my own twist, and curl up on my couch. I cry out all the tears I think exist in my body, my face gets puffy and red, and I think I depleted my tissue stash. Once I finish the drink, I lay on my couch watching comfort movies and reality TV to distract myself from the overwhelming amount of feelings inside of myself.

It brings its typical comfort, and by the time the sun rises, I'm no longer crying. I'm unsure about the future. Anxiety becomes the constant undercurrent instead of depression filling in any of the cracks. I shoot a quick text to the guys for them to come over later, barely checking their reply more than to see they said yes, before I throw on some cozy pajamas and curl up in my bed to sleep away the rest of my feelings.

* * *

Their words the next day bring their typical comfort. They reassure my fears about Britt, that Ric with a C is a creepy douche, and that Gabby will come back even though it hurts like hell. As my eyes stopped overflowing over a glass of one of their signature blood milkshakes, they went into premium distraction mode. Apparently, they are dating Gabby's best friend, and *she* will be at trivia night too. The stakes have just been raised; we are each on a mission to impress our humans. If mine ever talks to me again.

26

Sliced Bread

Gabby

Apparently, vampires can turn into bats. At least some websites say they do. Some say it's complete bullshit. I'm looking through every single story I can find about them and am trying to comb through it to find the grains of truth. Or grains of myth. I don't know really. Each one has another saying it is false.

None of the websites says *how* they were first created. I can't figure out why it bothers me so much, but I can't help but wonder what was the cause and *why* they exist. I've spent nearly a week locked up in my apartment researching. Every hour has been non-stop digging into the paranormal. I've read books on them, from fiction to supposed true histories. *Anything* I can get my hands on, to be honest. And yet I'm no closer to understanding than I was before.

My mind won't stop whirring. I haven't even picked up my paintbrushes. Instead, I've been locked in this hole of trying to decipher reality and fiction alike. I try not to go down this rabbit hole of what else could be real if vampires are. I don't think I want to know yet, but sometimes my brain goes there anyway. I try to shake it off and work on a piece, to focus on something other than what appears to be a wild goose chase. The painting is her, they all have been lately. This one focuses on her neck with fang marks in it and her jaw line, her lips, and her shoulders just in view. The bite mark leaves blood flowing down her pale skin.

I wonder if she was always pale. I think she was, but sometimes black and white photos distort that. She predates colored photography. I learned that in my research.

She is older than sliced bread.

I wish that was a joke. I'm dating a woman who is two years older than sliced bread, and yet she looks 27. My mind is completely boggled.

I want to see her.

I want to scream.

I want to hug her.

I want to stop overthinking.

I want to kiss her.

I want her to tell me it is a bad joke.

I want to *know* her.

I just want to be with her and to understand.

27

Dahlias

Josephine

Each day that passes is like a living hell. It has been almost a week, and Gabby has barely texted. I'm worried about her. I'm looking through her favorite restaurants and pull up the Chinese place, and add a bunch of her favorites to the cart and have it sent to her house. At least I'll know she is eating. Hopefully, she knows I'm thinking of her. I fill up my mug with more warm blood, trying to keep my heart rate down. It isn't working. I don't think I'll be able to exactly calm my anxiety down until I know she is okay. Not just physically, or even mentally. That she is okay with me. That I don't scare her.

The paintings from her are almost haunting in their torment of me. The large painting from her exhibition is hung in my bedroom now, a prominent display of her talent across from me whenever I try and sleep. I cleaned off a wall in my living room to fill with the small paintings she has made for me over the last few weeks, so even in there, I have no reprieve from how I have hurt her. How I scared yet another person I love.

I try to watch some shows and edit my photos. I feed the rays some snacks. Nothing is working. Nothing is okay right now. I decide I might as well wallow in it, and I bring out the photo albums from my human life. I turn through picture after picture of happiness and grief.

I guess my experience with grief started young. I remember my Mother and Father taking me to the cemetery to put flowers on the graves of the babies they lost on their death anniversaries. I still do it in place of my parents. I do it for my Mother, my Father, my brother and sister, Amanda and Margot too. More graves than that, if I'm being honest. Tomorrow is one of those nights. My sister Mary died when she was 83 in July of 2004. I already ordered the flowers. Every year, I get her favorite, orange dahlias.

I look at one of her pictures from when we were teenagers for a while, just looking at her. The two of us were going to a dance in town, they were always the best time. We were dressed in our nicest party dresses, hair curled to perfection. She was smiling so brightly she could have lit up the entire street. Mary was always so full of life. She was my best friend until the very end. Much to my dismay, she never wanted to be turned. I offered. I didn't want to live without her.

My heart skips ten beats when a thought of Gabby dying one day flashes through my mind. I don't want to lose her. Not to my vampirism, not to death, not to anything.

I wipe my tears away and turn through more pages of memories. There are lots of pictures from dances, both of myself and the other people at them. I miss being in pictures. There was always something so special about having a moment so completely captured, having that exact second of your existence frozen in time for eternity. I still like taking them for that reason, an impermanent moment made permanent. I just am unable to see myself in them. It stings. Life loves its irony. A vampire who loves photography, particularly self-portraits. My album is full of them.

De Medici didn't just take my mortal life; she took my favorite parts of my art and left me always searching to complete it.

* * *

Tonight is the night of my sister's death. The car ride to the quiet suburbs where the sprawling cemetery is takes forever. The night is unseasonably cool, so a light coating of mist settles over the hill. It looks downright Hollywood. I take a deep breath, my hand cinching around the dahlias a little tighter. My sister's grave is in the back, in the family crypt on the other end of the cemetery. Back when my family had it installed, it was new; the cemetery has slowly grown closer to the road.

The ground is squishy beneath my feet. I made sure to wear a chunky heel instead of my preferred stilettos, or I'd be sinking down into the earth. Reaching the crypt is always bittersweet. I miss them so much, but knowing they will never return is like a stab to my heart. Knowing I'll never join them there hurts just as much. The heavy stone door opens easily with my vampire strength. Once I have it open and the lamps from the pathways flood the crypt with dim light, I step inside. My parents had it built for them and their kids. There is a second one for my sister's family; she built it to last generations. She still wanted to be buried with our parents, though. I did too.

"Hi, Mother, Father, Louis, and Mary. Especially you, dear sister. I've missed you." I say, taking a seat on the bench in front of my sister's spot, holding the flowers for now. "I started seeing someone. You'd like her. She is beautiful, funny, kind, smart, and talented. She is like the sun. She even said she loves me." I run my hand along the smooth stone, giving her a sad smile. "I told her the secret. She says she is still processing. It's been stressful. I am hoping she is okay with it, with me. If she is, I'll bring her here for my next visit. I miss you, Mary. Not a day goes by that you're not on my mind."

I lean forward to put the flowers in her vase, arranging them so the circular pattern of the dahlias is showing out to anyone who may visit. I begin to hum our favorite song from when we were children. It was a little rhyme our Mother came up with about taking a boat to a new land. As a kid, I never realized it was the journey my own parents had taken as small children.

“And the boat comes up to the shore, the shore.” My voice breaks as I finish out the song. “A new land waits for us in the end, the end. A new adventure will begin, will begin. So I’ll see you on the shore, the shore.” I brush away the tear that has slipped down my face and blow a kiss to my sister. “I’ll see you soon, sister dear, I promise. I love you all.” I wave to them before exiting the crypt and closing it up. I call a ride share while I walk to the road, leaving behind my past yet again.

The loss never gets easier.

28

Bats

Gabby

I think I'm finally coming to terms with everything.

My girlfriend is a vampire. She drinks blood. She will never die.

It is a massive heaping pile of what the fuck, but I don't think I'm as scared anymore. I'm ready to learn more about it all, I think.

Almost.

I decide to take one more night to paint more, and I work on a personal collection. One I can't put on display because it shares her secret. Painting her again and again with her fangs out, the image of them is seared in my mind from her reveal. I have her in my typical sensual style; the eroticism is somehow only enhanced by the fangs. She is beautiful with them, like danger fully blended with grace. Even in the ones with a drop of blood hanging off the tip of the pearly spear.

I feel like I finally have my mojo back, like I am finally able to create again. I spend hours at the easel just sketching out various poses on different canvases and painting her body. I'll deal with the backgrounds another day. Right now, my focus is on her. I have been missing her like crazy. The other night she sent food here, my favorite order. My heart hurt when I got it, like I should be there with her instead.

I still needed more time.

I still do, I think. At least to paint my thoughts and feelings onto the canvas. No matter how scary the thought is, or was, I can't seem to paint her that way. Like some part of my soul is telling me not to worry, that she is still who I think she is. She is just not quite built the same as I am, or how I thought she was. With each painting I work on, a bit of the stress melts away. I go from a ball of anxiety to a woman who is simply missing the person she is in love with.

I take a quick break from painting to shoot her a text.

I miss you

Her response is almost immediate.

I miss you too. Are you okay?

Josephine

I think so. I want to talk about everything, I just have so many questions.

Anytime. I love you.

Josephine

I love you too. Does the day after tomorrow work? I have some paintings I want to finish before then.

Of course, I am always here for you

Josephine

Can I ask one stupid question quick?

Of course, it won't be stupid

Josephine

Can you turn into a bat? lol

Hahah, no. We do not turn into bats. It would be cool to fly though.

Josephine

It would be so cool. I'll see you in 2 days, love you.

I love you too.

Josephine

I smile for the first time in over a week. Josephine always knows how to bring light to my life, to my soul. And now I know she can't turn into a bat. It doesn't stop me from drawing some in the background of a painting. Or a bat necklace....and only a bat necklace on her body.

Painting her doesn't help with missing her, but my mind is finally clear.

The hours begin to blur together as I make piece after piece. At some point, Megan calls and I have to pretend like my entire worldview hasn't shifted. We talk about her boyfriends and how she cares so much about them. How she is excited for game night. I can truthfully tell her that I am too. She makes sure I go and eat food; the fixation on my art has been known to stop me from eating or drinking, from how immersed in it I get. Then the hours blur again. By the time I finish for the day the sun is high in the sky, and I nearly pass out in exhaustion. After I sleep for a few hours, I do it all again.

I paint and paint and paint until my fingers ache and time stands completely still while also racing a million miles a minute. It is impossible to describe the rush of painting piece after piece. They aren't my largest works by any means, but I love them. Each one is a piece of the understanding I have now, and I hope to make more once she clears things up for me. A collection on my view of her, of that part of herself she feels the need to hide. Each painting a piece to the puzzle of vampirism. How I somehow think it is still beautiful. Another day of getting lost in paintings ends, and I know that when I wake up tomorrow, it will be time to face the new reality and finally learn the answers to the questions I can't help but ask.

29
Monster

Gabby

I couldn't believe just how much I missed Josephine until she opened her door and I pulled her into the tightest hug and kissed her like my life depended on it. I never want to let go of her. We stay like that for a few minutes, craving the closeness of each other, before she pulls away, all smiles. It has been less than a week, and it still feels like too much time has passed, even when I was the cause of the distance.

"Hello to you too," she gives me one simple kiss on the lips. "How are you doing?"

"Better, I think. I just have so many questions." Understatement. I need answers to questions to be able to understand the world again.

"I thought you would. I kind of sprung a lot on you." She eyes me uneasily.

"I'm not scared of you. I feel like I should say that first. I just don't know what all goes into this." I grasp her hands as I tell her. She nods, smiles, and brings me over to the couch with her.

"You can ask anything." Her smile is easy and understanding; she looks so patient. So kind. So her.

"So, the whole no-showing up in pictures thing? Is that real? Some things have said it is, others say it only used to be true." I feel like I am rambling, but stopping is so hard when all I want is clarity.

"It's real," her expression drops. "I always loved self-portraits, but unfortunately, we don't appear. Christopher has been trying to create a camera that can. The farthest he has gotten is one that records our clothes, but not our bodies. He is a filmmaker, but this camera has become his obsession."

"That's why your pictures only feature clothing. The people in them are vampires." My jaw goes slack with surprise. The innovation is next level.

"That's the secret," she winks at me. I'm truly impressed; her technique seemed impossible to replicate. Now I know why.

"Mirrors too?"

"I haven't seen my reflection since 1950. Admittedly, your paintings are the most recent likeness of myself I have seen. Everything else is from when I was human."

"No one else had painted you?" I ask, and she shakes her head in response. "Well then, I'm honored that I could." I press a soft kiss to her lips.

"What else do you want to ask?"

"Silver and stakes. Are they dangerous?"

"Yes."

"The sun too?"

"Regretfully, I used to love sitting in the summer sun." Her expression turns wistful, like she is remembering a moment of happiness with the warmth of its rays on her skin.

"Are all vampires pale? Or is it a you thing?" I ask, and her laugh follows almost immediately.

"Not all of us are pale. There are vampires all over the world from all different races and ethnicities. We are an eclectic group."

"Can I ask how you turned?" It is a question that no amount of research could have answered. Her face loses the bit of the genuine humor that she had before.

"Of course you can. Unfortunately, it's not a happy story. I had just come from an event. It was the springtime, but a warm night. I was wearing my favorite blue ball gown. I'll have to show you a picture I took in it before leaving that night. But I was walking home, and I was grabbed. The Council leader for our city was replenishing our forces after the Second World War. A lot of men and women were taken off the streets to replace the numbers that were lost. No one asked us if it was okay. They wanted more power, more strength.

"Later, they found out that it was a terrible idea. We all came out...different than other vampires. We didn't handle the change well. Some of us, like me, feel the sounds and the lights of the world are too strong, like everything is turned up in volume or brightness. That's why mine are always dimmed, and the walls are completely soundproofed. Others couldn't tolerate blood; they rejected it. Some were more prone to blood lust; it's a dangerous state. Others couldn't take the mental burden and walked into the sun. The Council outlawed the forced conversions in 1955, outside of a few exceptions. The wars that happened after still required more new vampires. So instead of forcing it, they acted like your typical cult, and they draw people in now. It works. You wouldn't believe how many people want eternal life and youth without thinking it through." Her face goes through a range of emotions; the genuine fear on her face when she talks about that night blends with the grief. Then, the anger when she talks about how it has affected people. My heart is breaking for her. To be forced into a life like this? One so removed from your own normal? It must have felt violating, hopeless even.

"Vampires fight in our wars?"

"All of them. The governments have always known about us; they just like to keep us a little secret. So we can be weapons that the general public has no idea about."

"Wait, secret weapons? So the whole super speed and strength thing is legit?"

"It is." Josephine smiles my way again, but the unease is still left in her eyes.

"Can you prove it?"I challenge her, and she smiles and laughs lightly at the request.

"Do you want a bagel from that late-night shop?"

"Always." They are pillowy. Josephine likes to stock up on them for me, keeping them on hand for a quick meal.

"Be right back," she waves, and then the sound of the door shutting hits my ears. Within a matter of minutes, she is back with a bag of bagels for me and a few cream cheese containers. "Sorry it took so long, they took a while to get the order done."

"What do you mean it took so long? That place is *ten miles* away, and you were only gone for *ten minutes*. That is insanely fast."

"I do my best. You wanted to see strength, too, right?" She asks. I nod enthusiastically. The, she puts her pinky under the couch and lifts it.

"Legit superhuman strength. That's so fucking cool."

"Frankly, I rarely use the strength. The speed comes in handy, though. Especially for going over to your place." She lifts my hand to gently brush her lips against it. My cheeks flush immediately.

"It is a pretty cool party trick."

"It really can be," We laugh for a moment before the laugh fades away and the tension in the air rises. She leans in to embrace me but moves back far too soon, and I just want her lips on me again. But I hold back, for now at least.

"What about garlic?"

"That's a myth." Note to self: Italian is still on the menu.

"You can eat food. Does it help?"

"No. I usually don't eat, only on special occasions. Our digestive systems don't exactly work for food."

"Is it uncomfortable?" I ask. She shrugs.

"It's not the best part of the whole vampire situation."

"So you've been eating for me?"

"Of course." Her expression makes it seem like it should be obvious that she would set aside comfort for me. It doesn't feel like it should be, though. It shouldn't be expected that she would be uncomfortable for *my* comfort.

"You're extraordinary."

"I'm just myself. You're incredible. You are accepting me even though I'm this," she gestures towards herself while searching for her next word, "this monster."

"You're not a monster. You're a vampire, sure. You drink blood, sure. Not technically alive. But not a *monster*. You're kind and giving. That's not monstrous. Being a generous, compassionate, giving, loving, talented, and stunning person is not being a monster. It is being the woman I have fallen in love with. The woman I will always be in love with. The one I can't imagine not having in my life. The one I want next to me every moment. The one I *crave*." Her pupils dilate with the last words.

"I love you so much, Gabby." She says only moments before her lips crash into mine. Her kisses feel hungry, my own lips clashing into hers with just as much fervor. Gasped I love yous come from both of us as we lose ourselves in the moment. Her tongue gently exploring my mouth while my hand goes to tangle in her immaculate hair. She leans back slightly, and I let out a whimper from the lack of her lips against mine. "Can I touch you?"

"Fuck yes."

"You can too," She says breathlessly before going back to our kisses. Her free hand starts to roam across my body, the other cupping my jaw gently. She slides her hand up to my breasts, letting one hand engulf one. My nipple hardens under her touch, and she gasps into my lips as she feels the reaction in her grasp. She pinches my nipple between her fingers, and a moan leaves my lips while they crash into her own, the kiss growing more intense than I knew it could.

My free hand moves to her ass, I give the ample tissue a squeeze, and bring my hand back to leave a light slap behind before soothing it. She makes the most adorable little whimper when my hand makes contact. Josephine tugs at the hem of my shirt and asks between kisses, "May I?"

"Please," I whisper. She pulls back from our embrace to pull off my shirt. Once it's off, she quickly moves her attention to my jaw. Josephine peppers kisses along it, heading closer to my ear, whispering to me about how beautiful I look beneath her. She sucks my lobe into her mouth, gives it a gentle bite, then moves to my neck. She leaves love bites all down the column. I just know my skin will be left with little marks the next morning.

Her mouth strays lower and lower until she is leaving kisses on both of my breasts. She takes one small mound and licks across my nipple before closing her lips around it and sucking at it, her tongue flicking against the peak while in her mouth. My hands go to her hair and hold her in close while I moan out loud for her. One of her hands moves to play with my other breast, grabbing it and tweaking my nipple. After a moment, she switches to the other side and lavishes it with her attention. The moans exiting me appear to be never-ending. Her head lifts off my breast, and she peers right into my eyes.

“I’m dying to taste you.”

“I, I’m on my period.” My face flushes. My exes never liked going down on me during that time; her eyes only light up, though.

“Even better,” she smirks when she notices the shock that must be absolutely covering my face. “Darling, I’m a vampire.” The realization hits, and not long after I’m lifting my hips and she is helping take off my pants and panties, leaving me naked before her.

“I have a cup in.”

“You pinch and pull, right?”

"Yeah, they can get messy though," I tell her. So, she grabs a red blanket from her couch, I lift my hips as she slides it under me.

"Messes happen." She reaches inside and removes it from me, placing the cup on her table before licking her fingers clean. "You're so fucking delicious," she moans. Her fangs are peaking out from her lips as she lowers her face to my pussy, passing one long lick up the center, a moan of pure satisfaction leaving her. She takes her time with slow licks, her tongue taking casual flicks on my clit.

"More," my voice comes out in a breathy moan. She lifts her head from my center and kisses up across my body until she reaches my lips.

"Do you want to see another benefit of that speed?" Josephine asks between kisses, her fingers now softly circling my clit. I nod, unable to force myself away from her. "Use your words."

"Yes."

"Good girl."Her praise makes me melt more. I need her. She huffs a slight laugh before settling down between my legs again. She pushes two of her fingers inside of me, curling them to rub against me. Then the pace picks up, fast like a vibrator stimulating my g-spot. The moans leaving me make me sound wanton, and I simply can't control them. I didn't know I could make those sounds, or that anyone could, for that matter. Then I feel her tongue against my clit again, her lips circle around it as she sucks on it. Tiny pricks from her fangs add to the sensation, not enough to make me bleed, but the slight pressure adds to the sensation. Her tongue begins to flick my bud with increased speed. My hands go to grip her hair as I moan for her. I can't help but writhe under her; it's like I have a toy turned up to the highest setting, and it is overwhelming in the pleasure.

"Josephine," I lean my head back as my core tightens around her fingers. I can feel myself getting closer and closer to the edge. As soon as one of her fingers grabs my nipple and gives it a hard pinch, the stimulation is just enough to send me over the edge. I never understood what people meant when they said they saw stars until now. It is like time itself ceased to exist, and all I could feel was her.

30

Seated

Josephine

I keep touching her while she comes down from her high. I think I could become addicted to the sounds she makes, her whimpers, moans, and needy begging. The sound of her heavy breaths hits my ears as her body stops moving. I lift my head from her delicious pussy and lick my lips clean, my fangs still out. Then come my fingers, I peer into her emerald eyes and suck them clean. If I could live off her pussy alone, I would be a happy woman.

"It should be impossible to taste so good." I kiss her left hip bone. "The moans you make are like music, you know." Then the right. "I could listen to them all day." My next lands between her breasts. "And your body, it is a work of art." Another where her collarbones meet. "Even the best artists in history could only dream of making a piece so beautiful." I pepper a few across her collarbone. "You look utterly blessed by your gods." I place a one on her neck. "And sound blessed." Another right where her jaw meets her neck. "And taste blessed." One on her cheek. "And I'm here to worship." Then comes one final kiss on her lips. She kisses me back, and for the first time since she left my apartment last week, I feel like she is truly mine again. She loves me. She accepts me. She isn't afraid of me. And she comes for me.

"You're stunning," she pulls back from my kisses and strokes her fingers along my jaw. "But you're also way too overdressed. Clearly, the dress code is naked." Gabby smiles, lets out a little giggle, and I can't help returning the expression.

"Too overdressed am I?" I stand up and undo the tie for the halter dress I'm in.

"You are." Her eyes are locked on me and what I'm doing. I yank down the top of the halter, exposing the strapless bra beneath. “Getting closer,” I smirk in her direction before undoing the side zipper and slipping the dress down my hips. All that remains is a simple black set of lingerie. I turn my back to her and unclasp the bra and let it fall. Keeping her waiting for a view. Then I slip down the thong, so I’m naked while facing the other way. “Turn around, please.” Her words come out breathless. I can’t help but oblige. “I know it isn’t my first time seeing you like this. But it still feels so much more monumental.”

“I understand the feeling.” I walk to sit next to her on my sofa, and she holds me against her. “I can’t even begin to explain how beautiful you are.”

“That’s how I feel when I paint you. Every time, it is like all the things I want to say to you coming out through my brush. No actual words could describe you. It is like that quote about words and pictures. What is it again?" I smile and laugh lightly, my lips nearly brushing against hers.

“A picture is worth a thousand words.”

“That’s the one.”

I place a feather-light kiss on her lips, a breathy laugh escaping my own. "Each kind says different words, though. A painting shows how you see someone, a photograph shows how you truly are. And you are truly a living piece of perfection. Another lands on her soft, full lips.

"I'm happy to let you see how I view you anyday." She kisses me again, biting into my lip and causing it to bleed for a split second before healing immediately. She lies down flat on the sofa. "Your turn." Her tongue traces the seam of her mouth. My cheeks flush, and I place my thighs on either side of her head and lower myself so I'm only centimeters over her face. Gabby's hands grip into my flesh and drag me down further. "Josephine, my gorgeous muse. Sit on my damn face. You don't need to hover." With that, she tugs down on my thighs again until I am seated on her face, still trying to hold myself up at least a little.

The feeling of her tongue against my pussy has a low, soft moan coming from deep inside of me. She is gentle, taking her time exploring me. Every time she notices something makes me moan a bit more, she adds it in more often. Her mouth moves with such skill I can't seem to think straight, I'm simply lost within her.

She tugs down on my thighs again, evidently not satisfied with how much weight I've placed on her, so I put down a little more. Her hands go to grab at my ass. Gripping it in her delicate hands while her tongue continues to make me forget my own name.

I don't register when I begin to rock my hips, grinding against her face. Or even notice when she yanks me down more because all I can focus on is the way her tongue moves against me. The way she pulls pleasure from my body should be impossible. I feel myself being wound tighter and tighter. My fingers grip onto the sofa to keep myself up as I creep closer and closer to the finish.

And then I come loose, releasing on top of her face as my hips unconsciously rock against her, her fingers now gripped tightly into my thighs. I'm sure I'll have little half moons from her nails for a moment. I wish I could keep the marks she leaves. The one downside of healing so fast is not seeing the marks from a night of passion.

As I come down from my high, I brace my hands on the armrest of the couch and remove myself from her face before collapsing next to her. My legs feel like jelly, and I don't think I could walk right away if I tried. I lean into my love and kiss her softly, and I swear my heart soars again when she kisses me back. I don't know if it will ever stop soaring when our lips meet. I don't think it will.

"That was incredible," I half whisper out, like talking normally will break the serenity of the moment.

"*You're* incredible." Her hand goes to brush my hair out of my face, and I reach to cup her chin.

"I think we are, together." She kisses me again.

"I think you might be right."

We lay there together, lost in a place with no time, before I have us try to get up. "Let's clean ourselves up and climb into bed." I grab her cup for her and hold her hand as we walk to my en suite. We take a shower that I swear was meant to be short before actually cleaning up for bed and climb into the silk sheets, fresh from the wash that evening. I pull her over to me, and she lays her head on my chest, our arms wrapped around each other.

"I love you." Her voice is heavy with sleep.

"I love you too, and I'm so happy you came to talk to me today." I tenderly pet her hair.

"Me too. Don't think I've run out of questions, though." My laugh comes out more tired than I imagined it would.

"You can ask all of them in the evening. Sleep well, little owl." She mumbles a response as she falls asleep. I lay there for a few moments longer, just enjoying having her in my arms again.

31

Lycanthropy and Loss

Josephine

"So, vampires are real," Gabby tells me over our evening drink, her herbal tea with exactly one spoonful of sugar is steaming, the notes of ginger and turmeric reaching my nose. I have a coffee cup of blood, simple, sweet, a bit metallic, delicious, comforting.

"Very real." I flash my fangs at her, and she rolls her eyes, a smile peaking through even though she tries to hide it.

"What about other things?" She sips her tea, tipping the teacup back with both hands.

"You'll have to be more specific."

"Werewolves?" Her voice increases at the end.

"Real, but they don't tend to live in cities, vampires do...there is more food for us here."

"Do you guys really hate each other? Is it like in the movies where you just battle it out?" She places her tea down and pretends to throw some punches. My laughter is immediate.

"No, not at all. I think we get along pretty well; a shared secret keeps tensions low. An all-out supernatural war would draw *way* too much attention. Although we don't interact much in general." Her face drops in mild disappointment. Did she want me to have a rival species? Because I certainly do not.

"I suppose that makes sense. What about ghosts?" Gabby asks, picking up her cup, waiting to take a sip until her teeth let go of her bottom lip.

"Also real," I remember my shock of seeing a ghost for the first time. I had never believed in them. Granted, I had never believed in vampires either.

“Can you see them? Or like talk to them?” Her interest is piqued, she leans forward as she rapidly asks her questions.

“I mean, yes. But they really just end up being in the background. Like, think about the person who works at that hot dog stand near your place. You see him every day, right?”

“Well, yeah.”

“And you could talk to him. But you probably don’t, at least not often. It’s like that. Someone in the background, you see them, you’re aware of them, but you don’t seek them out. At least I don’t; some vampires make a career out of it.”

“Does everyone become a ghost?”

“No,” now it is my turn for my face to fall a bit. “Most people don’t. None of my family did. I would give anything to see them again. Not all spirits feel the need to stay.” She reaches out to take my hand.

“I can’t imagine all the loss you have been through.” She never fails to be compassionate to a loss she hasn’t experienced. She doesn't throw out platitudes like I have heard from others. Just genuine compassion. I love her for it. Still, I smile at her and try to change the subject. I don't want to cry tonight.

"For other beings. Zombies don't exist. Some people claim faeries do, some think it is a load of shit. No elves, gnomes, trolls, or goblins. Personally, I think the Loch Ness Monster is real, but there is no proof there." The tidbit about Nessie makes her grin. I wish I could bottle the feeling that her happiness gives me, pure euphoria. "No tooth fairy, no Santa, no Easter bunny."

"It is like there is a whole world out there I don't know about, and trying to make sense of what is real and what isn't seems impossible."

"I'd bring you to the Council building if I could, let you more into my world. But unless you're a familiar, it is a strictly no human zone." That and I don't want to subject her to the likes of Beverly and De Medici.

"What's that? A familiar, I mean." She goes back to worrying her plump lower lip.

"Effectively a human servant. They give their blood and serve vampires in hopes of being turned. They bring us drinks, anything we need, really. Just so they can try and have a shot at immortal life."

"Does it work?" She raises one brow.

"Sometimes. Other times, they waste their lives toiling away, never getting the one thing they want more than anything else." That is ordinarily what happens. If everyone were turned, we wouldn't have food. I have seen a few familiars live out an entire life only to never be chosen. They wasted the ones they were given.

"Why do they stay?"

"Hope. They simply hope one of us might change our minds." We rarely do. If a familiar will be turned the rest of us know almost immediately. It is like you can sense it, an intrinsic knowledge.

"And have you ever changed anyone?" She bites on her lip and leans as far forward as she can without spilling her tea. She looks honestly curious, not only in a let's-learn-about-vampires way. I don't know if she hopes to be turned one day or not. I'm not sure if I could turn her. The internal battle of wanting her near me for eternity and the desire to keep her safe feel thoroughly at odds with one another. I try to put the thought out of my head. I don't need to think about it quite yet.

"Two people. Christopher and Michael."

"Were they familiars?" I quickly shake my head no.

"No, they were my friends back then, too. It was 1995. The height of the AIDS crisis, but the coverage had already started to fade out. There were so many people who died, so many of my friends had died. I ended up telling them when they were ill. I offered to turn them, knowing that if I didn't, my two best friends would have ended up dead. A week later, they agreed. They watched one last sunset together before I turned them. I think they even recorded themselves watching it. One last touch of their humanity." I barely hold back my tears, thinking about that time never fails to hurt. It is a loss that I can't begin to process. Gabby looks like she feels the pain, too. The epidemic has caused a scar in the community: a wound that we all feel the effects of.

“That would have been terrifying.” She grips my hands.

“Have I ever told you my family’s way of saying I love you? It is one I had taught them too.” I feel the need to change the subject again; there is too much loss to have to navigate some days. Gabby shakes her head in response, and I squeeze her hand three times. “The first is for I, the second is for love, and the third is for you.” She smiles with her typical warmth and gives me three squeezes back.

“Are we still on for our date this weekend?” She changes the topic one step further, one step closer to my comfort.

“Of course. I have the whole thing planned out.” I smirk as I lift my cup.

“Are you going to tell me what we are doing?”

“No. All you need to know is to dress comfortably.” She scrunches up her nose and takes that lip in her mouth again. I want to bite it instead.

“I’m sure it will be fantastic, but I’m impatient with surprises.”

"Trust me, I've noticed. You're like those kids in the movies asking when you'll be there." I think back to the shows and films I've watched with tiny, impatient children in the back while the parents look ready to pop a vein. She bursts out laughing. "What? You are!"

"Oh, I totally am, I have just never heard of someone describing it as a movie thing." She places her tea down, her legs curled up against her as she laughs.

"It's not just a movie thing?"

"No." Her laughter continues. "Have you never gone on a road trip with a kid?"

"Well, no. Road trips are hard when the sun could kill you. Plus, my family that stayed close live in the city. The furthest I've gone since I was turned is the suburbs. And as a human I hardly ever traveled; it wasn't as easy back then." I shift awkwardly before taking a sip of my blood. Was it that common?

"I've been all over. It was the one constant in my life. Everything else was a new place, a new home, new food, new friends, new everything every month or so. I was *always* impatient to get to the next place. I think it was me trying to find some routine or a sense of a new normal. For other kids, it is pure excitement." Her laughter dies down, her own somber expression coming back as she thinks back to her childhood.

"What was your favorite?"

"Noxdale. It is my home base, the first place I've been able to settle in. I've stayed in my studio the entire time. Well, besides a few months when I roomed with Megan." She smiles again at the mention of our city.

"Would you ever consider a different apartment in the city?" I hold her gaze as I ask her, hoping she knows what I mean. Hoping she can tell how much I *want* her here *with me*.

"Yeah, I would. Not yet. But I would." Her words cause relief to crash over me; she might want to live here. It feels fan-freaking-tastic. "How long have you been here?"

"Decades. My mother bought me this place before I turned." I was thrilled when I moved in. It was the newest apartment building, completely modern and hip at the time. Now it is antique and luxurious. I've loved it in every stage; it is my own place of comfort. It is home.

"So over 70 years?" Her eyes widen.

"Yes, I haven't ever wanted to leave it. There are so many memories here." I run a hand along my couch, looking off into the distance for a moment. A slight smile graces my face as a few of those memories flash in my mind.

"Well, it's beautiful." Gabby begins to eye the rays in the tank. "Can I feed them a squid?" Her grin has almost this element of childlike glee to it.

"Yeah, go grab one from the freezer and thaw it out." She places her teacup down and jumps up to head to the kitchen. A few minutes later, she returns with the floppy squid for them to enjoy. I open the table tank for her, and she grabs the tongs from my fish supplies and lowers the snack in. Her expression turns to pure wonder at them enjoying their snack.

"They really are beautiful," she says.

“They are. I love watching how they move in the water.” She glances at me to give me a soft smile before turning back to them. Quickly, I snap a picture on my phone, needing to save the moment forever. Gabby looks at them with the same regard I have for her own beauty, while they swim around the tank unaware of the fluttering in my chest that I feel when I look at her. I’m just so happy she is back.

32

Trust

Gabby

Making up had never felt so good. My mind is still reeling from the other night. Josephine could finally open up to me, and every bit she told me, even the simple shit, is more and more important. Like I was finally getting to unlock her. Like we could be infinitely connected again. Then somehow we ended up naked and screaming for each other, and I felt closer to her than ever.

I hadn't realized all she had been through. I don't think I could have before I learned her secret. She had told me about having a lot of loss, but I couldn't have imagined it was a century of it. Who could have? No wonder she was scared in the beginning. I would have been from the whole death of a partner thing alone, but she is scared of *loss* in general.

Then her story of how she was turned. The lack of consent, how she was grabbed, and how everything changed in a matter of moments. I can't begin to imagine her fear of it.

It quite frankly pisses me off. Not that she didn't tell me, or that it hurts. But that she had to be hurt like that. It pisses me off that someone could *do* that to her. I can't imagine seeing someone and *changing* them so wholly without ever giving them a say. No wonder she views it as a curse.

Is it bad that I want to have that "curse" myself?

I don't want her to have to have that loss again.

I don't want to lose her to my own aging.

I grab the punching bag Megan gave me a year ago from the closet. I always feel this level of guilt using it. Like I should be able to keep my emotions in check better, but I can't. So I take a few swings. Some for her having to go through so much loss. Some for how she was turned. Some for how she feels she was cursed. Some for the guilt of needing to get it out. Maybe even a part of me hits it because she didn't tell me sooner.

It is like a revelation of sorts, and not one I wanted to have. This idea that I admittedly am upset that she couldn't have opened up quicker hits me like a truck. I wish she had told me sooner. I wish she felt like she could have. But I know *why* she didn't. I even understand it. The understanding makes me hate that it bothers me at all. Maybe it is why I hid it from myself. I decide to call Megan.

"Hey bitch," her voice sounds like relief.

"Hey. Weird question. If one of the guys didn't tell you something for a while, and they have a valid reason, would you feel hurt they didn't tell you sooner?" I pace back and forth while on the call, needing to work out some of that nervous energy. Trying to ask her what I want to without saying too much is practically impossible. Or at the very least, it is needlessly long-winded.

“What did she keep from you?” Her tone turns protective.

“It isn’t my story to tell.” I can almost hear her eyes roll. “Let’s just say I get why she kept it a secret. But I wish she trusted me sooner.”

“But she trusts you now.”

“Yeah, she trusts me now.” Thankfully, I can’t imagine the pain if she had waited a year or something.

“Then what’s the problem?”

I start to talk, but then halt. I can’t think of a real reason. “I guess I wanted that earlier.” The admission rolls from my tongue easier than I thought it would.

“Everyone wants trust earlier than they receive it. It has to be *earned*. You earned it.”

“When did you get so smart?”

“Oh fuck off. I’ve always have been.”

“Sure,” I drag the word out. She’s right, though. She always has been. She’s also the dumbest smart person I know. Intelligent, but not exactly wise. Maybe the wisdom is starting to kick in.

"Whatever. You know it's true. But I have to be heading out. Talk to you later." She makes a kiss sound and ends the call before I can respond. She is lucky that I absolutely love her to pieces.

I think about what she said for longer than I'd like to admit. Trust has to be earned, and I've earned it. What is there to be upset about? The feeling doesn't just zap away immediately, but it lessens. I repeat it like a mantra in my head and take a few more swings at the bag and wheel it away and paint some more.

33

Tassels and Turning

Josephine

I am in desperate need of more blood. I stayed holed away when she was still processing the news. I didn't have the energy to go out. Now I'm abysmally low on it. The rest of my stash gets used to fill up my water bottle before heading out. The city is overwhelming tonight; it's always harder when I don't go out as much. The traffic is backed up. They honk their horns like it will move them any faster. It won't. All their headlights create an overly bright view around me; it is blinding. I go as fast as I can, drinking my blood along the way.

The Council building is like a saving grace as I approach. I've been out of my supply for a while now. As soon as the door shuts behind me, I collapse to the ground and try to center myself. My breaths are rapid as I sink down, my forehead resting against my knees. I finally feel the full effects of my walk now that the blood isn't there to calm me down. Everything felt excessive. The absence of it all lets the anxiety crash through me.

A familiar gasps and runs to go fetch some for me. She is a younger woman. Barely 18 if I had to guess. My vision is blurred with panic, even with that I can tell she will be turned sooner rather than later. She is exactly the Council's type: young and pretty. The familiar rushes over while carrying a cup of thick, red fluid, and I down it, letting it calm my nerves and bring me back to a relative state of calm.

"Thank you," I tell her before finishing the glass.

"Chloe," She sticks her hand out to me with a bright smile. She is very new. Most familiars slip into the background, like a rarely seen force that keeps the building in motion.

“Thank you, Chloe,” I grasp her hand and give it a shake.

“What’s your name?” She sits next to me, pouring another bag of blood into my cup.

“Josephine,” I respond. The girl is too friendly to be stuck in a place like this.

“That’s a pretty name.”

“Thank you. Did you just start?”

“Is it that obvious?” She fidgets with her hair, her nerves palpable. I shrug in response. “I just hope someone turns me. Is that weird?”

“You and every other familiar here. You’ll get turned within a year or so, I would imagine. You’re young and beautiful, they always turn the pretty people.” With that, I stand up and walk into the rec room, leaving her on the floor.

The rec room is as busy as usual. Christopher waves me over to him. As I walk over, I notice Theo and De Medici talking in their secret Council language. Even Rex, a member of the Council who is less involved with politics and more involved in the perpetual discomfort of women everywhere. Something must be going on, probably something to do with Beverly and her spilling the secret.

"Where's Michael?" I ask my friend as I lean in to give him a kiss on the cheek.

"With Megan. They are acting like they are about to surprise me."

"Ahhh, I take it that it's almost your annual 'surprise' party?" Every year Michael attempts to surprise Christopher for his birthday; he has done it every year. He has also failed to actually surprise him every year. He might have better success if he waited to plan it at least a little closer to the actual day. That isn't him.

"That it is. I'd expect your invitation in the next few weeks. I hear it is western themed this year." Christopher grimaces as he says the theme. He may like western movies, but dressing like that? Never.

"He really sucks at keeping things from you. Does this mean I need to order boots and a hat?" I am equally unhappy with the theme; I simply don't suit the look.

"Some for Gabby, too. Probably something with tassels."

"At least she will look good in tassels. That western place on 88th still has late hours, right?" I ask him. He whips out his phone and does a quick search.

"Yeah, you should be good to go."

"Yay," sarcasm laces my voice. "At least I'll have an outfit for your surpiseless surprise party," I say as his eyes roll further back than I thought possible.

"Speaking of surprises, did you meet the new familiar?"

"She is very friendly."

"More than most. The new ones normally want to crap themselves in fear." Christopher says. I snort out a quick laugh.

"Can you blame them? We drink their blood." I shoot back my blood and flash a fang in his direction.

"Fair enough. Rex apparently wants to turn her." Christopher points to the vampire who used to be king of some small country. He changed his name after he had to abdicate due to the whole never-aging thing. Rex wanted everyone to know he was a king and should still be one. He is such a pompous asshole. Correction: a pompous asshole that fixates on young familiars.

"*Already*?"

"I mean, you saw her. Blonde curls, innocent face, young, that type of beauty."

"He is such a," I mouth the word "creep" so that Rex can't overhear.

"Oh, I know. Trust me, everyone has been pretty grossed out by the whole situation. I still bet she will be turned within a month."

"Then hopefully she will keep her distance." I grab a glass of blood from a passing familiar, Christopher does too.

"Hopefully." He tips his glass back. The door opens, and we turn to see who comes in. Chloe enters, and the creep is on her immediately. For someone pushing a thousand, he really doesn't look older than 35. Which would still be too old for her. Her demeanor screams naivety, just smiling like he isn't leering at her like she is a prized animal to *hunt*. He keeps getting closer, and the nerves start to appear on her face. He scares her.

"I'm going to get her out of there. I'll be back." I make my way over to the pair. "Excuse me, Rex, but I must talk to Miss Chloe here." I shoot her a kind smile and reach my hand towards her.

"Sorry, sir, I came in to help Josephine with something earlier." She hurries over to me and grips onto my hand firmly.

"Smart girl. You should stay away from him. He only turns familiars if they are *young* and willing to go to his bed to be turned." I whisper in a hushed tone. Her face blanches. "Christopher, I brought the new familiar over." I drop her hand, and he nods in recognition. "Where did you say you were from?"

"A small town about four hours from here. You probably haven't heard of it." She shrugs and shifts awkwardly.

"Try me. I've been in the area for a long time."

"Balance?"

"That isn't a common name to hear around here. One of my nieces moved there in 1966. Her children never kept in touch, but the two of us did until she died about 10 years ago, Susan McGreggor." A flash of recognition sparked in her face.

"I never knew Susan, but the McGreggors are a big name in town. One of her grand or great grandsons, I'm not sure which to be honest, was my first boyfriend in high school."

"What a small world." I take a sip of the blood in my glass and flash a fang-filled smile.

"Is he really going to try to change me for *that*?" She looks nauseous at the thought.

"Alarmingly, yes." Christopher chimes in. "What if I could make you a better offer?" He asks, and my brow hikes up in surprise.

"What do you mean?" Chloe can't help the curiosity leaking through.

"I'll turn you, but I need a favor first."

"What's the favor?"

"A trip. My boyfriend, Michael, grew up a few states away. He misses some of the things from his home area. It would be a shopping trip to retrieve some items that I, unfortunately, can't order."

"That's it?"

"That's it. I'd cover the expenses, I just can't do it myself." He likes to hide the softy in him whenever he can, but he isn't the best at it. Especially where Michael is concerned. She hands her phone to him to put his number in, and then she taps out a quick message.

"Text me the details." She smiles, realizing she has just secured her long life of immortality.

"Once I'm home for the night. Get ready, soon you will live forever." Her smile returns, and she heads off to the other side of the room.

"She doesn't know what she is getting herself into." I hiss at him.

"No, they never do. But she will be turned either way, at least I won't take advantage of her."

"I wish you weren't so right."

"Me too, me too." We both lift our glasses and let our conversation halt for a while.

34

Fangs Out

Gabby

Josephine took me shopping. Correction, she didn't *just* take me shopping: she got me an entire outfit for a surprise party happening *weeks* from now. When I tried to pay, she stopped me, "Let me get it." She said, handing over her card.

"Apparently, tassels were made for you," Josephine says, pressing her lips against mine as we walk back to my place. I can't help but smile, and her own lip curls in a smirk.

"Thank you for the clothes." I smile, still blushing from her kiss.

"It's no problem, we both needed some new pieces for the party." She grimaces whenever she mentions it. I can't tell if it is *just* because of the tassels or if the parties themselves are awful.

"Still, they weren't cheap."

"Well, you're my girlfriend, and I *like* to spoil you. And besides, I have more than enough. Benefits of vampirism, the Council provides well."

"Well then, thank you *and* thank the Council." I can't help but peek over at her while we walk. Her pale pink dress looks ethereal on her. "Will you pose for me back at the apartment? I've kind of been working on a personal collection. I promise it isn't going on exhibition." I can't help but wring my hands slightly, the nerves peeking through.

"Well, now you have me curious. What is this collection?" Intrigue coats her voice.

"A vampire one."

"Well, I can't wait to see your work. I have never seen my fangs. I think I'd like to." She smiles and squeezes my hand three times, her silent I love you. I return the gesture as we near the building. The elevator shakes on its way up. Something tells me I'll wake up to it being out again. Josephine eyes it with suspicion. She lets the look drop as we walk down the hallway. "Show me the new paintings," Josephine says excitedly when we enter. She grabs the bags from me and places them on the floor before perching herself on the armrest of my couch.

"Why are you so nervous?" She asks me when I come back into the room, sheepishly carrying my work. "You're never this nervous to let me see them."

"I guess I just hope you like them. I made a lot of them when I was still...processing."

"I'm sure they are incredible." Her smile is genuine, even with the tinge of worry I catch flashing in her eyes. My throat feels clogged, and I gulp as I turn around the paintings. Her jaw drops as she scans over them. "I was right, they are astounding, Gabby. Is that what my fangs look like? They are very pretty. Everyone has their own slightly different version of them. I've always wondered what mine looked like."

Josephine goes and kneels before a closeup I did of her mouth, her perfectly shaped lips with her iconic lipstick shade, mouth open in a wide smile, fangs out, with a drop of blood coming from one of them, her tiny nose only in frame until the bridge, her delicate chin filling out the painting, with the slight sloping of her neck blurred out in the background. It is a favorite of mine from the collection. She traces her finger across the fang with the blood dripping from it.

"The blood doesn't really do that; that was more of a creative choice," I explain, still nervous after her praise.

"I love it," she says while looking right into my eyes, utterly entranced. I don't know if she is entranced by me or the painting, but I'll take it either way. "I love you." She stands up and cups my chin as she kisses me. I can't seem to pry myself away, and my hands go to her hair. Our lips develop a heady rhythm, letting our emotions pour through them. I never want to leave her embrace. It might be the place I have felt the most at home.

Eventually, we manage to pull away, our labored breathing taking the place of our kisses. I still can't help giving her one more peck before taking her by her hand over to the painting area of my studio. I have pulled over a green velvet armchair. It is particularly luxe with its gold embellishments.

"What do you want me in?" She gazes at me with her eyelids lowered, pure seduction on her face. As if she needed a look to convince me that she is sexy.

"Whatever you like, you'll be a masterpiece either way." I mean it too. She is so incredibly breathtaking. Looking at her could nearly blind someone from her beauty alone. With a mischievous smirk, she starts to take off her clothing, leaving them carefully folded on a table just outside my painting area. She keeps stripping until all she has on is her simple gold jewelry and her black stilettos.

"Does this work?" Her eyes are trained on my features, looking at the blush I can feel creeping up my cheeks, and my pupils that I'm sure are dilated to the size of dinner plates.

“Perfection. I was thinking you could sit on the chair kind of like this,” I model the pose for her. I sit in it sideways, my legs hanging off one arm and my back arched across the other. One hand is on the back, the other is hanging down. Reminiscent of the first painting I did of her on the chaise. I watch her copy my position and turn her head to face me. “What do you need to have your fangs out?”

“Blood, I might have to take a few sips here and there to keep them out.” I nod and run to bring her the bottle. I open the cap and she takes a small taste of it; they are already out by the time she swallows.

“I’ll start with your face so we don’t have to worry about them for long.” Then I take my seat at the easel, painting the different planes of her face and body, the brilliant white of her fangs.

At one point, a rivulet of blood escapes the bottle while she drinks, forming a near-perfect bead going down her chin. I decide to add it in, the deep, rich red color adding an extra touch to the work. I think I could only paint her again and I would never be bored. She is perfection incarnate.

I put my feelings for her in each stroke of my brush. Love coloring every part of her from the flush on her cheeks that leads down to her chest, which is equally rosy, to the look in her eye as she watches me work.

"I love watching your expressions while you paint," Josephine says while hardly moving her mouth, trying to stay still for me.

"What about them?" I lift my brush from the canvas, placing the end between my teeth.

"You show every expression you're thinking of. Plus, it is adorable when you bite on the end of your brush or worry on your lip."

"What does my expression say?" I smile at her, pulling it away from my mouth.

"That you think I'm pretty." She can't help but let out a small smirk, but she quickly corrects it so her face is back in its original pose.

"Sorry, but you're wrong. I think you are earth-shatteringly beautiful, pretty doesn't come close." I toss a wink her way before diving back into the painting.

By the time the art is done, it is only half an hour left before the sun starts its ascent, so she dresses quickly to leave, shorter than I think either of us wanted it to be. But longer than it should have been given the time.

"I'll see you tomorrow." With one last kiss she is racing out my door, and I sit back at my easel to start the background.

35

Candles, Collars, and a Century of Skill

Josephine

I can't help but get a little nervous getting ready for our date tonight, it is our first time going out on one since she learned the truth. I try to follow my own advice and wear something casual, but it has never been my strong suit. I settle on some flowy linen shorts with a matching top. Cute, comfy, and casual enough. My fingers are decked out in rings, a simple gold choker rests on my neck, and I put on some matching gold pumps.

I never know if I want to do *more* and show off for her, or if keeping it simple is enough. I want her to think of me the same way I think of her, that she is the most beautiful woman to grace my life. Granted, she doesn't feel the need to put in all the extra steps; she is beautiful on her own.

I stop at the florist on my way to pick her up for our candle and picnic date. They are peonies, her favorites. Every date I get her a bouquet, something tells me she already has her vase out and waiting on the counter. I smile and breathe in the summer night, letting the warm air heat my skin for a moment before picking up my speed and ending up outside her apartment door.

The elevator was out, unsurprisingly, it had been making a sound I could only describe as *dangerous* last night. I tried to ignore how worried it made me, but I can't. I place a knock at her door.

"Hey there," she says with a smile, her denim shorts and flowy crop top looking unreasonably enticing on her. "Come on in." As she beams at me, I hand her the flowers that were behind my back. "Thank you, my muse, they are beautiful."

"I could never come to our dates empty-handed," I say. Gabby takes a deep whiff of the peonies as she puts them in the vase that already has cool water and a penny in it.

"I love them. You know, I have saved a flower from each date and dried it. I have a bouquet of them slowly drying out in my closet." She tells me as she arranges them in the vase.

"Do you really?" I puff my chest out a little, pride filling every fiber of my being.

"I do, the silica gel has taken longer than I expected to dry them out. But someday I'll have a beautiful bouquet to remind me of all of our dates." She smiles and places a peck on my cheek. I'm sure she has left behind a glossy imprint on my skin. I'm happy to leave it there. Who wouldn't be proud that she kissed them? "So are you going to tell me what we are doing tonight?"

"Not until we get there," I kiss her on her lips, and she gives me a suspicious glance as she grabs her bag.

"Well, how long does that take?"

"The ride share should be here in five minutes, so the ride plus five minutes."

"Sooo helpful." She rolls her eyes but still grabs my hand as we make our way down flight after flight of steps. "I knew the elevator would be out," she sighs.

"Does it go out often?'

"Once every month or so. It isn't the best one out there." Her breath rate picks up, and I just want to pick her up and carry her down the steps to save her from having to walk down all *ten* flights. Something tells me she would say she can do it herself. I settle for taking her bag for her instead.

"That is way too much. Is it safe?" It is the first time I've seen it broken, but I hate the thought of her being stuck without a working elevator. Or worse: stuck in a broken one.

"Enough." She shrugs like her elevator breaking that often doesn't matter. It matters to me.

"You know, my place is always available."

"Maybe tonight I can stay?" She tugs my arm slightly to have me turn and look at her. The want in her eyes is plain to see. Part of me wants to cancel our date tonight and take her straight home. But I won't do that, seeing her smile in the city lights is too special to give up.

"Any night you want." I give her a slow kiss before we finish the descent, making it outside right as the car arrives. I open the door for her, and she slides into the seat. The driver is thankfully not very talkative because all I want to do is focus on her. She tells me about the painting and how she got part of the background done before heading to bed. I'm hooked on every word. She talks about all the little details she has put in. I told her she will have to bring it next time she comes over so she can show me. Her talent leaves me in awe.

When we make it to the candle shop, I step out first and grip her hand to help her out. The car speeds away like it couldn't wait to rush to another job. She glances around at the small businesses surrounding us, different restaurants, art shops, activities, and photography studios. It is in an artsy section of the town. Streetlights dot the sidewalk, casting the area in a warm glow. The buildings are a mix of old and new, brick and sleek glass with metal.

"I still can't figure out what we are doing."

"Well, first," I squeeze her hand and lead her to the center of the row of businesses on the block to the Wax Bowl Candle Studio. The building is a few stories tall, the business is on the bottom, and a few apartments are above it. The red brick building with white trim shines at night, fairy lights brightening up the window with a variety of candles across the front window display. "We are making some candles together." She smiles with excitement.

"Hell yes! That sounds like a blast."

"It should be, Christopher helped set it up, one of his friends runs it." I open the door, and it has a sharp bell that rings out, and a woman comes from the back with black hair piled messily behind her head and a wide smile on her face.

"Welcome to the Wax Bowl, I'm Emma. You must be Josephine and Gabby. Come on over." She waves us to a wall with different containers we can choose from. "So basically, what we are going to do is have you pick out whatever container you want, then you can make your own fragrance blend. After that, we will assemble your candles and get them all packaged up for you. I'll give you a few minutes to pick." She shoots us another smile and walks to the front desk and taps away on her keyboard. The shop itself is fairly quiet. I can hear the hum of the lights under the soft music playing from the speakers and the methodical tapping from the computer. Nothing *too* strong. Even the fragrances are well kept inside of their packaging. It is peaceful.

'So, what are you thinking?" I ask as I scan the shelves with Gabby as I ask. My eye catches on a glass holder, it is an opaque green color, similar to her eyes. It has a rippling texture to the outside, simple but complex. Like her. "I think I'm going to go with this one?" I lift it up to gauge her reaction.

"It's perfect for you." Her smile melts my heart even more. My love turns back to the wall and grabs a simple cube-shaped holder made of a cream colored glass. "I kind of love this one. I know it is basic, but I can use it in my painting sets too that way. Then I have a piece of us in all of my work."

"That is an amazing idea," I tell her, and we set the holders down. With that, Emma comes back and brings us over to the fragrance area. It is obscenely loud for my brain, but I try to focus on each piece. It ends up being a blend of vanilla, lilac, and lilies, adding a small hint of cedar for a touch of something deeper. It should smell incredible. Gabby makes a blend with rosemary, mint, pink peppercorn, and a trace of cinnamon. It smells like her, and I'm half tempted to make my candle the same scent so I can always have her with me.

"Time to melt the wax," Emma leads us over to the wax melters and adds in the amount needed for each of our holders, placing our fragrance blends next to them. "Okay, so while that melts we are going to attach the wicks to the bottom of the holder. You're going to clean them out with rubbing alcohol and then glue them down."

"I'll clean them and you glue them?"

"Deal," she gives my hand a shake, and I start by cleaning out her container. She carefully glues each wick in place. My attention stays on her even as I wipe my own out.

"How are you so beautiful just gluing these down?" I whisper softly into her ear while she places the wicks in my own container. I can feel her shiver against me. I pull away with a light laugh as she finishes gluing and positioning them. We head back over to the wax pots and wait for them to melt, stirring in the fragrance blends once they are.

"Now we are going to carefully pour them in the vessels." We each pour our wax into the candles, and then all that's left is to let them sit and harden.

"Did I tell you about the thing Megan sent over?"

"No, what is it?" I lean forward onto my fist.

"She sent over, and I wish I was kidding, a bondage set she thought I could use for my painting. Rope, cuffs, spreader bars, and things I didn't know existed until she told me. I realize I paint some sexy shit, but not fetish paintings." The contents themselves aren't that funny, but her expressions of shock are. She is completely bewildered by the entire scenario that I can't help but have belly-aching laughs.

"I'm sorry. Can't. Stop." Thankfully, that ends up getting her to laugh, too. As the laughter slowly begins to die down, I wipe the tears from my eyes, a last few chuckles still escaping.

"Seriously, though, what is a posture collar *even* used for?" This time, only a giggle leaves my lips, and I stand up to go behind her. When I place my hands gently on her neck to imitate the collar, I feel her heartbeat pick up under my touch.

"It keeps your head up like this. So you stay exactly in position." Her face flushes, and I see Emma's does too from the corner of my eye. "You look so pretty like this."

"*How* do you know that?" Her words come out only after I drop my hands and sit down next to her again.

"I've been around," I glance around me, noting the company we still have, "longer than you." Gabby gives me a nod that she knows what I mean. "It has led me to learning a thing or two."

"Life gets boring, huh?"

"Not with you."

Once the wax had hardened, Emma had wrapped up our candles for us, and I put the boxes in the large purse I had brought for our date, knowing we would have a lot to carry. I take my girlfriend's hand, and we walk down the street a ways to a delicious Greek spot, according to the reviews, and load up on souvlaki, dips, pita, salads, a bit of wine, and baklava. I'm sure her mouth is watering at the smell. I'll admit it, it *does* smell delicious.

"Is this all for me?" Her eyes widen in surprise with that question as we walk hand in hand to our last location for the date.

"No," I say, and she looks mildly relieved. "I'm trying a bite of everything. It smells amazing. But the rest is yours." Her eyes widen again.

"It is so much food."

"That's what leftovers are for, little owl. You know I don't keep much at my place."

"Hmm, good point. Where are we going anyway?" She turns her head to glimpse at our surroundings, the inky sky leaving only the streetlamps to illuminate the spaces nearby.

"Somewhere pretty, we are almost there." We walk in companionable silence for a few more blocks until we come up to a large park in the city. In the middle, there is a pond that glimmers beautifully under the lamps that dot the place at night, the light breeze causing small ripples in the water. Lamps dot the paths through the park as we make our way to that little pond.

I set down our bags, and I lay out a blanket for us that I had tucked into my purse. Gabby helps me start to unload the food and pour the glasses of wine before we sit down, and she rests her head on my shoulder as she peers out at the picturesque view in front of us.

"This is beautiful." The awe comes through in her words. I wrap my arm around her and hold her close.

"It really is," but I'm not looking at the scenery, I'm looking at her. We stay like that for a while, but it is entirely too short. I could stay like that forever. "You know, one of the few places I had traveled to when I was human was Greece. I loved the food then, too. Beautiful country." I can still picture the warm sun on my skin, the smells wafting from the various restaurants with their outdoor seating, and the ruins dotting the visible landscape. That trip had me overjoyed for months after.

"Really? I had lived there for about two months, we stayed at a little apartment in Plaka, and just around the block there was a souvlaki place. I went probably more than I should have." Gabby grabs a bite of her gyro, a quiet moan leaving her as she enjoys it. The food may be delectable, but I know she is more delicious.

"Oh, I ate my fair share of food on that trip, too. I liked going to the different archaeological sites. I have heard they have found more since then. If I could go back and see them again, I would." I can hear the wistful tone in my own voice; whether it is from my memories or from my desire to travel again, I'm not sure. "I had always wanted to travel more. The opportunity just hadn't happened yet. I went to a few places before I was turned. Actually, I had a trip booked for Paris a month after my turn date." All that I can make come out after that is a bitter laugh. One month away from another place I had wanted to visit. I try to distract myself from the memory of having to cancel my dream trip with a pita dipped in tzatziki. It may not actually push away the pain, but it tastes good enough to provide a moment of respite.

"I'm sorry you didn't get to go. I can show you my own pictures from Paris, they aren't as good as yours would have been. But they would let you see the city." She offers with a sad smile, she knows how hard it has been for me not have my humanity. I wish she could have met me back then. I was more vibrant, more full of life.

"I would love that." I feel her squeeze my hand three times, I immediately return the gesture.

"I did tell my parents about you." She quickly takes a bite of tzatziki on some pita, as if she revealed something bad. I like that she wants to talk about me. I want her to think of me as much as I think of her. I want to consume her every waking thought like she does mine.

"What did you say?" I make sure to keep the amusement in my voice to relax her, her heart rate lowers.

"That I met this beautiful woman who looks like she is straight out of either a golden age movie or a pinup picture. That she treats me incredibly well. That I've fallen in love with her. That she has bad ass stingrays in her penthouse, which is like the most unhinged pet I've heard of in the best way," a small giggle leaves my lips. "I also told them that she is kind, generous, and very close with the people she cares about most. That she is incredible." I can feel the affection in her gaze.

"Well, whoever she is, she sounds pretty amazing."

"She really is." Her lips crash into mine, and I hold her in a tight embrace. Once we come up for air she says, "She is the best." With a small smile, she turns and grabs a piece of baklava and moans with her bite, a trickle of honey flows down her chin. "This one you have to try." I wipe it off her face and lick it off my finger with my own moan. "Actually try it." My eyes roll, and I pick up a piece and bite into it.

"Well, you're right, it is delicious." The honey flows from between the nuts and the phyllo dough; it might be my favorite thing I have had tonight. I put the rest of the piece in my mouth and clean off my fingers.

"How the fuck did you eat it without a mess?"

"A century of skill," I wink at her, and she rolls her eyes as she tries to stifle a laugh.

36

Well Shit

Gabby

The date was perfect. Josephine is always so beautiful under the starlight. She would look beautiful anywhere. The night just suits her with her cool-toned, pale skin and shiny black hair. She looks like the night itself. Walking up to her apartment building sends waves of peace through me. A night of going home with my love, carrying a bunch of delicious food, and replaying the night in my head. I really can't think of anything better.

I want this to be regular life, not just a perfect moment after a perfect date. I want to simply be home with her every night. When she opens her door, she quickly goes to put the food away, using her speed to have it all done in seconds, all while coming back with a bit more of the wine. The casual conversation flows so easily with her. It is like I've known her my entire life; we simply fit. Then I open my stupid mouth.

"Have you heard from Britt recently?" I ask, thinking she *should* have gotten back to her by now.

"No, last I heard, she is still planning to screw all of vampire kind over. I just keep replaying the worst-case scenario over and over in my mind." She takes a long draw of her wine as she rubs her temple with one hand.

"What is the worst possible outcome?" I leave three squeezes on her shoulder. It is like I can feel the tension dissipate from her body, that small touch of affection having an immediate impact.

"Britt gets herself killed by the Council, the world finds out we exist and we get hunted down or experimented on, we lose our sense of safety, and all-out war breaks out."

"Well, that was more than I expected. Did you say she could get killed?" My own anxiety spikes as I really process what she said. The Council *kills* people. Could I be at risk?

"Yes, if they can't make you be quiet, they either force turn you or kill you if they can't scare you into submission after a close call. If you spill the secret it is automatically elevated to one of those more extreme options." Note to self, don't even think about sharing the whole vampirism thing.

"Well, shit."

"Well, shit indeed." She leaves to pour herself more blood.

37
Blood Lust

Josephine

My night with Gabby did not go as expected. I thought we would be getting naked under the sheets again. Instead, I went through most of my blood supply, and we talked through my anxieties. And hers. The Council can be a terrifying prospect, especially for humans. It's terrifying to me too. The normal vampires and the benefits are fantastic. The leaders, though? They thrive on cruelty. So much of it has been committed against me.

1950

Leaving the Council building was hard. It took me weeks to be able to go home because just existing was beyond difficult. I would scream and cry, clawing at my skin only to watch it knit itself together. I felt like an abomination, like I would be doomed to hell if I ever died. Or maybe that was *hell. Enough decades passed that my faith did too. But back then, it was its own form of torture. I mean, who can ever handle being something that would be considered evil? Something that would doom them to an eternity of torture?*

Some people broke. They would run screaming from the room. Later, I learned they went outside into the sun and burnt alive. De Medici had the best time telling us whenever someone didn't make it.

"Remember James?" Her laugh that followed sounded sinister. I did *remember him. A head of dark brown, curly hair, a nose that looked like it had been broken a few too many times, and a scar across his cheek. I couldn't tell you if he was kind, or had a vicious streak. Only that he was out of his mind from the turn. "He was weak. He couldn't take the* gift *I have given you. Eternal life." She threw her hands*

up in the air like she was some goddess there to be worshiped. All she was, all she is, *is a stone-cold bitch with a love of torture.*

"He ran out those doors," another dramatic motion had followed as she pointed to the simple wooden door that kept us in the room to transition. "And out of the building. Do any of you know what happened after?" No one made a sound, we all laid there in our agony, not trying to draw her attention over to us. De Medici's eyes rolled at our lack of engagement. "It was daylight. *He burned alive. Have you ever seen someone lit on fire? Every last part of him burned. He kept burning until, for a moment, only his bones were left, and even they were lit ablaze." Her smile was serene. Like it was a happy sight for her, you would have believed she was talking about a regular campfire and roasting marshmallows over it.*

I remember feeling sick to my stomach. "If any of you think about going out those doors too soon, you should remember James. If you quit like him, if you abandon *us like him, then you'll* burn *like him too." De Medici had walked out of the room in a flourish of material. In that moment, I wanted to burn too. Anything would have been better than the bone-deep pain I felt.*

I try to shake the memories out of my system before picking up another round of blood. I don't plan on staying tonight. But I need the sustenance; I drank too much yesterday. Plus, this weekend is trivia night. I need enough to get me through that. And if I know one thing for certain, a room with three vampires in a high-stakes game of trivia requires it to be flowing.

I push through the door and embrace the silence of the hall. I sneak through the building, trying to avoid anyone and everyone. Woefully, I have no luck. Beverly rounds the corner, scurrying past with her own bags filled to the brim. She sticks to the shadows like she is trying to hide from any prying eyes.

"How is your human?" I ask her, happily standing on the fact that *I* didn't almost fuck up. And hoping Britt doesn't either.

"He isn't a human anymore." Her eyes narrow at me; she knows I know that already. But sometimes it is so much fun to twist the knife when she has spent decades putting everyone else down to feel more important, to feel better than everyone around her. The rage literally glowing in her eyes, the bright red color shining enough to cast her face in the same shade. Her fangs already descended.

"Are you in blood lust?" I ask. Beverly rips open one of the blood bags and takes a deep draw from it, letting her fangs go back in, although they stick out a bit more than they should. Her eyes lose some of their glow, but she appears almost lost to the feelings.

"No." She's lying.

"And your new vampire?"

"Still in custody, if you must know." I can see the energy coiling through her; she is skittish, like a rat that's ready to bolt. Something feels entirely *wrong* about this.

"It is important to stay up to date on security risks. And those suffering with blood lust." I give her a cautious glance and speed past her. I'm sure her fangs have descended fully again. The world can't handle Beverly in that state; she is terrible enough without it. Adding it in would make her impossible to handle. It could make her deadly.

Once I make it to the blood room, I pull out some shopping totes and stuff them full of bags, tucking some wine bottles on top to hide them from any humans before heading back home.

I grab my phone and text the guys.

We have a problem. Beverly is in blood lust.

I wish I could say I was surprised. The hateful bitch was always going to end up that way eventually.

Michael

Did you tell the Council?

Christopher

Absolutely not. I may hate her but I'm not going to be responsible for her staking.

If the Council can't bring her back they will kill her; the longer it lasts, the less likely it is to be fixable. They'll find out soon, blood lust can't be hidden for long. I just don't want to be someone's death sentence. Beverly may be terrible, but I'm no killer. A shiver runs down my back as I remember the glowing look in her eyes. I try to relax with a mug of blood, taking a half hour to just...exist.

It wouldn't have mattered anyway. Look:

Christopher

He attaches a link to a video from the news. Posted a minute ago. I click on it immediately. The title reads "People found in park, drained of blood," and the video only gets worse. They depict people in the park from my date last night, with fang marks left on their necks. This really isn't good. Beverly may have fucked all of us over.

And yet, a part of me is relieved.

Britt isn't the one to do it. She is safe.

38

Stay

Gabby

The anxiety has wormed its way under my skin; it is electric and alive there. I feel like I have found my stability, my home, my family, my future. Then Britt doesn't just cancel it right away? She threatens all of it by being selfish? I can't take it. I can't take fearing for Josephine's safety.

My little punching bag does nothing to help.

I need a drink. So, I pour myself a shot or three of vodka and down the glass. I try painting my feelings out, but seeing Josephine's face and knowing this could be her literal life at stake makes it impossible to paint her. And I can't seem to want to paint anything else.

Then the night gets worse.

Lock your doors. Stay inside, I love you.

Josephine

What do you mean?

While I wait for her response, I lock the doors and windows in my studio. Anxiously pacing back and forth in front of my window once I finish. Then she sends me a link. People have been left drained of blood in the park, the same one from our date the other night. The sight is shocking. I see the picturesque little pond that we held hands by. Except instead of the landscape we enjoyed, it is now littered with bodies. People scattered across the lawn with every last drop drained from them. I clutch at my chest, my anxiety spiking high enough that I feel like I could be dying. My breathing comes in more rapidly, but my eyes stay glued to my phone.

What's going on?

A vampire from this area went into blood lust.

Josephine

I don't understand

It's when a vampire loses their mind. They can only focus on the kill. Full predator, no humanity.

Josephine

Well shit. A scream rips out into the air, and my gaze breaks from my phone. Whipping my head around, I look outside my window to see someone being grabbed by another individual, their neck being bitten into.

They are outside my apartment. I'd show you...but...

,

I'm going over there. Stay inside.

Josephine

My mind races. I keep my eyes locked on the action below as my girlfriend comes into view and I say a silent prayer to my gods to keep her safe. I *need* her to be safe.

39

Origins and Endings

Josephine

As soon as I receive Gabby's text, I'm off. I run over to her building and see Beverly outside draining a man of blood. The guilt from letting her go is unbearable; I didn't want to be responsible for her death, but now I think I might be responsible for all of them. I won't be for Gabby's.

"Beverly, what are you doing?" I yell out into the night, she removes her fangs from the man as she still holds him close. Her eyes are glowing bright red, she is entirely gone now. All that is left of her is her hate and aggression, fueled by the insatiable hunger of blood lust.

"*Go* away." Her words come out garbled, like she is unable to really articulate anymore. She has gone past the point of no return. I had already texted the guys while I ran so they could contact the Council. I just need to keep her here long enough for them to handle it. Keeping them from knowing before the killing started was one thing, but she's a risk to everyone and everything now. And it's my fault.

"Beverly. Calm down." I have my hands out to her in a pacifying gesture. She tosses the man to the ground, leaving him barely alive, only small rivulets of blood leak from the puncture wounds. He will die unless he is turned. I'm sure the Council won't waste an opportunity to "save" a life and beat their own forced conversion rules. Hopefully, he survives *that.*

"And I need you to leave. Or should I go up there?" She points to Gabby's window where she stares out at the scene. "That's your little *human,* isn't it?" Fury boils inside of me. My own fangs descend and I quickly swallow some blood from my bottle, unwilling to end up like her if for no other reason than to protect Gabby.

“Don’t fucking touch her.” I don’t think I’ve ever meant something more. The idea of anyone hurting my girlfriend? Unimaginable rage fills me at the very thought of it. Another mouthful of blood.

“Aww. Have you become attached to the little blood bag?” She taunts. The air fills my lungs as I take a few deep breaths, determined to keep the full rage inside me. I let out a little of it by running up to the demon in physical form and punching her in the face, a crack reverberates through the air from where my fist meets her jaw. My knuckles split and stitch themselves back together in a matter of moments; her jaw does the same.

“Don’t speak about her like you could ever understand what it is like to sincerely care about someone.” I practically growl out the words. She swings and strikes my cheekbone. I feel a crack in my face. The pain flares up before dulling with the start of healing. I reach for a fallen stick on the ground and hold it up to her. She backs away like a caged animal. In a way, I guess she is. “Stand down, Beverly.”

The air moves faster next to me, so loud that I can hear it, and the members of the Council appear, weapons in hand. They surround Beverly; she doesn't even have the chance to react. Theo drives a silver blade into her heart before turning to me. She disintegrates into a pile of ash while he stares right at me, the breeze blowing her away.

"She was too far gone," Theo says, voice as cold as ice. Then they leave, like it was business as usual. Nothing felt like it was normal. Hearing about blood lust and seeing someone lost to it was something else entirely. Now all that is left are the memories of her hate.

The man is no longer there. The Council never wastes an opportunity.

Pack your things. I am taking you home with me. I need to see that you're okay.

She immediately sends a thumbs up, and I run up to her door. The lock clicks, and I run to bring her into my arms, tightly embracing the woman I love. I kiss her like it is the last moment in the world, like she could breathe life back into it through my lips. I hold her close to me so long that time seems to have stood still, like this moment could stretch for eternity while she is in my arms. She pulls back, and it feels like my heart could shatter at the loss.

"Are you okay?" Gabby's voice is timid and unsure as she asks me.

"I'm not sure. Are you?" I force myself to pull back a bit and examine her. No injuries. I thank anything that could be out there for her safety. For keeping her in my life.

"I am worried about you. She hit you." Her eyes have a rage behind them I had only seen flashes of before, her even temper dissolving just a tad. I caress her cheekbone and smile up at her.

"I'm okay. Vampire healing." I lift her hand to touch the cheek where I was hit; it isn't tender anymore.

"They killed that vampire." She points to her window across the apartment.

"They did."

"Couldn't she have been saved?"

“No. Once you reach the point of blood lust where you kill like that... that’s the end. There is no getting better.” The sight of her draining that man, fully submitted to her animal side, is haunting. I think I’ll have nightmares for weeks. She gives me a tight nod, her lips drawn in a firm line.

“I need to grab my things,” Gabby says, quickly running around the studio, throwing things into a bag and swinging it over her shoulder, her easy-going pace abandoned for a flurry of motion. “I’m ready.”

“Can I carry you? I want to get home fast.” She nods again and loops her arms around my neck so I can scoop her up in a bridal carry. I place one soft peck on her lips and walk out her door, locking it behind us. Then run full speed home and bring her into my apartment. I make sure to lock it securely. “Are you okay? Was the ride alright? I’ve never carried a human before.” I say sheepishly. Her hair has been mussed up by the wind.

“I’m okay, maybe a bit motion sick. You can go really fast.” She wobbles as I put her down. I keep my arms around her so she stays steady enough. The two of us walk over to the couch, and I lay her down on it.

"I have some of that ginger tea that you like, that should help." I go and make her a cup of it, and myself one of blood. I smile at the brand new kettle I ordered just to make her drinks exactly how she likes them, before I pour her a cup of tea and add the sugar. Exactly how she likes it. I carry the mugs back and give her hers.

"Thank you, love," she takes a slow sip and lies back on the couch. "I think driving might be easier for me." She says, and I let out a soft laugh.

"I can see this. I needed you to be safe at my home. To make sure no one could touch you. She threatened you, and I saw red like I never have before." The anger is still pumping through my veins. The *thought* of anyone wanting to hurt her burns.

"I was safe upstairs." She smiles gingerly, before clutching her stomach and drinking a little more of her tea.

"I *know*. I just—I couldn't handle the thought of anyone hurting you. I broke her face for a moment, though." I can still recall the sound of the crack of her jaw beneath my fist. Her giggle brings a bit more life back into me.

"That's pretty hot."

"Hot?"

"Yeah, my bad ass vampire girlfriend fought with an out of her mind vampire and broke her jaw for me. That's hot." She says. I roll my eyes while I shake my head and laugh. I'm not exactly sure how my outburst was attractive, but I'm happy to have her think so. I take a sip of the blood, letting it help bring me back to normal. I need the calm it can provide. "What does the blood do for you?"

"A lot of things. It gives me energy, keeps me full, it can calm anxiety, or anger, or sadness. It feels like magic half the time."

"Turning into the undead is kind of magic."

"I guess you're right," the corners of my mouth turn up, and I let out an unexpected laugh. She views my curse like it is fantastical, not like it is evil. I wish I could do the same.

"How did you guys become a thing? Like, who was the first vampire?" I slip down onto the floor and hold her hand, rubbing circles with my thumb along hers.

“Do you want to hear the story?”

“Yes, please,” She sips her tea and looks into my eyes. I can feel her love in her gaze. She bites on her lip and waits for me to start the tale.

“There is an old civilization, the name has been lost to time. We are talking a few millennia ago. They had a level of power we don’t have today. I’m not sure how they got it, or how it got lost. But they wanted to beat death. Like Egypt, they had their mummies; they attempted to hold off death through preservation. Except their power helped make the bodies look *perfect*. Like they could come to life at any moment.

“One day, the most powerful woman in the civilization thought she could birth new life, just not in the traditional way. She made a concoction and fed it to her daughter, a beautiful young woman. The stories always call her Vita, life. Then the mother drained her daughter of blood. She chanted, she prayed, she did countless tasks over the next few hours in the deepest room of her home. Vita woke up.

"But she had changed. Now she craved the blood of other humans. She could no longer go out in the sun. Silver burned her flesh. She was entirely different. But she did not die. People lined up to be turned into creatures exactly like Vita. Her mother did the same process on each of them, not realizing it could be accomplished with the blood of a vampire. People from other areas were brought back, bound up, and given as gifts of food to the new creatures in hopes that they would be chosen next.

"Over the next few years, most of their community had been turned. They could no longer just bring in their enemies for feeding on. The vampires had to spread out. Vita's mother had died in the move, so no new vampires could be made. Until Vita fell in love. The story calls him Mors, death. The pair apparently had a wild love affair. Vita couldn't bear the thought of eternity without him, so she came up with an idea. She fed him her blood like it was the mixture her mother made, like the very recipe she took to her grave. Then she drained him of his blood, drinking every last drop. She prayed to her gods, she chanted, she wept, she held him close. He woke up the same as her.

"That is the story we have all heard from the Council." Gabby's eyes had held mine the entire time. She is completely enveloped in the story; her eyes are shiny with emotion. I was too, when I first heard it. Who couldn't wonder why we were made? How we were made. And who wouldn't understand wanting to turn someone they loved so dearly?

"Is it true?"

"Yes."

"Do Vita and Mors still exist?"

"They do. They are technically in charge of the Council, but these days they only send out staff to do their bidding. They choose to stay secluded. I'm sure living thousands of years would drive anyone to isolation."

"That's so sad," her eyes have softened, the green somehow looking more vibrant with the sheen of unshed tears in her eyes.

"I don't know. They clearly still love each other. What could be sad about that?" My own heart hurts when I think about me and Gabby like that. I want her for eternity. But I'm not sure I could ever curse her like that. Her hand squeezes mine in the one two three pattern I taught her. "I love you too."

"How have you all stayed hidden all this time?" She asks. I huff out a laugh.

"No one wants to believe the things that go bump in the night are real. They definitely don't want to believe they look just like them. They come up with stories to try and hide the truth, or fiction to make themselves feel safe if they know it. People will do anything to not really have to face the unknown. Anything to not face their fears."

"You're not wrong. Realistically, nothing is more terrifying than the unknown."

"It's why people who want control keep information inaccessible. If you don't understand what is real, then everything is a terrifying possibility. You're left to trust whatever they tell you. So vampires and the people who know about us keep it a secret. You're left to either be considered crazy and believe we exist, or sane and believe that we are fiction." I lean my head to the side and rest it on her stomach. She moves her hand from mine to stroke my hair. I feel like I could almost purr like a cat at that; it is just so calming.

"Anyone who would know you could never be afraid. You're too incredible."

"I pale in comparison to you." I nuzzle into her. We lay like that for some time. Her hand in my hair, my head resting on her as it lifts and sinks with her breath.

"I know it's early," her voice breaks the silence, but is heavy with sleep. "But I'm exhausted after the...excitement from today."

"Me too, little owl," I somehow pull my head up from her stomach and finish my now cool blood. "Let's go to bed." I glance at the time; it still won't be daytime for another two hours, but the events of the day have left us both worn thin. I take our mugs as she goes to change. Her fuzzy little shorts and soft cotton tank top are adorable on her. Her hair is pulled back in a silk scrunchie. She is only half under the covers and asleep by the time I come in. Her breaths are even, and she lets out the smallest snore. Absolutely adorable. Quickly, I change into my own pajamas, wash off my makeup, and climb into bed with her. I place a gentle kiss on her nose and curl up next to her, drifting to sleep before the sun starts its ascent.

40

On Beating Vampires

Gabby

I can't believe everything that happened yesterday. I feel like I cycled through a million different emotions and had an entire season of some drama on TV played out in real time. And yet, none of it mattered as much as being able to fall asleep in the arms of the woman I love after she ran to my side to protect me.

I've never been weak. I have never needed saving. I still don't. I would have stabbed that bitch with a silver knife if I had to. But it felt nice to have someone *want* to protect me, to want to keep me close. I guess I had never really had that. Not in full. My parents protected me enough, but they always expected I would do most of that myself while they were out on their adventures. I think I like being taken care of. It is kind of nice.

Unfortunately, it doesn't stop my head from spinning. Just hours ago, I was watching everything unfold from my window. I could have sworn that man on the ground had died, but he disappeared with the group of vampires. When I asked Josephine about it in the evening, she told me the Council would have turned him; saving a life is one of the only reasons they can force convert now. I was shocked that they could do that at all. She told me I shouldn't be, that they will use any loophole they can find to bring their numbers up and still follow the rules.

I want to know more about her world. I want to be a part of it one day.

I have the rest of the night free before game night tomorrow. Truthfully? I can't wait. I have to prep my 20 questions for it, though. I scour through different websites, rack my brain, and write out my list and the answers.

Avoiding anything history feels like a necessity. If I'm competing against vampires, the past would only expedite my loss. Which makes me wonder what topics she will cover. I want to know more than anything. What does she find the most interesting?

Sadly, I have to wait an entire day to get my answers, or my questions, I guess. The hours spent focusing on it have me working on the collection of paintings in front of me later than I had hoped. I only wish there were a world where I could display them. She looks so beautiful, so powerful.

41

Warnings

Josephine

Today should have been easy. Sadly, I was mistaken. I received a summons to go to the Council to talk about the situation with Beverly. I rush through getting ready, knowing they aren't exactly patient. The outfit barely has me looking my normal, less polished than I'm comfortable with. It will have to do.

I run over to the Council building, its internal silence not causing its normal comfort. Instead, anxiety spikes in my chest, and I swear I can hear it. One of the familiars is waiting for me and leads me over to De Medici's office.

The door opens and her, Theo, and Rex are waiting at one end of the room. The heavy door shutting behind me sends dread through me; it sits bone deep like they are handing me a death sentence. Perhaps they will.

"Sit," De Medici's icy voice commands, and I sit down on the chair facing the three of them. She is dressed for intimidation today; she wears some of her bone accessories. The fingers hanging from her necklace click together when she moves, bracelets and a crown made of more bones make her look more like the queen of death and cruelty rather than the local Council leader. "We have word that you *saw* Beverly only hours before that little *vermin* went on her killing spree."

"I didn't know she was at that stage. I had assumed someone would have seen her in the blood room." I try to keep my voice level, taking a sip from the cup next to me. I try to stop the shaking in my hand, but the blood doesn't calm my nerves enough to hide it.

"Someone should have. The familiar is in my possession now." Theo says with a grin that sends a shiver of fear through my spine.

"It does not matter if someone else should have seen. You did and failed to report it." De Medici's fangs pop out slightly, and she takes a drink from her own cup. Rex just sits there leering.

"You're right." Why bother hiding it? They will only be more and more angry the longer I hide that truth, and I will still have to suffer those consequences. I truly hate the Council, not that I could ever say that out loud here.

"Of course I'm right, you stupid little human lover." She essentially snarls in my direction, looking like the rabid dog she is, the bones swing and clash together. "Theo, punishment." De Medici snaps her fingers in his direction, not sparing a glance his way.

"No. It should have been reported in the blood room." De Medici immediately tips her chalice back, her fist clenched in rage. "*But*, if you *ever* fail to report blood lust again, I can assure you that your punishment will be *severe*. Remember Tiffany?" I can feel my face pale. Who could ever forget about her?

1970

Tiffany's punishment was public. They had her in the auditorium of the Council building. The floor and walls had been covered in plastic. The bell-bottomed suit in bright colors and the patterned shirt that Theo wore contradicted everything around him.

She was secured with silver cuffs to a table. She had let her long-time boyfriend, another vampire, go full blood lust without saying a word. She picked up blood for him, let him stay home, hiding his condition. If she had shared it, they would have tried to treat him, but I'm sure she didn't want the chance of losing him.

She did anyway.

It was forced attendance. De Medici presided over the whole thing, sitting in the corner and staring at Tiffany being tortured. Watching her body restitch itself. Theo never let her die.

It didn't matter, though. The same night she was released, she drove a stake into her own heart. I'm not sure if it was her boyfriend dying or if it was the torture. Probably both, I know I wanted to stake myself after my loss to be next to Amanda again. She couldn't handle life after that moment. I can't blame her. The loss alone is enough to want to go with them. But what she went through? What we all had to witness her go through...it was indescribable.

"I understand," I say. My shoulders threaten to slump forward, and my limbs are like jelly from the fear of that ever happening again. "I won't fail to inform you."

"Dismissed." De Medici says, her attention focused on Theo. She doesn't speak a word until I leave the room, but I can tell it won't be good. She never liked him being lenient. Yet, sometimes he was. Sometimes he was crueler than her.

I stop in the blood room before heading home. I have enough for the trivia night set up for myself and the guys, but with the stress of tonight, I feel like I might end up on an absolute blood binge with some trashy TV about humans getting up to pointless things while I write out my questions for the month. I can't wait to see Gabby tomorrow. It feels like an eternity away.

I'm sorry Auntie, can we talk?

Britt

I am not sure how to feel receiving a text from her. Part of me is relieved that she reached out, that she has apologized. The other part of me doesn't know if I can trust her yet.

The evening after trivia night.

Thank you

Britt

After her text, I pick up some blood and run to get settled at home. I make a massive mug of the blood to try to relax from the Council and from Britt reaching out. I narrowly escaped without some form of punishment, and it would have been severe. Somehow, the anxiety of talking everything through with Britt is worse.

I try to distract myself by placing an order for delivery for tomorrow night from a restaurant that specializes in appetizers. Their whole menu is snack-based, and I know it will be a fantastic spread for the humans at game night. The guys *still* haven't told Megan. Luckily,

Gabby is aware. I don't know how they have hidden it for this long, but it will be an interesting night full of lots of opaque water bottles for us.

I drain my blood and pour another giant mug of it and throw on my reality TV show and scour the internet for some new questions. I would love to redo some of my best ones for Gabby, but I can't. I want one of us to crush those two. I think we just might succeed, as long as I *don't* reuse any. Within a few episodes, I have drained a few bags of blood, my nerves have settled, and I have all twenty questions finished.

I spend the rest of my night going through the pictures for my exhibition. I narrow it down to the ones I'll use and have enough time before bed to edit one of them. Only forty-nine to go. I think I groan at that realization. My favorite part of the process is taking them, not so much the editing part.

After that first edit, I finish my blood and tuck myself into bed, preparing for a fun day of competition to start tomorrow.

42

Trivia Night

Gabby

I woke up later than I had anticipated. I have barely enough time to get ready, grab my things, and hop into a ride share and have them speed over to Josephine's place. Naturally, my own elevator was out *again,* so I had to *run* down all 10 flights of stairs. By the time I make it to her place and the elevator carries me up, and I reach her door, the fatigue is setting in. When she opens the door, I can barely even recognize how beautiful she is; the exhaustion is dire.

"Tea, please." I reach my hand out to her like I'm weak and in need of some serious aid. Josephine rolls her eyes, gives me a kiss, and heads to the kitchen to make me a cup. Brewed strong, just like I like it. She always knows exactly what I like.

"Didn't sleep much?" She calls through the opening.

"The exact opposite. I got too much sleep. When I woke up, I only had a few minutes to throw some clothes on, and then the elevator was out."

"Again?" Her voice is filled with shock. Honestly, I wish it were different. But I swear that thing stops working if someone *looks* at it wrong. It is infuriating.

"Unfortunately."

"I have bread? Or one of those soups you like? The rest of the food will be here in an hour, but you need to eat something." I can't help but laugh.

"I would love some bread." Her sigh of relief is palpable.

"Good, because I have to go shopping for some more food for you." Her stance is apprehensive as she shifts her weight around, like she is nervous about what I would think. She always has a few things on hand for me, but buying food is still new for her; she hasn't had to in decades. When Britt comes over she brings her own, or Josephine orders it in. But shopping? That gets her a bit nervous.

"Well, I happen to love those things," I say, and her face lights up.

"I got a baguette." She runs off to go fetch it and brings it to me with some butter on the side. "I remember liking my bread buttered." I smile at her.

"Buttered bread is great. Thank you." I say. She has her own cup in hand, the metallic smell wafting over to me while I enjoy my tea and eat the snack she must have bought today. It tastes too fresh to have just been sitting here.

"Are you ready for trivia?" She asks.

"Hell yes. I just hope one of us wins. Although I kind of hope it's me."

"Oh, I'm going to win," She says confidently. "But most importantly, the guys are going down."

We spend the rest of the hour curled up with our drinks and my breakfast. We talk, we laugh. It is everything I want. I want this forever. I want *her* forever. I open my mouth to tell her, and the doorbell rings through the house. Josephine excuses herself to let the others in. They flood into the house with a mess of hellos and kisses on the cheeks. Megan squeals and runs over to me for a quick hug.

"Ready for trivia night bitch?" She asks

"I'm taking you down." I narrow my eyes at her.

"We all know I'm the master of taking things down here."

"Maybe in your throat." She fakes offense, and we end up snort-laughing as the others make their way over.

"What's so funny?" Michael says as he loops his arms around Megan and gives her a peck on her forehead.

"Her oral skills," I tell him as Josephine reaches for my hand.

"Now that is *far* from funny. More impressive than anything else." Christopher adds in and gives a quick kiss on the lips to each of his partners. They are *adorable*. It solidifies the idea of spending forever with Josephine. We could have that kind of love forever. Like Vita and Mors, and Michael and Christopher. My muse drags me out of my thoughts with three quick squeezes to my hand.

"I think my little owl here should read first, then you," she points at Megan. "Give our newcomers the first go."

"I'm down." The guys say in sync. We all exchange glances in silence before someone breaks out into a burst of laughter, creating a domino effect across the group. The doorbell cuts through the laughter, and my stomach rumbles. The bread was delicious, but I'm *hungry*.

"That will be the food." Josephine drops my hand and races to the door, bringing in a bunch of different boxes. "The snacks have arrived." She says as she carries the mountain over to the table. Jalapeño poppers, potato skins, garlic bread, wings, nachos, soft pretzels with beer cheese, and a variety of other snacks cover the table. Everyone goes and grabs a plate, even the vampires, since apparently they haven't told Megan yet. I wonder if they ever will. I hope they do, she will *love* it. With our plates loaded up, wine poured, and water bottles essentially strapped to the vampires' sides, the game is about to begin.

I take my place in front of the group and pull up my questions. They are a hodgepodge of different categories, ranging from "What shaped poop does a wombat have?" (cube) to "What town was Romeo and Juliet set in?" (Verona), and question after question was answered. Normally, by one of the vampires. Apparently, you pick up a lot of random knowledge from having decades of trivia nights. Then it is Megan's turn. In a very Megan fashion, hers are all about sex. And unsurprisingly, her boyfriends get a lot of them right. So does Josephine, though. I think my cheeks stayed permanently red for the entire set of questions, flushing even harder when my girlfriend had the answer.

Josephine does a set about photography and rays. I got 10 of them right. Before knowing her, I wouldn't have. Sometimes we sit around, and she gushes about her passions, the love for them thick in her voice. Her face lights up as she asks hers, her feelings plainly on display. The guys have general trivia questions. Megan and I are trailing far behind; the vamps have really collected their knowledge. I wonder if one day I'll collect just as much.

"Time to tally the scores," Josephine says with a grin. Since I'm definitely out of the running, I hope it is her so I can give her a congratulatory kiss.

43
Confession

Josephine

Everyone begins to tally up their scores. Gabby has 14, not bad for her first game at all. Megan came in at 12. Michael has 20. Christopher has significantly more at 26. I bite my lip trying to suppress my grin. Then I clear my throat and read my score to the group.

"28." Then I fully let my smile through as Michael groans and Christopher flips me off with his own cheesy grin.

“Congratulations,” Gabby says as she comes up to me, placing a hand softly against my jaw and kissing me. It is like the whole world zooms in on me and her.

“I love you,” I mutter into her lips as we pull apart. I feel her smile against me as she returns the sentiment.

We spend an hour or so talking with everyone. Megan seems like a great fit for the guys. She has Michael’s off-the-charts horniness and is quick-witted enough for Christopher. Hopefully, they actually tell her soon so they can see where it goes. I just hope she sticks around once they do. I know firsthand how delaying the news can make it more difficult. And then there is Gabby. The lights make her hair shine, the brown almost turning gold. Like she is some ethereal being. My heart threatens to beat out of my chest anytime I look at her.

When everyone says their goodbyes, I am thrilled. I get to be alone with her again. We clean up the food, stocking my fridge for her. And I remove the blood bags littering the floor, the guys and I kept slipping into the kitchen to fill up our bottles. I think we went through five or six bags each. After the cleanup is finished, I feel her arms wrap around me. She leads me by my hand over to the couch and sits me down.

"I really want to tell you something." Gabby bites her lip; her heartbeat increases. She meets my eyes, but they are only filled with nervousness.

"You can tell me anything." I hope my words reassure her, and I give her those three little squeezes.

"I guess it is really more of a question."

"Ask away." My thumb makes circles on her hand, my own heart beats faster with her nerves.

"Will you turn me?" My eyes widen, and the motion with my thumb stops. "I don't mean right now. But in the future. I love you, Josephine, and I want to spend eternity with you." Her words barely reach my brain.

"I'm not cursing you," I tell her. She stands up, the world feels out of balance, and everything sounds like it is underwater. It is all distorted.

"Being with you isn't a curse." Her tone sounds angry, I think. All I can feel is panic. The conflicting feelings of wanting her by my side forever and also not wanting her to go through the pain of being a vampire and the loss and loss and loss she would experience. Upsettingly, I can only seem to blurt out the second part.

"I love you too much to turn you." I have to hope she can understand what I mean because the words refuse to come out right. Gabby's face is covered in tears; her expression breaks my heart. It's like I have rejected her, like I've broken her. I just need to try to explain, and I can't find the right words.

"So you want to watch me *die*?" Her voice is raised, cutting through the distortion.

"Gabby, of course not. Please, just listen," I reach for her hand to try and explain, and she rips her hand from mine. I become aware of the droplets running down my cheeks as they fall onto my shirt, the fabric becoming wet.

"I'm going home." She grabs her bag and storms out the door. I call after her, but she doesn't answer. I fucked up. I fucked up badly.

I just want to protect her.

44

Crescents

Gabby

My blood is boiling. She loves me too much to turn me? Loves me too much to have us be together forever?

That's such bullshit.

The tension is tight in my chest as I run from her apartment. The world blurs past me; it's like reality has disappeared. It has to be fake. I get a few blocks away before stopping, my hands are down on my knees as I take heaving breaths. Somehow, I manage to request a ride share through the fog of emotion.

I think I could throw up. I imagined that conversation going so many ways, but not like that. I never expected her, the person who has wept in my arms about loss, to say no. That she views it as love.

How can it be loving to choose to watch someone grow old and die in your arms if you can have them with you forever? How can it be loving to say no to eternity? Not right now, just *someday*.

I feel something wet dripping down my fingers. Looking down, I see blood flowing from my palms. I unclench my fists and red crescents are lining them, the crimson liquid pooling in the fresh cuts before trickling once again.

"Fuck." I rummage through my purse for something to clean it up, a few crumpled-up napkins at the bottom of my bag will work for now. I hold them to the wounds as the car pulls up. The driver looks concerned as I hop in, the napkins colored a bright red now. All I can do is flash an apologetic smile as they start driving...and looking at the back seat with worry. I try to keep my mask of calm on. Wanting nothing more than to scream and lash out. Let go of the facade I always try to have on. The one I let slip earlier.

The one that *deserved* to be let loose. Not even a "let's talk about it," no, instead I am told that it would be cruel to me to spend that long with someone I love. I don't *have* close family, my other friend is dating two vampires, and I don't think *they* would say no. So who would I lose? How would my existence be cursed? Does she not see how the circumstances are different? I *want* this. She got forced, I wouldn't be. My whole body is hot, like someone could burn themselves if they touched me.

The feelings in my chest and the stinging in my palms feel like a complete contradiction to the colorful sunrise coming up over the horizon. A bright sun peaking through the bottoms of the buildings, bringing light to the darkness. I've only plunged deeper into it, and I can't seem to find the light. Like a cloudy night sky during the new moon, no light to be found.

45

Protection?

Josephine

The sun is rising now, its golden hue shining through my windows as I watch, hoping to see Gabby come back. Wanting to talk to her, to tell her everything that is truly in my heart, that I couldn't get out. Let her know I *want* her forever. I just don't want her to suffer, and I don't know what to do: be selfish and keep her close or let her experience less loss and heartache, even if it means I suffer more of it. I take out my phone to send her a message.

Gabby please, I promise I didn't mean it the way it came out. Talk to me. I love you more than I can ever put into words.

Gabby opens it right away; no three dots ever show. I place an order with the florist where I buy all her flowers at and have some sent to her house in the evening when I know she will be up with a simple note that says "I'm sorry -J." I want to make it right. To talk about it somehow, and I can't think of the best words to say to her. I pour myself cup after cup of blood, trying to make my heart stop breaking from my own stupid actions, and it isn't working.

I have monumentally fucked up.

I drain a few mugs, couch-locked from my own actions. I stare up at the gallery wall that Gabby painted for me. Tiny tokens of her love, shoving it in my face just how phenomenal she is, and how I screwed up. I couldn't tell her how I feel; I choked. I couldn't tell the Council that Beverly was in blood lust. I messed up. Now several humans are dead, and my heart feels like it has been stepped on and ground down into the dirt.

My doorbell rings and drags my attention from my own self-hatred, a feat I didn't know was possible unless the interruption was from Gabby herself. When I go to the door, I see Britt there. I had completely forgotten that she was coming over; the hectic nature of trivia night and my fight with Gabby overshadowed the anxiety of the meeting.

"Come on in," I tell her between sniffles, my eyes still brimming with unspilt teardrops.

"Auntie, what's wrong?" Britt comes in behind me before pulling me into a hug.

"I made a mistake." I wipe the tears from my eyes and seat myself back on the couch. She nods, concern coating her features as she sits across from me. "What did you want to talk about?"

"I—I wanted to apologize."

"Go on."

"I shouldn't have upset you with the interview." She picks at the skin by her nails, a nervous tick she has had since she was young.

“That’s not why you shouldn’t have taken it. My anger shouldn’t be the reason, Britt. The risk to your *safety* should be. And if you don’t care about your safety, then mine.” I don’t have the energy in me to be angry, not tonight. I just want her to *get* it.

“I just thought that maybe—maybe this would help you out. That more people would go to your exhibition, so that they could discover your talent.” She says, I know she means well. My niece has always reached for the stars, and I love that about her. But I wish she would keep it from my own work.

“I’m not worried about accolades.” I reach for her hand to give her three squeezes. “When I make art, I do it to enjoy the process.” She nods, it’s as if she is being eaten alive by guilt. Her fingers look raw from her picking at them, and dark circles hang under her bright blue eyes.

“I’m sorry for how things happened.”

“I am too. No matter how angry I was, I shouldn’t have yelled like I did. I’m just worried about you. I want to keep you safe.”

“I know, Auntie.” She grasps my hand with our signature three squeezes before standing up. “I had just wanted to take the time to apologize for scaring you. I will see you at your gallery?”

“You know I won’t be there, but come visit me after. Okay?” I stand up to drag my niece into a hug. She examines my face, blotchy and swollen from my tears, and gives me a sad smile. I wish I could hide the remnants of crying.

“I will. If you need to talk, please reach out, Auntie.” She says. I nod, trying my best to put on a real smile. She turns and walks out the door, the expression of guilt never entirely leaving her face. No matter how mad I may be, I can’t abandon the last piece of family I have left.

Once the door clicks shut and I lock it securely, I hurry to the kitchen to pour myself as much blood as my cup can fit and drain it. I try to enjoy the feeling of reconciliation but the hurt from what I did to Gabby eats me alive. Mug after mug of blood seems to stop the worst of it, but the guilt lingers there like a ghost.

Eventually, the golden rays that swept across the ground are coming from high in the sky. The midday sun beating down on the humans skittering across the streets. I text the guys to come over once it is dark out. I need their advice. The only person I really want, though, is Gabby. I think my heart may have just been ripped out of my chest.

Sleep decided to evade me for the entire day. My thoughts are stuck in a loop of self-hatred and guilt. She never messages me back either. Not about my text. Not about my flowers. Nothing. Silence has never been so loud. Minutes after the sun has set, I hear my doorbell ring, and the guys are there looking worried. I refused to tell them what happened over text. My face is stained with tears, eyes puffy, and lips swollen and red on their own.

"Oh, Josie, what happened?" Michael says. I can't begin to gather the energy to correct him. I just walk into his arms and hug him and cry.

"I fucked up."

“Let’s sit down, okay?” Christopher says, and they lead me over to the sofa. Their expressions say it all; the worry is etched deep within them.

“She asked if I would turn her.” I relay the rest of the story, and Michael’s hand goes to his mouth in shock. Christopher’s eyes widen. The dam breaks, and my eyes flow again, the blood no longer containing them.

“And what did you mean to say?” Christopher asks.

“That I love her more than I think I have ever loved anyone. That I’m conflicted; part of me wants to be selfish and turn her, like I did with you two; another wants to protect her from the pains of immortality, from a world she isn’t a part of. I want to save her from being cursed. I also want to keep her next to me for eternity. I don’t know why I couldn’t just *say* that.” My words are split up by the sobs coming out harder than I can control. I try another taste of blood, and it’s not helping. I am half tempted to smash the glass against the wall.

“You know, it definitely could have been phrased better. But Josie, I think she will at least hear you out. She is upset right now. Give her time to cool down.”

"Try to realize, it isn't a curse to her. It is *life* with someone she loves." Christopher adds in. Part of me hates that he is right. I know it isn't a curse for her, but I don't know how to separate how I feel about vampirism from the equation. It has taken *so much* from me. Maybe it has given me some things too, the traitorous thought leaks into my mind as I look at the friends here with me.

"But how will she feel when there is more loss?" That's the real question. How will she handle that grief? How does anyone handle it?

"You can't know that until it happens. But she would have you." Christopher gives my hand a squeeze, his voice calm and reassuring.

"And you have us," Michael says. My tears just continue to flow as I pull them in for a hug. "Josie, how much blood have you drank?" He glances at the floor littered with bags.

"A lot."

"I see that, soon, I'm dragging both of you to the Council building." Michael gives me another squeeze and Christopher a kiss on the cheek. They look so happy together. They always do. Even when they were human they looked like the ideal couple. Seeing them made me believe in soulmates for the first time.

Could I live with myself for being selfish enough to keep her with me? Because I want that more than anything, an eternity of chats going late into the day in bed, kisses, art, dancing under the stars. I realize that I do want that, maybe even despite the consequences. Why didn't I tell her that? Why am I so stupid?

"You're not stupid." Christopher's voice cuts through my thoughts.

"Did I say that out loud?" My eyes widen in shock.

"Only the last sentence." He says, I sigh in relief. "You are not stupid, though. You are in love, and people in love sometimes make terrible decisions when they think they are protecting someone."

"I *am* protecting her."

"I know you think you are. But she is strong. She can make those decisions for herself."

I ignore his comment and force myself off the couch and get myself dressed as quickly as I can to go to the Council building for some more blood. I come out carrying a box for each of us, ready to fill them to the brim.

"Just how much are we getting Josie?" Michael's eyes are wide as he takes in the boxes.

"Enough to last me a while under extreme stress."

"She'll respond soon. It is almost your exhibition, she won't miss that." Christopher says sadly as we speed over to the Council building and into the blood room.

"I hope you're right. I have to finish the pictures tonight, and then frame them, and send them to the hall. They ship out in the morning." I say.

"Well, that's exciting. I can't wait to see how hot my clothes look." Michael's grin lights up my mood a little as he slings his arm around me. "I already know Christopher looked sexy as hell in his." His eyebrows wag and I actually let out a laugh. I needed this, I think, time with friends when everything is so unstable. It feels good.

"If you need any help, let us know."

"I will, but you know I like getting them ready myself." I had finished the editing in my spiral of self-pity, desperate for anything that made me feel like I have even a shred of a redeeming quality. So, the workload should be light... albeit more last-minute than normal. My attention has been hooked on Gabby since I met her.

It still is.

We load up the boxes with as many blood bags as we can, managing our precarious piles as we head back to my apartment so we can unload them into the fridge. Bag after bag gets taken out. It's like I'm stocking up for a war. In a way, I am, a war of my own mind.

"Thank you," I give them each a hug. "Not just for the boxes, but for being here. I needed it."

"We know. Are you going to be okay?" Michael says with a raise of his brow.

"I think so? Maybe? I don't really know."

"Well, be prepared, we are going to your exhibition. Michael got a green velvet suit, and it is...something."

Christopher says, his face pulled tight as he tries to disguise his horror over the velvet number.

"I can't wait to hear about it." I flash them a genuine smile, if not a bit small. I miss going to my own exhibitions; I just can't take the risk.

"Not going this time either?" Christopher always thinks I should attend.

"No, I like my anonymity. I want to create. Although if it wasn't for eternal life, I would go. I used to love going to them. They were always a great time."

"They can still be a great time, you'd just be a normal patron."

"He's right, Josie. Come with us." I shake my head violently.

"No, and it is still Josephine. There is too much stress this time, let's not add to it."

"*Fine*." Christopher's voice is full of drama, like he wishes he could push more. Usually, he would, I think he can see the worry that might be permanently etched into my face.

"Now, both of you get out. I love you and appreciate you, but I have too much work to do for this weekend." They respond with light laughs and quick hugs. Once they leave, I pour out some blood and drink it while I start.

The pain may have been dulled by their reassurances, but I have never felt worse. I have been trying to stay distracted by editing more and more pictures. Distracted from the exhibition and what people will think. Although I said I don't want accolades, it doesn't mean I want my work hated either. Distracted from Gabby and how much I hurt her, from how much I would do *anything* to make it better.

I shake my head and refocus on the images before me. They are of myself and the guys in various outfits. The collection is "Undressed" with each image being of us, although we don't show up, in various places in lingerie or more revealing pieces. Stripped down to that level of vulnerability. Shooting the collection had felt...different. I have always loved lingerie pictures, but they had never been in public before, not on a street or in a park, like this time.

I took countless whenever I was away from Gabby for a night, or even part of one. Nights when the guys were busy with Megan were filled with me capturing my own lack of image, the ones of the guys reserved for our nights together. They turned out exactly how I wanted them to. The pieces of clothing show up in intricate details, holding the shape of our forms without our skin showing through, the city lights shining through any translucent fiber. It has become my personal brand. Clothing without the body. No one has been able to figure out how they are made. I don't think they would believe it if they were told.

I finish up the last of my edits and print out all of the images so I can frame them. Picking the right color backdrop for each picture takes another few hours of my time. I made the palette different shades of green, like Gabby's eyes. A detail that's now like a stab in the heart.

I spend the rest of my night putting each picture with the best shade for each shot and placing them in the shiny golden frames. Some in the soothing, deep forest tones that surround her pupil. Some with the sage green that shines the brightest. Some with an earthy, mossy green that adds so much depth. Along with countless shades in between. They are all *her*.

I finish just in time, delivering the work to the front desk to be picked up as the golden rays of the sun light up the town.

46

Running

Gabby

I *hate* this. I hate that she said those things. I hate that I miss her. I hate that I want to reach out even though it has hardly been a day. I hate that it *hurts* more than I thought it could. I hate that the flowers she sent me are so beautiful. I hate that I feel bad for storming off.

Processing feelings has never been my strong suit. When I was a kid, I would run off to whatever park was nearby in whatever place we were living at the time. I'd stay until my parents found me hidden away, just trying to think. Trying to cope with our unstable reality. I think I was always expected to be happy; we had a “great life full of adventure,” but it didn’t feel happy. It felt tumultuous. When those emotions would run too high, I would leave or burst out into anger.

I hate that I still do.

I feel like I should have a better handle on it than I do. That by 25 I should be able to talk rationally right away. That anger shouldn’t show its ugly face before any other emotion. And yet, the sadness doesn’t hit right away. The rage is just starting to ebb. I spent the last day in a blind rage, and now? I want to cry. And honestly? That’s exactly what I plan to do. Cry, eat some pizza, binge-watch my comfort show, and try to not think about life. I hope it works for once.

Just checking in. I hope you’re okay

Josephine

I open the message and close it again. She has checked in twice now. Quick messages that I *should* be able to respond to, but I can’t yet. Tomorrow I will. I think. I want to. I don’t know. I hate feeling like this, like life is out of control. Like I've been rejected, my feelings being smashed down yet again.

2010

I was ten years old. We were spending a summer on the coast of France. It was beautiful. I loved the ocean and the food; the gulls would squawk and dip to try to take bites from people's food. I would spend hours at the beach just painting the ocean.

Even in a place that beautiful, I was still unhappy. I remember begging my parents to find one place to live; I didn't care where. That I was hurting. I wanted normal school, friendships that lasted. I wanted roots. *They didn't understand it. They still don't.*

"Don't you realize how lucky you are? Most kids would kill for this life!" My mom had screamed at me that day, when I had begged for normalcy. For stability. "You get to see the world. You have friends everywhere you go. What could possibly be wrong with it?" I held back tears as she berated me for wanting what any child needs. It wasn't the first time I had tried either. Every time, my feelings were

negated. They weren't valid. They weren't theirs, so how could it be true?

It was one of the days I ran away. There was a little park on the seaside with a large tree. The tree had a little hole in it, and I crawled inside and hid there the whole night. My parents looked all over, screaming for me. If they wanted me close, they could have listened. *Maybe they could have done what parents are supposed to do and make sure their child is okay.*

They would never do that.

The memories grip me like a vice. There were so many moments like that. This is apparently another. Like she *decided* my emotions for me. That she knows best. But it is also my life, my body, my choice. It just hurts.

So I do what anyone else would do. I shove another piece of pizza in my mouth and click "next episode" and try not to cry.

* * *

I think I might be ready to talk to her. I don't want to miss her exhibition; she has been taking her photographs since we met, planning the shoots for longer still. Sometimes I would sit with her while she got ready for her self-portraits. She would dress in exquisite pieces of lingerie that complimented her marvelously. Josephine is always so beautiful. Like she had been blessed by Aphrodite herself. My heart races when I think of her. I miss her. I want her back by my side. I want to hear her explain.

I think I'm scared.

Scared that she might say she doesn't love me like *that*. In the way you do when you want to spend forever with someone. I love her like *that*.

It is like I can picture us in the future, holding hands, looking this young and beautiful forever, this happily in love. Friends surrounding us, going through years and years by each other's sides, and just existing in our own type of happiness. Stability, love, family, friends, security, happiness, night after night of twinkling stars. That's what I can see in our future.

All I want is to have her with me like that for eternity. I'm fucking terrified that she doesn't. That she only loves me enough for at most a mortal life when I want her through every season. I would happily paint her for thousands of years if I could be that lucky.

I brew myself a pot of tea, the same way I taught her to when we first started dating. It just makes me think of her, how she hums to herself without realizing it as she preps it. In those early evening moments, she would have her hair slicked back into a neat bun with a silk robe tied loosely around her waist. How she always looks at me with hopeful eyes, wanting me to love it. Even if she did it poorly, I would love it.

I feel a tear trail down my cheek. I hate the unknown and being away from her. I think I'm finally ready to talk to her, give in to my desire to see her again, even though my fear tries to argue that it would be easier to simply not know how she feels.

I love you Gabby. I'm so sorry I hurt you.

Josephine

Deciding to actually swallow a bit of my fear, I message her back this time. Writing out a few words and then backtracking over and over again.

I guess it is my turn to be sorry I ran.

No, it isn't. I messed up. Please give me the chance to explain.

Josephine

I think about responding, but I don't think I can yet. Not like this anyway. I think this might be the time for one of those movie moments. How often do you get to have one of those? I quickly change out of my sweats that I may or may not have been wearing for the last few days and quickly shower. Washing away the tears, the anxiety, and the fears for what she *might* say.

I'm going back to my girlfriend and I'm fixing this shit because I don't think I can live without her. I scramble through my shower, thankful I put it on a shower cap to avoid having to dry my curls. I'm on a damn time crunch to get to my girlfriend. I throw on an outfit, and I can't genuinely say I have paid attention to what it is. Just *something* so I can leave.

Grabbing my purse and keys, I run to the elevator. Naturally, it is out of order again, so I speed down flight after flight of stairs, my breath heavy by the time I reach the bottom. I bolt across the street the very second I make it outside. I run to the little corner shop halfway down the next block.

The heavy door barely pushes open, but once it does a sharp ring comes out. I think I might genuinely run through the shop, but somehow I manage to contain my speed and make my way over to the snacks and rip a big box of sandwich cookies from the shelf. Her favorite. My impatience runs high as the kid at the till struggles with the machine. I bite my tongue; it isn't his fault I'm in a hurry, but dammit, I need to be next to her, to have her in my arms again. I already called a ride share, and they are approaching any second. As soon as I have the receipt in hand, I'm bolting out the door with the cookies tucked under my arm.

The ride seems to take forever. My leg is bouncing nonstop, and I think the person driving thinks I have lost my mind. Maybe I have. I don't care.

I just need to get to her.

47
Collapse

Josephine

I stare at my phone for a while. Gabby texted me. She isn't as mad as she was. But then she had stopped again. She opened my message, and nothing. That was ten minutes ago. I can't seem to put down the phone. Hoping for another shred of contact, something that tells me she is still mine. That she still loves me. That I haven't destroyed everything.

I manage to pull myself away and pour a mug of blood. I think that's all I have been doing this evening. The whole night has felt off, I woke up with the evening sun still in the sky while in a panic. But then she messaged, and I'm left to hope the off feeling was just anticipation for her words.

Until my phone rings. I dash to it to see if it is Gabby. Then my stomach plummets when Britt's name is there instead. The feeling of offness creeps up my spine stronger than before.

"Hey." I try to sound relaxed, but all I want is to talk to Gabby.

"Auntie, I fucked up."

"What do you mean?" My heart immediately starts pounding in anxiety, I can't even throw up anymore, and I still think I might from the immediate surge of emotions.

"I rescheduled the interview. I know I shouldn't have, but it was such a good opportunity. I thought you'd be happy once it was over. He asked how long you have lived in the city." Britt's words come out so fast they virtually become one.

"No." My head is spinning, and the world blurs around me.

“I fucked up, I said around 100 years,” her voice is laced with panic, but it is fading into the background. A ring of black closes in on my vision, and my body begins to sway.

“Get over here now,” I somehow manage to force out, my voice sounding weak to my own ears as I collapse to the floor. Everything goes black.

* * *

I can’t tell quite how long I have been out, but the call has been ended, and Britt sent me a text saying she is coming right over, and not to open the door. Or look at the news.

So naturally, I pull up the broadcast immediately. The anchor’s face has hints of fear in it.

“Tonight on Noxdale News, we are covering an ongoing situation. One that I’m not sure we ever thought we would have to cover. Local art podcaster Bradley Fayne released an unedited interview this evening.” The video begins to play, and it is Britt’s face.

"How long has Sage lived in the city?"A smooth male voice comes from the other end, saying the artist name I'm using currently.

"Around a hundred years now," She says confidently before the look of shock and anxiety comes across her face. "Wait, don't include that. I want it taken out."

"I thought you said she was 33?" He leans forward.

"She is." Britt could never hide her emotions well; the panic was written so clearly.

"That's a bit less than 100 years." He jokes, a light-hearted smile on his face. Britt looks too panicked to register that he found it ridiculous. She could have kept the secret even with her slip. Except she kept talking.

"I said I want that part removed." Her voice takes on an uncharacteristic hard edge.

"It can't be that serious, it isn't like she is a vampire," his voice sounds joking, but the panicked expression comes through clearer.

"You can't tell anyone, please," She begs. Giving it all away. The video keeps playing, and she revealed the secret.

She *told* him on camera. I zone out for a second, my heart making me feel like I could be *dying*.

"We have reports that a crowd is outside of the alleged vampire's apartment building. Are the things of our nightmares real, or is it all just a horrible publicity stunt? We will have to wait and see." The news anchor finishes off her segment as the screen opens to footage of the front entrance of my building. People are screaming at the doorman to let them in, but he is keeping firm with his denial. The mob of people are seething with rage. But two women push through. Britt and Gabby. *Gabby*.

I need her right now, both to hold for my own anxieties and to keep her safe from the crowd that appears ready to kill. Her face is full of concern. The doorman lets the elevator operator bring them up, the group rioting even more that someone else could be let through when they are hell-bent on getting inside.

48
Viral

Gabby

The sheer number of people outside her apartment has me shocked as the car arrives. It is like an angry mob is surrounding it. What the fuck is going on? As I climb out, cookies now safely tucked in my purse, I cautiously head towards the crowd and see Britt.

"Britt!" I call out, trying to be heard over the riotous group demanding to be let in. "What the hell is going on?" When she turns around, she looks like is overwhelmed by a mix of fear and guilt. This can't be good.

"The interview. You were all right. I fucked up. The interview was this morning. I thought he would delete the footage, but he didn't. By this evening, it went viral." That's when I listen to them.

"Show us the vampire!"

"Let us see that monster!"

More and more calls are shouted out, wanting to kill her. Wanting to hunt her down. Wanting proof she exists. Others are going for blood. The anxiety spikes so high that I throw up on someone's shoes. When I manage look up, he is holding a stake in his hand. I rinse out my mouth with my water and spit it at his face. He glares at me with pure rage, but fuck this shit, he is trying to kill my girlfriend.

"We need to get to her *now*," I say, grabbing Britt's arm. We start to push through the crowd, shoving people to the side. The doorman sees us and ushers us up, recognizing our faces. The ride up the elevator is tense and silent. Britt now has her key clutched in her hand, ready to not bother with ringing the doorbell. As soon as we reach the door, she opens it. Josephine is crying and pale. I run to her, and she meets me only a few steps in. I lean down and kiss her with every bit of passion I can muster.

“Are you okay?” I tell her at the same time she says, “I’m so sorry.”

“We can talk about that later. I just need to know that you’re alright.” I hold her face between my hands, needing to see that she is safe and unharmed after everything I saw outside.

“For now,” she nods as I cup her jaw, kissing her one more time. Then she pulls away and turns to Britt. “You, however. You have royally fucked up. Do you get what you have done? There is a literal *mob* outside my building ready to kill me! You have risked your own life because the Council could take you for questioning at *any* moment! You have ruined *everything!* Everything, Britt.” Her anger is palpable; she reaches for her blood to chug, trying to calm herself down and will away the fangs that popped out in that moment. “I have been there for you from the second you were born! There to protect you from a family that only wanted to shame and change you! I have been the one there for you! And this is how you repay me?

Telling the *one* secret you could never tell during an interview, you told me you *canceled*?" Britt is sobbing at this point.

"I'm so sorry, Auntie. It was an accident, I swear. After that clip, he asked me questions, saying it won't be released if I did. I shouldn't have trusted that."

"That doesn't help us right now, Britt. It being an accident doesn't stop my attempted murder or you possibly getting murdered by the Council!" Her phone begins to ring. "Fuck," She mutters and leaves the room while answering the call, an uncharacteristic curse leaving her lips. We both sit there in silence, except for the sound of Britt's sobs, as we wait for Josephine to return. Her stomps give away her return as they echo down the hall. "That was the *Council.* They have told every vampire in the city to lock down. No one can go anywhere. Two of them were out. And can you guess who else you just risked?"

"M—m—mi—"

"I'll put you out of your misery," I have never heard her so angry. Josephine is borderline feral, like a predator intimidating its prey into submission. She chugs more blood, her anger visibly reducing...but barely. "Yes, it is Christopher and Michael, they just texted they are on their way here to go through the angry mob with stakes outside my building! All because you couldn't keep the one most important secret. Because you *lied* and said I didn't have to worry." She downs an entire bag. "Luckily, they are bringing more blood and a very shocked and upset Megan with them because you also outed them to their girlfriend. I can't even look at you right now. Get the fuck out of this room. Find a guest bed and *stay*. Unlike you, I'm not willing to risk a life just because I want something." Britt leaves the room quietly, a lone sob exits her mouth once she turns the corner. I don't feel bad; she risked the life of the woman I love.

"Are you okay, love?" I walk over to her and take hold of her hand.

"No. Nothing is okay. I'm sorry you had to see that."

"You don't have to be sorry, I understand." I wrap my arms around her, and she begins to cry into my shoulder.

"About the other night—"

"No. That can wait. Let's handle this first. I need to know that you're safe. That you'll be safe long term. I love you too much to lose you like that."

"I love you too." The doorbell forces us from our embrace. Josephine peeks through the peephole. "It's them." The door opens, and the night won't get any easier from here.

49

Torture Room

Josephine

I don't know whether to be happy, relieved, pissed, or any number of other emotions at the guys coming...and bringing a human who is still reeling from the revelation of vampires being real to my apartment, as my life is at risk. Still, I think I need them more than ever. I run to pull them into tight embraces, forgoing our usual la bise greeting. My tears soak their shirts. Gabby's is already drenched. Megan runs over to Gabby to hug her friend as well. They talk in hushed tones. Megan is visibly freaking out, and my sweet Gabby is trying to calm her down.

"Are you both okay?" I scan my friends for any injuries from the crowd violently trying to force their way into my home.

"Yeah, we managed to get through unscathed. I think they are taking it easier on people getting through, just in case they *live* here. Luckily, *we* hadn't been specifically outed. How about you? Are you okay?" Christopher takes his turn to check me over for injuries, either on my body or on my heart. Much to my dismay, I think the internal wounds are plainly visible.

"Physically. I just don't know what we are going to do."

"Lock down, apparently. We got the call as soon as we picked up Meg."

"Did they call you yet, Josie? The Council said they are investigating. You should make sure Britt is safe." I can't help the scowl that comes across my face. Britt knows how important family is to me, and she gave away the most important secret to me like it was nothing; she gave away my safety.

"The traitor is in a spare room. I won't let my family die, even if their actions might end up with all of us dead. She apologized *yesterday*, claimed she canceled the interview. She *lied* to me and then outed us." The guys go silent; the gravity of the situation isn't lost on anyone. After a pause, I ask in a whisper too low for the humans to hear, "How are things going with Megan?"

Christopher sighs and runs a hand down his face. "Well, she is mad that she had to find out vampires were real from the news. Then, when we picked her up to shelter here, she was unhappy that we waited so long to tell her. And now she is having to process everything while a mob is threatening to break in." He says, gripping Michael's hand until his knuckles go white.

"So bad, it's going bad," Michael adds in, everyone keeping their volume low. "I'm hoping Gabby can talk to her."

"Me too, telling humans is *hard*. But right now we have more pressing issues to attend to. Let's go get some warm drinks started for our little group, and we can sit down and plan." The guys nod and we walk to the kitchen. I start to work on Gabby's tea while Christopher handles the blood, and Michael tries to start the hot chocolate. I end up pushing him aside before he butchers my family recipe. Soon we have mugs full for everyone, the comfort is needed with the chaos of the day. Michael runs a glass to my traitorous niece and then comes to sit in the living room with the rest of us.

"We need a plan," Gabby says, taking the lead. "The news is out, and clearly, the people are pissed. Actually, scratch that, the people are scared, and it is coming out through rage. Now we just need to show them that you're not dangerous." Her hands are wrapped around her cup of tea; this time, it is a soothing blend with chamomile in it.

"How are we going to do that?" When I speak, the defeat in my voice is overwhelmingly strong. I hate sounding so weak, but I am at a complete loss. But Gabby? She sounds so strong; she amazes me more every time she speaks.

"That I don't know, ideas?" She glances at each of the other people in the room.

"Don't look at me, I just learned that you *exist* from the news instead of my *boyfriends,* who have been hiding this from me for over two months now." Megan shoots daggers at the guys. I can't blame her. I waited too long to tell Gabby, but at least she heard it from me.

"I wish I had a camera that worked with us, so they could just see that we are safe and normal-ish. I don't think the Council would be down for allowing people into the building to see how we really obtain the blood." Christopher rests his chin in his hand as he tries to think.

"I think the torture room would also hurt our chances," I say before taking a sip of the sweet blood.

"I'm sorry, did you say the torture room?" Megan freezes mid-bringing her cup up to her lips.

"What about the humans?" Michael throws out there, purposely ignoring his girlfriend's question.

"What do you mean?" Gabby leans in, drinking her tea as she stares right at him.

"The other humans would be more likely to trust one of their own. What if you did a media campaign? Tell them how vampires *really* are. Our involvement in the arts, how many of us have fought for the same causes as them, how we are peaceful."

"It could work," my voice perks up. This could be what we need.

"I'm going to ask the Council about it. With how tumultuous things are right now, we need their approval. Otherwise, it won't just be Britt that is at risk."

"Are we seriously not going to talk about the *torture* room?" Megan's cup is now on the table, her voice rising in agitation.

"While you wait on that, I think each of us couples needs some time to figure out our own," I gesture around at all of us, "issues." Everyone nods. "I have a guest bed for you all to share. Michael can take you to the unoccupied one. We can reconvene out here later." The group nods, except for Megan, who is still left there in shock.

"Those issues had better involve addressing the torture room."

“Well, love, you have to understand the Council has rules.” Christopher starts, trying to figure out how to broach the subject with the fuming red head.

“So they torture people? What kind of shit have you two dragged me into? A bit of kinky fun is one thing, but *torture*?”

“Only if you break the rules.” Michael points both index fingers at her. “Realistically, the secret has already been exposed, so you should be good.” Megan continues to go off on the two of them for everything they have hidden from her, while Gabby and I drain our mugs. Afterwards, we rinse them quickly before sneaking off into my room.

“Well, that was certainly something,” Gabby says once the door has shut behind us.

“It was something indeed. I can’t blame her, though. I should have told you sooner, I know that, but finding out like this...she has every right to be mad.” After a beat of silence, I step closer to her, needing to close the gap between us. “I missed you so much.” I lean in to kiss her, not seeing her or talking to her for that long felt like hell.

“I missed you, too. It just hurt so much.”

“I’m so sorry,” I grasp her hands and lead her to the bed, we both perch on the edge of it with our hands clasped together. “I wasn’t saying what I should have-what I wanted to say. Let me try again: I love you. I want to spend every lifetime with you. I want to watch the sunrise as we go to bed, as the cityscape changes time and time again. I want to make art with you every day. I want to kiss you, hold you, and love you for eternity. I want you in every season. I want *you*.” My hands are gripping hers tightly, my eyes welling with emotion. I hope she *feels* how much I mean it. If I could rip my heart out of my chest so she can see it beats for her, I would.

“Then why did you say no?” Her voice breaks, tears threatening to spill from her own emerald eyes. It breaks me.

“Because it feels selfish to want that. Being a vampire has only caused me pain. I never want you to hurt, I never want you to experience that kind of repeated loss. I want you happy and safe in my arms, just without that pain.” The drops start to fall from her eyes. I am tempted to pull my hands from hers, to wring my own after wiping away the streams that are running down her freckled cheeks.

"I wouldn't be losing anything, I'd only be gaining a long life with you. My one friend is dating yours. My parents already only see me once a year, if that. They don't text. I'm already alone besides you and Megan. I *want* that long life with you. I want to dance under the stars with you, have magical dates in the night, everything. It isn't selfish to want someone you love in your life for the rest of it. That's just love." She kisses me, our salty tears wetting our lips. "I love you, Josephine."

"I love you too. Are you sure it wouldn't be—," the words catch in my throat. "Are you sure it wouldn't be a curse to you?"

"I promise. I. Want. That. Life. With. You." Gabby's eyes are glued to my own. When she looks at me like that, I feel powerless to say no to her.

"I'm not turning you yet, not with everything happening."

"I'm not asking you to." She leans in, her lips only a breath away.

“But in the future, I think we can do that.” I finally say, having been frozen under her stare. Her kisses crash into me, letting her hands trail across my body.

“I need you,” Gabby says between kisses, she leaves them down my neck as she unzips my dress. “And I need this off of you.” She pulls back just enough to slide it off my shoulders so she can start to undo my bra. “Your body is perfect. I’ve always thought you looked like a pinup girl or an actress from the silver screen. Just incomparable, timeless, pure beauty.” With that, she helps me take the bra off my arms and moves her attention to my breasts. Her tongue flicks against my nipple before taking the bud into her mouth.

“I wish you could leave marks.” There is always something so intimate about them. Hickies, bites, scratches, all the marks of passion from the night before lingering on your body. The memories of the pleasure surging whenever you catch a glimpse of them. I’ll have to settle for looking at the ones I leave on her instead.

“Me too, I want you to be able to look at them and see my affection across you.” She bites down softly, and a moan escapes my lips. Her other hand goes to grip me and tweak my other nipple. She moves her mouth to the side and places a hard bite on my breast, the pain quickly dulling to pleasure. “Imagine seeing that. Beautiful.” Her kisses and hands begin to move lower across my body. I lift up my hips, and she tugs my dress and thong down, leaving me exposed for her. “Let me show you a piece of our eternity.”

As she ends her words, she lowers her mouth to my clit. Flicking her tongue against it, tracing lines up and down and around the sensitive bundle of nerves, pulling a quiet moan out of me. Taking a break from my clit, she leaves me to whimper as her attention changes. She passes her tongue across my sex and audibly moans as she tastes me. I can’t help but thread my fingers into her hair and push her head right where I need her.

Gabby huffs out a laugh and gives me what I so desperately want. She licks and sucks on my clit, trying to make me forget my own name, I think. I’m pretty sure I almost *do* forget everything but her. My hand tightens in her hair to keep her in place. Her fingers gently go into me, stroking the walls of my pussy, making my moans turn into whimpers of need.

"Gabby, fuck. More, please." I plead as she continues her movements, honed in on my every need as my body begins to tighten.

"Come for me," she leans back barely long enough to speak, her lips still brushing against me, before she dives back in. Within seconds, I'm coming undone on her face. When she moves away from my core, her face is covered in my own release. "How do you taste so addictive? Getting to make you come with my mouth could inspire a thousand paintings, my muse. You should taste yourself too." She places her wet fingers in my mouth, and I clean them off, tasting myself on her. "See, delicious." She licks her lips and pulls me into her. I'm about to trace my hands down her body when my phone ruins the moment with a call.

"Yes?" I can't help the breathless tone in my voice.

"Get dressed and stop fucking. The Council got back to us." Michael says before the call disconnects, and I groan and flop back on the bed.

"I don't want to leave this bed, but I think we have to." I turn towards her, her hair mussed up, and her pupils dilated in arousal. I want nothing more than to bury myself in her tawny thighs. "The Council has a plan."

"Ugh, I don't want to either. Let's get dressed, I guess," she groans. "I'm thinking comfy clothes? Maybe something easy to take off?" I immediately smile at her; she is so carefree with clothing. She doesn't feel the need to be perfect. I love it. I could take a lesson from her book every now and again. Maybe I will tonight. "I have to borrow something because I really didn't prepare for a lockdown."

"You can borrow anything you want, little owl." I head to the bathroom while she rummages through my closet before coming out and throwing on my own pj shorts and top. She does the same. I can hardly believe how good she looks in my clothes; they hang loosely on her, and all I really want to do is pick her up and throw her back on this bed. If only that were in the cards.

"Ooo! I almost forgot!" Gabby yells and darts off to dig through her oversized bag. Out of it, she grabs a pack of sandwich cookies. "I brought you your favorite snack! It was kind of meant to be an I'm-sorry-I-ran-away-instead-of-talking present." She gives me a sheepish grin as she brings them over. I smile so wide that my cheeks hurt.

"I love it, thank you." I pull her in for one quick kiss before popping a cookie in my mouth. "Now I have to hide these or Michael will eat them all." I tuck them into my vanity drawer, take Gabby's hand, and head out into the chaos.

50

Press Release

Gabby

Heading out into the living room is like going to a war room to discuss battle strategies. I guess we kind of are. Josephine's hand tightens in mine, and she stands still. I follow her line of sight, and then I see it, well, I see *who* is causing her reaction.

"What is she doing out here?" Josephine hisses at the intruder. Christopher immediately comes over with placating gestures while Britt, the she in question, shrivels up about two sizes.

"I know you're mad at her, we all are. But this plan involves her. She *has* to be here."

"Fine." Her voice comes out icy. My own eyes drop in a glare as I look at my manager. Britt has threatened my girlfriend's safety, and it fills me with my own heated rage.

"Come on, Josie, have some blood," Michael says, holding out a pink colored milkshake to her. Would a blood milkshake taste good? I can't imagine it would, yet they are all sipping on them. There is a plain, vanilla shake left on the table, and I take it for myself. *That* tastes good.

"It is still Josephine." Her eyes roll, and she grabs the glass and settles in on the loveseat. I curl up next to her. Our legs intertwine. She is so soft. Her skin is like velvet. "What did the Council say?"

"They like the plan. The word is already out; now they are on damage control. They have reached out to the local news station to have the videos the girls make put out there. If you three are okay with it?" Christopher looks each of us humans in the eyes expectantly.

"Of course I'm in. These bastards are threatening her life, and I won't watch my girlfriend get staked because someone blabbed." I grip Josephine's hand three times as I turn to glare at Britt. My love returns them, and my stomach flutters with butterflies, even with the intensity of the moment. It does with every I love you, verbal or not.

"I'm in. Even though you two hid it from me," Megan glares at her boyfriends, her words come out sharply. "I don't want anyone to die either."

"Me too. It is my mistake, I should help fix it." Britt says, her voice is filled with regret, and she doesn't lift her gaze from the ground.

"Then it's settled. Tomorrow night we start recording the videos and send them out. Oh, before I forget, the local Council and Vita released statements." Christopher announces.

"What do they say?" Josephine asks. He takes out his phone and clears his throat.

"The local Council release says: We understand this may come as a shock to our Noxdale community, and the world at large. Vampires have been here since the founding of our city. As soon as there was shelter, there were vampires helping build it. We have long been patrons of the arts, a sector of Noxdale that has thrived. We have been a part of this community for generations, a part of your lives. Thank you for your understanding. - Sabina De Medici."

"Well, that doesn't sound like her at all." Michael scoffs.

"It's because she actually has to talk to humans for once, for her own safety. If she called them blood bags it wouldn't work. What did Vita say?" Josephine leans forward to hear the response. She had told me the vampire hadn't been heard from directly in over a century.

"I am called The First or Vita by vampires around the world. I am the first vampire. I have witnessed our species exist across millennia. I have also seen yours. While you may feel fear in regards to me or my children I can assure you we are no different. We have had our periods of violence, yes. But so have humans. I have seen more atrocities committed than anyone should. Cities have burned to the ground, people have starved beyond recognition, and I've seen them burned. From *both* of our species. I have also witnessed moments of tremendous hope and change. People who have fought for freedoms, communities that have come together to help when things go wrong, and incredible pieces of innovation. From *both* species. It is my hope that with this revelation, albeit a very unexpected revelation, that we may forge new understandings and bonds. That we may both grow better as a result. -Vita, The First, Supreme Head of the Vampire Council." Christopher reads the release from his phone; every vampire in the room listens with laser focus. From what I know, it is monumental.

"And we are supposed to do better than that?" I ask the group.

"You just have to be honest. These are statements from vampires. They don't trust us. They trust *humans*. No matter what you say, it will mean more." Josephine says to me as she grips my hand in hers.

"She's right. But for now, we have humans to feed and nerves to calm. What do you have?" Christopher glances over to Josephine, and my own stomach rumbles at his words. I hadn't noticed I was hungry. I was too wrapped up in her, and tragically pussy doesn't fill the hunger.

"Bread, soup, and leftover appetizers from game night." She says, taking one of her hands to run it along my leg. The guys nod and head to the kitchen to grab some of the food for the other humans and myself. They bring out the cold food for tonight: a few trays of dips, and various fruit.

"So, what are we supposed to say tomorrow?" I break the silence after the meal; it was too quiet for far too long. Josephine kept glaring at Britt the entire time. The guys were drinking their milkshakes, and Michael ended up rubbing Christopher's shoulders to ease some of his tension. Megan stared into her dip while Christopher gripped her knee. It was just too tense. Something had to give.

"Great question," Christopher clears his throat and sits up a bit straighter, releasing his grip on his girlfriend. "Talk about our good traits. How we only source blood from people who *choose* to donate to us, not ones that donate to the medical system. That we participate in the arts and charity. Talk about how we treat you, how there is love," he glances over at Megan and Michael, his eyes full of affection. "Just humanize us. They need to think we are safe and normal, not evil creatures."

“What about the people who had been drained at the park?” Megan asks. I hadn’t thought about that; in fact, I had done my best to keep the memory hidden in the depths of my mind. As hot as it was watching Josephine fight for me, it was still terrifying. She could have been hurt. I could have been killed. Life could have been altered forever.

“She was sick, the Council fixed the issue as soon as they had been alerted. Blood lust doesn’t happen often anymore, not with our access to blood that we have now. Plus, it is typically caught early, so it can be treated. It was the first true case in decades.” Josephine’s voice comes out detached. She told me how she hated Beverly, but watching the Council *kill* like that brought out her own traumas. What they had done to other people was...inhumane. At least that was what she told me; she refuses to go into detail in her stories by claiming some things are too terrible to repeat.

“I have been around vampires my whole life. My mom and grandma were close to Josephine, and I was too. Then the guys were turned the same year I was born. I spent a lot of time with them, too. I can focus on angles going back to childhood.” Britt still can’t talk without sniffles of tears, the guilt visibly eating her alive. Good. I would have thought she would have cried them all out by now. I was wrong. "This is even the first time she has been mad at me, if that doesn't prove the capability for kindness, I don't know what does."

"It is going to work. We are going to figure this all out. For the rest of the night, I say we relax, we can watch some shows, talk, drink, whatever we need to do to deal with the stress of the day. Tomorrow we will fix this problem." Christopher says. The group mumbles their agreement as I stand up to peer out the window. The crowd is growing. It continues for a few blocks, ready to attack if they get the chance. The building has the doors locked by now, I'm sure. Police are there to try and push people away from the building, their flashing lights painting the crowd in hues of blue and red. It feels completely unreal. "What does it look like now?"

"Worse. The people keep flooding in. The cops are setting up a barricade. They all look so angry." I get it. I am too. Just for another reason. I'm angry they are threatening people because they don't understand them. I'm upset they want to hurt someone I love because she is *different*. As if that's a crime. She didn't choose this; she was *made*.

They are angry that their small view of the world was shattered. That they couldn't see things as they truly were. As if their ignorance is her problem. They are angry that there is another difference, another group other than themselves. Typical humanity, hating things that are different because they don't try to understand.

I even understand being afraid. I was scared when Josephine told me. But I never would have thought of murdering her. I would never *hurt* her. Fear of the unknown happens, but that's when we have to choose to learn.

I chose to learn.

They are about to as well, whether or not they want to. I'm not letting them take her from me.

51

Sunshine

Josephine

I think I would have collapsed into bed this morning if Gabby and I hadn't had some unfinished business. My lips are on hers as soon as our door is locked. I bring my hands to her ass and grip her tight, letting my sharp nails press into her skin. I lightly nip at her lip with intense need. I kiss her for so long I think we might meld together. Her own hands are raking down my back, leaving invisible scratches on my skin. I move my kisses to her neck, her breathless moans coming out when I touch just the right spot on her. I take my time kissing her, wishing I could leave my own marks on her neck, but those will have to wait until after the video.

"I have a request."

"Whatever you want." I lean back enough to remove her shirt, her bare breasts underneath it. I lick and kiss across the small mounds, frantic to touch every part of her that I can. Hickies bloom across her bust.

"Bite me," Gabby says, her voice heady. I immediately whip myself back in shock and look up at her.

"What?"

"Don't turn me, not yet. But bite me." She looks deadly serious, even as she pulls her plump lip back into her mouth.

"I've never fed off of someone before without turning them, plus you'll be on camera tomorrow, you can't have marks for this to work." Her smile is anything but wholesome, like she knows something I don't.

"They expect you to bite here," She moves her hair back and shows off the graceful slope of her neck before extending her wrist to me. "Not here. And you have enough bracelets that we can cover it." I think my eyes must still be wide because she encourages it again by moving her wrist just a tad closer.

"Are you sure?"

"Deadly."

"Only one taste."

"Only one taste." She reassures me. I nod, dropping to my knees in front of her. I yank down her shorts, peppering kisses along her hipbones and thighs, leaving a few marks of my possession on her as I go. Her noises encourage my attentions lower. I trace two fingers across the apex of her thighs, and a smirk crosses my face.

"You're already wet for me. What a good girl." I praise her. The crown of curls bobs as she nods, her pupils dilated. Her heart is pounding. I push two fingers inside of her and place my thumb on her clit. "Look at me, keep your eyes on me." I start to move them, stroking her inside her warmth and circling on her bundle of nerves. She tips her head back, and I stop until she refocuses her gaze. I lift her wrist with my free hand and gaze deep into her beautiful eyes as I graze my lips across it, her pulse thumping under them. “Last chance to back out before I bite.”

“I trust you.” Her words come out with a moan. I swear she is addictive.

I take a deep breath to steel my nerves, then push my fangs into her wrist. She makes a hiss of pain that dissolves into a low moan. She struggles to keep her focus on me as she almost tips her head back again, quickly correcting herself. She tastes so damn good. I can’t tell what is better, her pussy or the sweet metallic flavor on my tongue. The warm blood coats the inside of my mouth. It has never tasted this good. It is everything she is, warm, sweet, with a spicy edge to it. It is happiness, it is love, it is life. It’s the sunshine on a hot summer day. Just like she is.

She begins to rock her hips as my fingers continue their intense pace, her pussy clamps around my fingers as her rocking gets more and more insistent. I slip my fangs from her wrist as soon as she is falling apart on my hand, not wanting to take too much. I lick her wound, helping it to close. Her moans still echo in my room as her orgasm slowly starts to subside.

“That felt so damn good,” She looks at me with awe as she places her hands on my shoulders so she can balance. “I’ve never come so hard. Who knew the secret was a bit of bloodletting?” Her laugh sounds lighthearted. My own joins hers; we needed this, I think. We needed to laugh today.

“You’re not too faint, right?” The realization that I drank from her kicks in, as does the need to make sure she is okay.

“I’m alright. Did you enjoy it too?”

“More than I can explain. You’re incredible, Gabby. I can’t wait to spend eternity by your side and between your legs. Now, let’s get you cleaned up.” I slip my fingers in my mouth and clean them off before helping her walk on shaky legs to the bathroom. “You are so beautiful. I never knew it was possible to be so damn pretty.” I give her a kiss on her forehead, and she melts from the touch of affection.

“That’s only because you haven’t been able to look in a mirror for the last seventy-some years.” My face flushes bright red, and I have her sit on the edge of the tub. I turn on the water, my hand feeling for the right temperature before plugging it.

I pull out a box of bath items I bought for her. Bath bombs, Epsom salts, bubble bath, and lotion for after all in her signature scent. Gabby's smile grows even wider seeing the selection. I want to take care of her tonight. With everything going on I can't be sure that it won't be my last. She deserves everything I can give her. She nods enthusiastically when I ask her if she wants to use them.

While the tub is filling, I pour in the bubble bath and the salts, letting it fill until she can submerge up to her shoulders. The herbaceous scent of the rosemary and mint wafts into the air as she settles in the soapy water. Her delicate fingers drop the bath bomb in, the green and blue colors swirling in the tub with sparkling glitter floating on the surface.

She tells me stories about her as a child, how she would run when she felt overwhelmed by emotions, how she would try and make friends everywhere that she went. Even one where she made friends with an elderly lady on the corner who would give her sweets. She seemed precious. I gave her some of my own stories, like when I fought my mom to let me cut my hair in the bob style that was popular when I was a kid, to the food drives my mother and I would do, and the little fights I had with my siblings.

"This feels amazing, babe," she reaches a wet hand up to pull me closer, the herbaceous smell of the bath filling the room intensely.

"That was the goal." I smile against her lips, and she kisses me one more time before letting my face go. I turn around to get a washcloth from the cabinet and wet it in the water before taking slow, methodical swipes of the cloth along her skin, cleaning away the night and our time together that evening. She makes content noises as I clean her with the cloth, her eyes closed in pure relaxation. I want nothing more than to capture the moment forever. "Can I take your picture? Just a simple one. You look damn near ethereal right now."

She nods, keeping her eyes closed to enjoy her bath. I pick up my phone from the counter and take her picture while she is relaxing in the claw-foot tub. Her head, shoulders, and arms are above the foamy water that has been tinted cyan. Her face is one of pure bliss, her muscles slack in relaxation. She is the most beautiful woman I think I have ever seen. Maybe that the world has ever seen.

52
Pillow Talk

Gabby

The bath Josephine drew for me was *luxurious.* Everything smelled and felt perfectly relaxing. My skin came out softer than I think it has ever been; no wonder her skin is like velvet. After she helped me dry off and get dressed for bed, insisting on carrying me back to her room. And now, as I lay next to her, I don't think I've felt this complete before now. She is everything I could ever want.

"What did you want to be when you were a kid?" I ask as she rubs her thumb in repetitive circles on my exposed hip.

"A photographer. But I didn't know if I could. It was a different time. My father was happy to support my hobby, but realistically, I was expected to get married and settle down. Once he died my mother took up that cause. Except, I never did." She lets out a short laugh. "I think eventually my mother gave up on the idea and figured I would just be a spinster. Instead, I turned into a mega spinster with an art career. Father wouldn't know what to think of the world today." She looks lost in memory with her words. Like she is picturing what her father would say about the differences in the world.

"Do you think he would like the changes?"

"It depends on the change, to be honest. He would have liked the technology, I think; he loved buying new inventions. Our house was absolutely covered in them. It was like an eclectic little museum of modern marvels. I'm not sure what he would think about rights changing. He was a man of his time, and that time was oppressive. I had to hide who I loved for decades. Now it's different; you can be out, and you won't be arrested or seen as evil. You can be yourself, and its life changing. It wasn't the same then. I had many 'close friends' back in the day, but I couldn't call them my girlfriend. My first kiss was actually a boy."

“I have to hear about it,” I say. She laughs and throws one of her small pillows at me.

“It was terrible. We were at a dance, this is during the great depression. I was in one of my sister’s hand-me-downs that night. It was such a luxurious fabric that we weren’t really supposed to buy with the war effort. I felt gorgeous though, and I was hoping to have fun with my friends, some of who I *may* have had a crush on. But instead I was asked to dance by this boy, Elmer.” Her face scrunches up.

“Like the glue?” I can’t help but snort out a laugh. It seems like such an outdated name compared to the youthful beauty of the woman next to me. It is easy to forget just how old she really is.

“Yes, like the glue,” her own smile is humorous. “So, we were dancing, nothing too close, and he got fresh.”

“Fresh?” My mouth quirks up in a smirk.

“Old story, old slang. But yes, he got *fresh* and kissed me right on the mouth. I was not prepared for that at all. I think I looked at him like he had two heads, and he backed away quickly in embarrassment. I left soon after. I couldn't risk being kissed by some random boy again."

"You're adorable." I place a soft, tender kiss on her cheek. "I'm sorry he did that, though; you should have had a say."

"Thank you. I don't think anyone has told me that until you." My face drops, the amusement leaking out of it.

"They should have."

"Have I told you how much I love you?"

"You've mentioned it once or twice," I say. She rolls over to plant another on my lips. I swear her lips are like pillows; they are so incredibly plush. "I love you too."

"As much as I want to talk until the sun sets, we have a busy night coming up. We should rest." I nod and press my lips to her once more, her forehead still against mine. "Let me hold you." She turns on her side and holds me close, my ass and back flush against her. She places a quick peck on the back of my head.

"Good morning, my muse."

"Good morning, Gabby. I can't wait for you to be my first view of a new evening." She nuzzles into my back as she gets comfy, and soon the cadence of her breath slows as she falls asleep. I drift off not long after.

53
Set Up

Gabby

Today is the day. Somehow, I'm supposed to try and convince a fuckton of angry and scared people that my girlfriend and all of her kind are absolutely safe and wonderful instead of blood-sucking demons who will murder them all. No pressure. My anxiety is through the roof. I try to look put together and still like myself, using whatever is in Josephine's closet and vanity, with the instruction from Christopher to pick as much white as possible. Something about the subliminal messaging of innocence.

It's going terribly. Her prim and proper styles look fantastic on her, but where she is business casual, I'm beachy vibes. And where she has luscious curves, I have...nothing. I manage to find a linen wrap dress that fits my figure and is similar enough to something I would pick out myself. I throw on a thick stainless steel bracelet over my bitten wrist to keep it hidden from the camera. Paired with a simple touch of eyeliner, mascara, and lip gloss, and I'm all set.

Josephine and the guys have been setting up her photography studio to record the videos while us humans prep in Josephine's room. When I walk in after getting ready, I can see all the changes to her studio. A plain, white backdrop sits behind the lens. Christopher is fussing with the settings and grumbling about how his camera would be better for a video, but he can't get it with the lockdown going on. Michael is helping Josephine set up lights, making sure everything will be balanced on the film.

"You guys have been busy," I say to announce my presence in the room. Josephine's face brightens in a smile, and she climbs down from her ladder to pull me in for a kiss.

"We have been, it is almost ready. Well, after you are done eating. I don't want you getting hungry during filming. You have to keep your energy up after last night."

"It is moments like these that I'm thankful you have soundproofed your walls." Michael throws in the quip over his shoulder.

"Afraid I'd show you up in skill?" Her eyes sparkle with amusement at him.

"Quite frankly, I'm afraid I'd throw up at the sound of my pseudo-sister getting off."

"Besides, you would have been frustrated with us, too. With three people, the acts can get...lengthy." Christopher chimes in, his voice tense with the focus on the camera. "I wish I had thought about bringing my own. This is not ideal."

"It is better than most people have; it will be okay." My girlfriend's eyes roll back.

"Well, it still isn't the same as a film camera. This is top-notch for photography, but we both know mine is best for film."

“It will turn out amazing, I’m sure. People aren’t going to be focused on the quality as much as they are on what we are saying anyway.” My nerves flare again with that. I have never done big speeches or spoken in front of a crowd in general. It just isn’t *me*. And now I’m doing a video that will be broadcast on the news? An *important* video at that. I think Josephine can see my panic because she grips my forearm and tilts my chin down so she can look me in the eyes.

“What’s going through that beautiful mind of yours?”

“I just am nervous. This is so important, and I don’t want to mess it up.”

“No matter what you do, I believe in you. Speak from the heart, and it will be okay. You’re more awe-inspiring than you could ever know; the people will recognize it just like I do. I know it.” Josephine seals her words with a peck on my lips.

“Finished!” Michael calls out, climbing down from the ladder and moving it to the side.

“It is as good as it is going to get on my end, too.” Christopher sounds far less excited about his outcome. But at least we have a break before having to dive into filming. I don't know what I'm supposed to say yet, but I keep that worry hidden to myself as I clasp Josephine's hand and walk with the guys to the living room, where the others are already sitting.

"I'm feeling like wings," Megan says as she lays on the couch, her head dangling off the edge and her feet up and over the back of it.

"No wings until after, you need to look clean and angelic." Christopher rests his hand on her knee as he talks, running his thumb along her skin.

'Fine. Garlic bread then?"

"Garlic bread and soft pretzels?" Josephine throws out into the room. The three of us agree and dive into our meal while the vamps consume an obscene amount of blood.

54

Action

Josephine

The guys and I haven't wanted to admit our worries to the girls. If this goes badly we will need a new solution, and I don't think any of us are ready for that. I sure am not. How would we come up with one? We wouldn't want the Council to resort to their methods, who knows how badly that could go. Not that it would work either, it has gone *international.*

People across the world know about our existence now, and the vampire world is in an uproar. Councils are scrambling to get ahold on things. Even Vita has released a statement to the press, the wider vampire community hasn't heard from her directly in a few centuries. It all feels unprecedented.

The girls are all in the photography studio now, lounging on some chairs we dragged into the room for when one of them is recording. Gabby is gripping my hand, her knuckles gone white. She turns towards me as she bites her lip.

"It is going to be okay, little owl." I give her three squeezes; she is clenching mine too hard to return it, but she sends an uneasy smile. "Just pretend you're telling a friend about us."

"Talking to a friend? Yeah. I think I can do that." She gives me a fake smile, her hand still gripping me tight. I wish I could ease her nerves for her.

"Who wants to go first?" Christopher calls out from behind the camera, his director skills kicking in.

"I will, I made the mess after all." Britt stands up, fidgeting uncomfortably as she gets seated. I'd be surprised if she couldn't feel the ice in my gaze as I glare at her. I love my niece, but I can't forgive her that easily. Not for this.

"Action," Christopher calls out into the room.

"Hi, my name is Brittany Johnson. I'm the one who accidentally leaked the existence of vampires to the world. I want to start by apologizing for any fear my statements may have caused you or the people you love," her PR voice is in full swing. "I was so excited to promote my great, great aunt Josephine's art that I forgot to have her back, like she has always had mine." She continues her speech, covering her childhood and how I stood up for her, how the guys and I had played dress-up just to make her happy. "When my mom died, she was there for me more than anyone else. When I wasn't perfect enough for the rest of my family, she told me I was perfect the way I was." Her words have me tearing up. That was such a hard moment, my great niece was such a fantastic woman, and mother. I hated watching her go. The worst part, though? Watching Britt go through what I did with my father, no kid wants to lose their parent young.

She moves on to talking about vampires as a whole, about how we are safe. That our blood is donated specifically to vampires. That blood lust is rare, and how Beverly is no longer a threat. By this point, I can't stop the tears from streaming down my cheeks. Her earnest efforts to correct the situation thawing the icy rage I have been feeling.

"I know this is a scary time, but I hope that you will join me in my Auntie's teachings about opening our hearts and minds to those we deem as other, so we can all see just how similar we are. Thank you for listening." She hunches over as soon as Christopher yells cut, a few rivulets running down her own face. I run up to give her a hug. We don't need to say anything; we hold each other tightly for a long moment. Everything she said tugged at my heartstrings. Hearing the impact I have been able to have on her felt so heartwarming. I hadn't realized it before now.

"I'll go next," Gabby says, shocking me to my core. "Britt inspired me. I got this. I think." I walk over to my beautiful girlfriend and press a long kiss to her lips.

"I know you do. You're incredible, my love." I give her one more peck and sit back to watch as she takes her seat. She shakes out her nerves before looking at the camera.

"Action."

"Hi Noxdale, I'm Gabriella Young. I am here to talk to you about the vampires I have come to know. Starting with my beautiful girlfriend, Josephine." She takes a small portrait she has made of me from her pocket. "Since she can't show up on the camera, I thought I would let you see her like this. I carry this portrait with me everywhere, like my own version of having her as my phone background." Gabby's laugh sounds like music. I don't know how anyone couldn't enjoy the sound of her. The painting she pulled out reminds me of the gallery wall of small paintings she has given me since we met, except this one is a close-up ending just under my shoulders.

"I have been with her for a few months, and I have never felt so much love. When I first saw her, I thought she looked like she could have come from the golden age of cinema, or have been a pinup girl from the 50s. Much to my surprise...she was actually from that time.

"I remember finding out she was a vampire. Like you all, I was scared and shocked. I didn't know what was real anymore, or what that truly meant. I also, like I'm sure plenty of you are right now, researched until my fingers gave out. I looked up vampire myths, history, and what they supposedly could do. But I was already in love. I knew that she was sweet and kind. I knew that she felt deeply, grieved deeply, and loved deeply. I knew that these stories about evil beings couldn't be true. And they aren't. I went to her and asked her what was true and what wasn't. Fun fact, the bat thing is definitely not real."

My heart swells. She lets her face display every emotion as she goes through her memories of that time. From her peaceful smile, to the genuine fear and anxiety when she found out, to her beautiful grin that she gives when she is joking. I think back to my own feelings from that moment. I think we were both terrified. She was scared of the unknown, and I was scared of losing her.

"She never seemed different to me, even after the news. She was the same kindhearted and giving woman I had fallen in love with. She was the same woman who had danced with me under the stars and made me feel like I had found my family. She was still the woman I knew I wanted to spend my life with. She still is." Gabby turns her head away from the camera and to me. She flashes me a smile and makes a heart with her hands.

"Then I met her friends. Men who she changed out of compassion during the AIDS crisis. Friends who she changed so they didn't die. She saved them, albeit in an unconventional way. But she did. They are just as kind and as caring as her, coming over at the drop of a hat to be there by her side, like any friend would do during a hard time. Because at the end of the day, they are just like us." I glance over at the guys; their arms are wrapped around each other and Megan. Maybe changing people isn't always a curse. I think I would be alone if it weren't for them. Maybe it wouldn't be a curse for Gabby either. Maybe she would truly be happy.

I think she could be.

"Please keep the ones I love safe. Get to know them." The tears are flooding down my face by this point from the emotions in their speeches; Gabby has her own trailing down hers. Her lips becoming swollen and a barely noticeable shade of brighter red. I don't think I have ever been more in love. I run to her to pull her into a hug, salty tears soaking our clothes. When we sit down, I drag her into my lap and hold her.

She watches her friend attentively but I can't be bothered to pay attention. I'm looking at her more in awe than ever. I would worship at her feet if she wanted me to, and I would love every second of it if it made her happy.

55

Toleration

Gabby

The next evening is an early wake-up for all of us, the sun covering the city is shimmering its golden light over everything. The alarm on Josephine's nightstand blares to life. She still keeps one of the old school style clock radios with the blaring beep of my nightmares. I wake up with a start, and she just casually turns over to shut it off, a sound she clearly is used to.

"How can you handle that noise?" I ask her in complete shock.

"I've had this alarm for *decades*, I'm used to it by now." She simply shrugs before leaning over to give me a kiss. "Let's get ready to watch your videos." Her smile flashes my way, and we quickly slip on some clothes and head out by the others, after she sneaks another cookie, of course. She makes me my cup of tea and her mug of blood, and we cozy up on the couch for our own little viewing party. The news anchor comes up on the screen, her polished look a stark contrast to our sleepy eyes and blankets strewn about.

"Tonight, we bring you a special segment. Three friends of the alleged Vampires of Noxdale have sent in their own footage about their stories. Let's take a look." Her face disappears as the videos play one by one. As far as this room is concerned, there isn't a dry eye to be seen. I'm not sure if we are crying from the emotions in the video or the overwhelming hope for this to work.

Josephine grips my hand tightly, one two three. I squeeze hers back again as the news anchor comes into view once more. She has a glimmer of her own tear in her eye. "That was touching. Later tonight, we will show you the reactions of the public." Someone mutes the TV at that point, keeping it on to wait for the protesters to appear in a later segment.

"Well, that went well, I think." Michael looks optimistic, if not convinced.

"One down, a lot more to go," Christopher adds in, bringing a touch of realism. I wish he didn't, we need the hope today. The tension in the room is electric. We need to send one of us out to buy food and clothing for the people staying, no one was planning on being locked down. At this point, we are just hoping the mob disperses with the press release so we can.

"I'm sure it will go well. You all did a fantastic job. Especially you." Josephine turns to look at me, her mouth in a delicate smile as she presses her lips to mine. When she pulls back, I can see the guys and Megan curled up together, comforting each other. Then there is Britt, sitting there with her hot chocolate, staring out into the room.

"Are you doing okay, Britt?" I put aside my anger with her; she seems so alone. Not just because she doesn't have a partner holding her in this moment, but emotionally too.

"Awesome." Her smile seems forced. I know I should press more, but I'm not ready. I get she is trying, but she still hurt the person I love the most. I can't forget that so easily.

"Lies. Do you want to be honest?" Josephine does it for me; her brow is raised, challenging her to try and test her bullshit detector.

"It has just been rough lately. For all of us." Her look directed at Josephine gives pure don't push it vibes. Josephine levels at her with another I know you're lying look, but without another word.

"I for one want this lockdown to end. I hate being in one place for too long. I need to *move*. Or at least get back to the play room." Megan gives a sultry glance at her boyfriends with an expression that makes them ready to drool and chase her through the daylight just to reach said play room. I don't want to know what could be in that room. Britt grabs the remote from the table and clicks the mute button. I snap my attention back to the screen as Josephine's building comes into view.

"I'm coming to you from right here in Noxville to the protesters outside the vampire's apartment building." The field reporter walks over to one of the people in the now darkened street corner. The crowd is less enraged tonight than they have been before. It is like something in their fire has died down. "What do you think of the new press release?" She holds the mic in his face.

"I think we want to judge them for ourselves. Let them plead their case." Person after person repeats the same sentiment. They aren't utterly murderous, but they're not ready to forgive either.

"Fuck it," Josephine says as she gets up and puts on a pair of pumps placed near the door.

"What are you doing?" I rush over to her, my heart is pounding.

"If they want to judge me to see if I'm *worthy* of their toleration, then I'm doing that. We aren't going to be prisoners in my home." Her determined face softens when she looks my direction and pulls me in for a passionate kiss. It is like I can feel her soul, like she is giving me every ounce of love she can, just in case.

"Please, stay.'

"I can't, I love you. Stay in here where it is safe." With that, she runs away. I feel like I'm dying.

56

Enough

Josephine

My anxiety is flaring, but apparently so is my courage. I don't know what got into me, but I *can't take it*. I can't take the idea that I need to be afraid to exist, or that my girlfriend has to be afraid because of my existence, and I definitely can not take how these people are protesting my life right outside my home, keeping all of us trapped inside. I push open the doors to the building, keeping myself behind the police barricade that has stayed in place for the last few days.

"Well. You wanted to judge me. Judge away." Questions and comments come in like an avalanche, too many words swarming around so fast that I can't hear them at all, only a big wave of sound. "One at a time. Line up." The crowd is still in a surge of chaos, and the reporter and cameraperson are trained on me. Not that I'll show up.

"Have you ever killed anyone?" A clear voice breaks through the crowd. I contemplate my answer for only a second. I would have said yes before, that I had made Amanda fall from that roof. But I didn't; her fear did. Not me. Maybe I'm finally coming to terms with that.

"No. Unless you count turning two people, but they are alive and talking." I try to make my tone come through jokingly, throwing on an uncomfortable smile at the end.

"How do you feed?" This person's question comes out with vitriol.

"Like my beautiful girlfriend said, from donations meant for us."

"How do they know about you and not us?" Their tone is still suspicious.

"Some people figure it out, and they want a taste of immortality. They donate time and blood in hopes of being turned." The person doesn't really seem convinced, but at least they back down.

"If your kind is so normal, then why hide it?" Another demands.

"Because of this," I spread my arms out to gesture at the crowd. "Because we were scared of the fear and the hatred of humanity. I mean, we have had to hide in my apartment for fear of our lives since this came out. Not just vampires, either, our *human* loved ones have had to as well. From *you*. From the people holding weapons that could kill us. No one wants to feel unsafe, even if that means they have to hide so they aren't at risk." My temper rises, and I wish I had my blood with me because I could use the wave of calm that it provides. My fangs are still tucked in, but it is intense; they want to protrude from the stress. I can't let them.

"What happened at the park?" Their tone isn't accusatory, but my face still falls.

"It was a tragedy. Sometimes vampires get ill; we call it blood lust. It has been virtually eradicated because of an easy supply of blood; one sip can stop it at the first symptom. But sometimes breakout cases still happen. Beverly was one of them. Of all the vampires in the world, and we are across the world, she is the first case in 55 years. And that case has been handled." Some of the crowd is beginning to disperse as more and more questions are asked and answered. Each time I notice the crowd shrinking, I feel a rush of confidence that at least *something* has worked. The fear of the human world had been overwhelming.

"How many of you are there?" A man asks. His blond hair is immaculately styled, looking put together. He looks a lot like some of the friends my father had; all of them kept their secrets close. My own walls are raised, his demeanor seeming *off*.

"In Noxdale? I genuinely don't know, I'm not on the Council, so I don't have the records."

"Can we go visit this Council?" I let out a bitter laugh.

"Can't answer that either, but it is generally considered a vampire safe spot, so I'm not sure." With that, he says "hmm" and walks away. Something feels off about the interaction. But I shake off the feeling, letting the ball in the pit of my stomach stop so I can go back upstairs and tell everyone what happened.

When I reach the door, Gabby is pulling me into her arms and giving me a kiss so long we nearly gasp for breath at the end.

"I was so worried." Her eyes glimmer with unshed tears.

"So was I, but look," I point outside the window, "they are all gone." I send a smile her way.

"The lockdown hasn't been lifted yet." Christopher cuts into our reunion. "So I'm having Megan get the clothes and whatnot for everyone, she has their sizes and what they want. We were about to order a bunch of food for the girls before she heads out."

"Whatever they want, my treat," I tell him before holding Gabby close and slightly swaying side to side with her. I whisper in her ear, "You are so beautiful. I'm sorry I scared you." She just holds me tighter. I love her more than anything, more than my own life. I needed her safe. Now I think she finally is.

In a moment, she pulls away from me and starts to place her order for at least a few days of food, some groceries, and some restaurant items. I swear, we are placing orders over half the city between the girls. But soon Megan is out the door, yelling that she is finally free. I'm holding my girlfriend's hand, the guys are wrapped up together, and Britt is checking the headlines.

"Your answers have all been released. The public is responding well. I think we may have done it." Britt says while still scrolling her phone.

"The Council sent a text, three more full nights in lockdown to make sure and then we can exit. So four counting tonight." Christopher chimes in, pulling up his own text.

"They also said they are running blood deliveries each night until then if needed. Apparently, it is safe enough to risk a few familiars," Michael's eyes roll, "Do you want more blood, Josie?"

"Let them know we want some, just in case." I run my fingers through Gabby's curls, detangling them as I go. They are so beautiful, just like her. Brown with strands highlighted in gold tones, bouncing around her head when she moves. I can never get enough of looking at her. I never will. I need to find a way to have her be mine for eternity. I smile to myself as we are cuddled up on the couch, thinking about how I can do exactly that.

The rest of the night goes smoothly. We all talk, laugh, play games, and the humans eat a meal that Megan cooks for them. It is like one big family. With the stress from outside gone, we can fully enjoy our time together. I feel light, like the world around me is shining in golden rays and warming us all like the sun. Like I am back outside on a summer day, feeling the heat through my body. And it is perfection.

I really could do this for the rest of my life. I *want* to. And I will. I look over at Gabby again while she laughs. The sound is truly magical, and her smile never fails to make me smile in return, like her joy permeates every cell in my body. I even love her enough to turn her, despite my fears. I want to kiss her so bad, but I hold off and let her take her turn at the game before us before I steal one. I needed her lips against mine so badly. I don't think there will ever be a time when I *don't* need them.

Bed that morning is idyllic. I get to hold her next to me, talk to her about our night, place kisses on her nose, and play with her hair once more. All I can feel for her is love. It is like I'm looking at that emotion distilled and concentrated into its purest form. She simply *is* love. And when she falls asleep in my arms? I think I just might be the luckiest woman on the planet.

57

Stay

Gabby

The last few nights have been so much fun. It has been a nice time to hang out and enjoy each other. But I'm also happy for everyone to leave so I can enjoy my girlfriend alone. As soon as the door is shut and they are out of the apartment, I feel a different level of calm. Like I can just unwind and be with the woman I love.

"Can I stay tonight?"

"You can stay anytime you want. I'm getting you a key tomorrow night." She admits, stepping close enough to me that we are pressed against each other, her arms wrapped around my neck.

"A key sounds amazing." I smile so big my cheeks hurt as I wrap my arms around her waist, pulling her closer.

"You can always move in, too." Her face shows every ounce of nerves she must feel asking that. My own emotions have their own minor fight. I love stability, keeping things the same whenever possible. So moving cuts deep like a loss, like I'm back to being a kid again. The other side of the battle tells me that I can have new stability here, that I can stay by her side forever, no more moving. Just eternity, together.

"That sounds even better. But slowly, a bit by bit." My voice comes out more tentative than I wanted it to. Her expression is so understanding, like she knows where I am coming from. Feeling seen is one of the best things I think I have experienced. She never fails to do that. Whether it's her compassion, or the way she makes my tea, or even the items she bought me for the bath, she *sees* me, and she pays attention.

"Bit by bit. I like that plan too. I have an extra room we can turn into a painting studio for you. We can set it up however you like." Her face is closer to me now, her eyelashes flutter against my face.

"You're incredible," and I close the distance, letting my lips crash into hers. Her tongue sweeping against mine only makes me want to clutch her tighter. Sharp bites to each other's lips, my hands messing up her flawless hair, hers tangling in my curls, and a stumble towards her sofa happen in a way that seems both fast and like time isn't moving at all. I don't stop kissing her until it hurts and we are out of breath. Her already lush lips are left swollen from our kisses. I did manage to actually mess up her hair, though, an achievement I never take lightly. Soon, she is back to fixing it, though. Getting every single hair back into place without looking. Every little thing she does impresses me.

"Come on, let's watch a movie and just cuddle. I want you in my arms all day." She says, lounging back on the couch and beckoning me over. I cozy up to her, laying my head on her chest as she puts on some old film I have never seen that she swears is mind-blowing. Like with most things, she's right.

I can't wait for countless nights spent like this. There will never be enough.

58

Save or Destroy

Josephine

I have three things I have to get done tonight. Step one: have a key made for Gabby. Step two: pick out the most important part of my surprise for her. And step three: stock up on more blood because that lockdown has me severely low on my stash, even with the deliveries. Well, low *enough*. I try to have a bit extra put aside just in case. What if there is an emergency and I need stress relief? Or another lockdown? Blood is always needed.

The first step goes easily, I choose a key that is the same shade of green as her eyes. I put it on my keyring for now, before racing to the small, artisan shop to select the perfect piece for her, I tuck it away in my pocket for safekeeping. I head out into the night before racing to the Council building. Once I'm there, I pull out a large tote bag from my purse to fill up with the blood bags. De Medici is in the hall. I brace myself for any sort of encounter; she wears her necklace of bones.

"Just who I wanted to see. Come into my office." Her smile is predatory. I wonder if she can even wholeheartedly smile. I walk into the office and sit on one of her uncomfortable chairs as she perches ahead of me. "Shall we start with the good?"

"Yes." At least there is good.

"You fixed the issue. We are out of lockdown. Well done to you and your little friends. The humans did fine, too, I suppose." She can't hide her disdain when she says humans; her face contorts into a grimace.

"Thank you."

"Now for the bad. One of the people *you* told is the reason we have this issue. After *millennia* of secrecy, your poor decision-making has caused vampires globally to be outed. *You* caused *humans* to know we exist." She is visibly shaking with her rage, her head turns as she tries to gain some composure. She quickly decides she needs blood and drains a crystal chalice filled with the crimson liquid.

"I told her not to do the interview *several* times. She assured me she wouldn't say anything. It was a genuine mistake." I try to plead my case, hoping she doesn't take her rage out on me. Or worse, to take it out on Gabby or Britt.

"Oh, I know. How long had she kept the secret?" De Medici taps a stiletto nail against her cheek.

"30 years."

"More than most who break it." She writes something down on her notepad, in their little Council code. "You won't be able to read it."

"I know."

"Do you know what the language is?" I shake my head, keeping my eyes locked to hers, scared that if I move them for even a moment, she will attack. "I figured. You never paid much attention to our history. You at least know about the first?" I nod, recalling the story of Vita, some call her the first. I like to humanize her. "This was their language. Their tablets were destroyed after her mother died. All of them. No one wanted to have records on how *we* were created. Or that we existed. When you have this type of strength and speed, it is so *easy* to *destroy* anything that could harm you.

"The entire civilization was destroyed. To the point where archaeologists haven't found a trace of it. Buildings were ground down to nothing, used to help build other countries. Tablets went through the same process. Everything else burned or melted. Do you know how difficult that is? To make a civilization vanish from the annals of history? But Vita remembered the language, the language of the Council. We can also *save* what we choose. But it is often so much easier to destroy them. Don't you think?" De Medici's glare is pure maliciousness. I gulp, the knot in my stomach growing at her clear implication. Her threat against my niece permeates my body. I can feel the worry growing.

"It is easier to destroy. But isn't it more satisfying to save?"

"Interesting position. You may leave my office." I stand up quickly and head out the door. My phone is burning a hole in my pocket as I quickly stock up on blood. Downing a bag right there in the room. As soon as I speed away from the Council building, I have Britt on the phone.

"Hi Auntie, how are you doing?"

"My apartment ASAP. Pack everything you might need for a while. You're on lockdown."

"What are you talking about?"

"The Council, they are investigating you. I'm heading to you. Pack."

"O-okay," she mumbles before disconnecting the call. In moments, I am at her door using my key to enter. "What did they say?"

"They said they can destroy every trace of something or save it. They meant *you*. You have to stay safe where I can protect you."

"Okay, Auntie. Will you help me? I need my bathroom things. I'm getting clothes, and then my laptop, phone, and stuff like that." Her normally bubbly personality is replaced by an almost robotic sense of order. I take a real look at her, dark circles under her eyes, fingers left scabbed over from her picking at the skin. She looks like hell. I decide to focus on the task at hand for now; safety has to come first. Then care.

"Okay, I'll get those taken care of. I have food still at my place, plus Gabby is moving in, so there will be more. You can make a list for whatever you need; one of us will bring it to the apartment."

"She's moving in? Congrats," Britt flashes a smile my way, the unease still showing through her masked emotions.

"Thank you." I go to her bathroom and put her items in the bag until it is full, and come back out and pack up all of her electronics. She is still working on clothes, so I help her, and within a few minutes, everything is done.

"I'm just grabbing my blanket, and we can go." Her hands shake as she reaches for the soft comfort item, a gift from my sister to her. I remember sitting with her, we would talk for hours while she made it for Britt. It was one of the last things she could crochet before her hands gave out from age. The 30-year-old blanket still looks brand new. She had bought the best yarn she could as she made row after row until it was big enough to last her for her whole life. A nostalgic smile crosses my face for a fleeting moment before I snap back to the severity of the situation.

"I'll call a car." We pack everything up into the ride share and ride in silence. My hand pats the gift in my pocket, holding onto that one piece of the future, trying to distract myself from the concerning present. It isn't working so well. My heart is racing, and I think my palms might be sweating from the nerves. I shoot Gabby a quick text to say that Britt has to stay with us. She responds quickly to tell me she hopes everything is okay and that she will be over tomorrow night, but she is working on packing right now.

Getting home makes it feel like a bit of the weight has been lifted off my shoulders. My door had been fortified to withstand other vampires years ago; just that extra touch of security feels immense. I carry her items to her bedroom for the stay and help her unpack. I start by organizing her bathroom and hanging up her clothes.

"Do you have everything you need?" I ask.

“I think so,” Britt says, not sounding fully convinced.

“I’m here if you need me or anything else. I love you, Britt.” I walk to the door, ready to try to calm myself down and get my own things put away.

“Thank you, Auntie, I love you too.” She says, but her words sound hollow. I turn back, leaving one hand on the door frame.

“Anytime.” I give her a tight smile, the nerves too tightly wound around me to do more than that. I shut the door and make my way back to the living room. I unpack my blood and take the gift to my safe behind one of the photographs from my human years, one I took of my parents before the cancer. Once it is safely tucked away, I work at calming down. I have a few mugs and binge my favorite show again. My nerves only begin to settle by the time the sun rises. Every time the blood began to work, I would think again, and suddenly I needed more. At least the TV helped to distract my mind.

59

Unstable

Gabby

I hate packing. Not only does it take forever, but it reminds me of all the times we had to pack up our couple of suitcases and leave again. I think I cried five times just packing up some of my clothes, and now I'm knee deep in my extra art supplies and the boxes I'm putting them into. My apartment is in a state of chaos. I may be moving bit by bit, but figuring out what to pack at each moment is harder than it has any right to be. I take a deep breath and begin to load in about half of my canvases into some boxes, wrapping them carefully as I go.

Britt is staying with us for now

Josephine

I hope everything is okay. Packing up right now, I'll be there tomorrow night.

I send her a kiss emoji with it. I can't help but wonder what is going on with Britt. She has her own place, we had a meeting there before my first exhibition a few months ago. I shrug away the curiosity; it must be something with the building. A quick survey of the room around me has me heaving out a deep sigh at how much I have to do over the next however long. I start carefully packing away all of the extra paint brushes, palettes, and duplicate paints, filling up more boxes with those little odds and ends. I make sure to put my backup easel, the one from my parents is staying here for now. It is one piece that seems so final, like if I take that, then I'm really gone from another place.

Another rush of tears flows down my face, and I take a moment on my couch to just feel the emotions. I hate that leaving is so hard when I *want* to be there with her. I want to be next to her every morning and night. On the other hand, I also want nothing to change, nothing like this anyway.

Once they stop flowing, I start to pack up additional things I don't need quite yet, giving myself a slow introduction to yet another move. I pack half of the dried flowers from the bouquets Josephine has brought me; the other half I'll keep here until I lock the studio door for the last time. Once it gets too hard again, I pause and rent a truck for tomorrow to bring the boxes to her apartment. The endless task of moving looms over me too much to continue after that. It just makes those feelings of instability rise inside of me again. I take some time to paint my muse once more.

60

Fears, Fish, and the Forbidden

Josephine

I spend my evening planning out a date for Gabby and me to go on, wanting an idyllic moment to give her my gift. Every little detail ends up written down and stored in my safe to keep it at the perfect level of surprise. Once the picture is put back in place, I pour myself a steaming mug of blood and curl up on my couch as I wait for Gabby to arrive with her first load of things. Britt has been in her room all day sending out emails to her clients about an unforeseen emergency, and that she will not be able to attend any events, including my exhibition tomorrow night. It will be the first one that I'll attend since the 50s. This will be the first time I can hold the hand of someone I love at one of them; it feels monumental in ways I can't explain. I placed a rush order on a gown from my favorite local designer; she already has my measurements and is simply the best for having it ready within days.

Finally, my phone rings, Gabby quickly telling me that she has arrived and needs help with the boxes. Within moments, I'm by her side and pulling her in my arms; a night away from her is practically an eternity.

"Load me up, little owl." I smile at her, although there is a touch of apprehension in her eyes as she bites on her lip. "What's wrong?"

"Nothing." She tries to smile to ease my anxieties as her gaze drifts to the side.

"You're lying, when you're worried you bite your lip like that, and your eyes dart around. What's wrong?" I ask, but she rocks on her feet back and forth for a moment before responding.

“Moving is hard for me. I did it so much as a kid and those feelings are coming up again. It will be better once I’m settled here. It just is…difficult.”

“I’m sorry, love.” I place a gentle kiss on her forehead and pull back. She smiles at me, that hint of sadness still peeking through. But she starts loading me up with boxes in spite of that, as she grabs an easel I haven’t seen her use before and a box herself. “That’s a new easel.”

“Not really, it is pretty old. It’s my backup. The one I typically use is the one from my parents. I am starting with the extras. Make it a little less overwhelming,” her voice is shaky, not her normal, easy-going smoothness.

“I get it. This was my first place of my own. My mother got it for me when she realized I was never going to marry some rich man like she thought. Packing up an entire life felt like a lot. I can’t imagine how hard it would be to do that all the time, have a stable place, and then do it again.”

“You’ve only lived in two places?”

“Mhm, my brother’s lineage still has my parents’ home. They got it when my mother passed. Of course, they didn't stay close to me, but I keep tabs on them. I have the entire family tree laid out. Some have even reached out since the vampire reveal thing. They didn't know I still existed; now they do. I think most of the ones reaching out want me for their history papers or something like that, though."

"That's exciting." Her tone comes through a bit more cheerfully.

"It is. Do you talk to the rest of your family?" I ask her.

"There aren't really any to talk to. My mom and dad were both only children, and my grandparents have already died. It's not like my parents feel strongly about keeping in contact, so outside of a conversation once or twice a year, it is just me." Her eyes dart to the ground from my peripheral, her fingers playing with the tape on the box. We reach the door, and I have her unlock it, my hands busy with balancing the mountain of boxes.

"That sounds lonely." I place them on the ground and start to split them into piles. Some marked studio and others marked bedroom. She places her two boxes in the studio pile, and we turn around to grab what should be the last load.

"Yes and no. They were the two constants in my life; I never got to have long-term friends until I moved here. But I have new constants now, ones that are less," she pauses, looking up at the ceiling while she thinks for a moment. "Emotionally distant. In a lot of ways, I am less lonely, even if I do miss them."

"Maybe one day I can meet them," I say. Her smile appears a little more genuine this time.

"Yeah, I hope you can too." The next load of boxes is done in much more silence, the truck safely parked on the street until the next evening, when it can be returned before the exhibition. Once we are back upstairs, lounging on the sofa, she is attempting to toss bits of popcorn into her mouth, hardly catching any. Her face scrunches up when she misses, it's adorable. She pauses her failed game of catch and looks at me, "Are you excited for tomorrow?"

"Nervous, actually. I haven't been to my own exhibition in around 70 years. I've never been able to go to one with a woman on my arm either." I say. I swallow the lump forming in my throat. I don't know why it is so terrifying to go to my own exhibition, I should be *excited* to be able to again. Especially when I've dreamt about going, even if I refused to acknowledge it. I fidget with my hands, needing to do something with the stress.

"It'll go smoothly, people love your art."

"I hope so, they haven't known it is *vampire* art before now. That could change everything." I pick at invisible dirt under my nails.

"Maybe they will find it more fascinating. You never know." She tosses another popcorn kernel up in the air, and it hits her cheek; her mouth contorts into a shade of disappointment.

"Open," I grab one of the kernels and toss it into her mouth on the first try. She sticks her tongue out at me and giggles.

"I bet you can't do it again."

"Try me," I pick up another one and raise my eyebrows. She opens her mouth, and I make it in again.

"Completely unfair. You don't even *eat* popcorn, and yet you're a master at this." She sits upright and reaches forward to try and tickle my side. I jolt away from her with a grin.

"I can't help it that I-"

"Auntie, I need you to see this." Britt interrupts my words; her face is contorted in worry, and she picks at the skin around her nails. I sit up straighter. Gabby shifts, her stance going from relaxed and playful to rigid.

"What's wrong?" I ask. She says nothing, just comes closer to hand me her phone. It is a message from a number that is new to her, sadly not to me. De Medici. She is being summoned to the Council building for her actions. I snap my gaze up to meet hers. "Don't go."

"Isn't it worse if I don't?" Britt's brow furrows.

"No. If you go, they are detaining you. We can hide you here until it blows over." I hand the phone back to her, my expression flat.

"They aren't known for forgiving people, Auntie." Britt protests. Forgiving or not, I'm not sacrificing my family.

"I don't care. The answer is no."

"Would anyone like to tell me what the hell is going on?" Gabby's confused tone brings my focus back to her.

"Well, you know how I said Britt was staying with us for awhile?"

"Yeah, I thought it was for building maintenance or something." Her words come out slow, unsure of where the confusion comes in.

"The Council told me they are investigating, with the threat that they could destroy her. And now Britt wants to turn herself in." I turn towards my niece, my hands clasped together. "Trust me when I say this is a bad idea. I have a lot of experience with these people; please trust me." Her nod is resigned, like she doesn't believe me. I don't know why she wouldn't. I have *always* looked out for her best interest. If she had listened to me before, then she wouldn't be in this mess to begin with. Perhaps that's why she agrees, even when she clearly doesn't think she should.

“Are you okay?” Gabby looks genuinely concerned as she focuses on my niece. “Having them out for you has to be hard. I am here to talk if you need me.”

“Thank you. I-I-I’m going to go lay down for a bit. I think I’m getting a migraine.” Britt rubs her temple and turns around slowly. Once she leaves the room, Gabby turns her sights back on me.

“What will they do if they capture her?” Her voice sounds tense.

“Nothing good. Theo would be in charge. He is a sadist; he tortures these people for fun, I think. He would be there to extract a confession and to give her a punishment. Whatever they see fit. It could be *anything,* but none of it is good. Gabby, I’m worried. She can’t go out there.” I grip her hands tightly, not bothering to hide my expression. I let the tears well in them.

“We will keep her safe.” She brings me into an embrace, her arms holding me tight as she hums a soothing tune into my hair. “Let me get you some blood,” she mumbles before pulling away. She stands up with a stretch and walks her way into the kitchen and heats me up a mug of my go-to drink. I never told her how, but even her first attempt is perfect. *She* is beyond perfect for me. I sip on the warmed-up beverage, letting it flow down my throat, the metallic liquid soothing some of the worst bits of stress. "What does it taste like?"

"The blood?" I ask.

"Yeah. What am I going to be drinking for eternity?"

"I don't think I would have found it good as a human, but now I do. You can taste some sweetness and iron. Different people have different diets, and those cause subtle flavor changes too." I stare into the deep red liquid, thinking of all the subtle variations. It is like a wine sommelier, you can notice those flavor notes that others can't imagine, ones that words fail to describe.

"Then what do I taste like?"

"Like the sun. You're warm and bright. It is like pure happiness and summertime with you. You're *delicious*." I lick a fang, still out from my recent sips of blood. She truly is the best I have ever had, no matter which version of tasting is used. I won't feed from her again, at least not until it is time to turn her. I told her as much when she asked me to drink from her again. I think I'd become addicted otherwise.

"You're delicious yourself." She flicks her tongue out in front of her a few times. Something about her pulls out these genuine bouts of laughter right from my core. I'm not sure I have laughed this much in years.

"As much fun as that is, I have to add some more food to the ray tank. They finished their month of prep."

"Why do you wait that month?"

"It makes sure they are healthy before I feed them to the rays." I give her a peck on her forehead, and I scoop out the little fish from their separate tank in another room into a transport container. Gabby lifts the lid on the coffee table and restocks their food. I have more coming in a few days to repeat the process. I buy enough that the fish last a month with the rays. I pop in a frozen squid to the mix as well. Watching them swim and investigate their new tank mates is always fascinating. They still had a few left, so they aren't hungry yet. Just curious. I replace their lid, and we both sit to watch them swim in their circles, bodies rippling as they circle the enclosure.

"They really are gorgeous. I never thought I would have pet stingrays." Gabby says as she stares at them in fascination.

"Just an owl?"

"Ha. Ha. Ha." She jokes. I smile and nudge her with my shoulder; her humorless expression fades, and she lets a grin escape despite herself.

I'm so happy that she is by my side.

61

Exhibition

Josephine

My anxiety is through the roof. I have to go to my own exhibition today, the first one in decades. The guys are having a car come to pick us up in a bit. I put the finishing details on my outfit until then. The silk gown in the same red as my lipstick hugs every one of my curves. The material stays tight to me until my mid thigh before it flares out more, a shallow v-neck shows off my ample chest. Paired with a gold bag and heels makes the look good enough. But the last pieces of jewelry I add to it make it complete. Gold rings on my fingers, and a simple locket with my mother and father in it are all I needed yet.

My hair is curled and pinned in an elaborate hairstyle, something I haven't done in forever. Something I haven't had a reason to do.

But Gabby, she steals the show. Her gown comes up to her neck, still sleeveless to highlight her shoulders. The chiffon fabric is cinched at her waist until it flows out, with a long slit up her leg. It is my favorite color on her, sage green. The color makes her eyes pop so beautifully. She uncharacteristically has on eye shadow, a deep brown, which only highlights them more. She lets her beautiful head of curls down, their brown and gold tones only accentuating everything else she wears. The matching accessories tie it all together. Looking at her makes me want to confess my love all over again. She looks so breathtaking, I can't help but take my camera out photograph her. She poses by the door; she doesn't have to try, though. Her candid shots are just as stunning. I swear I have to pinch myself to remember that she isn't a dream.

"The most beautiful models in the world pale in comparison to you. You are beauty incarnate." I place a soft kiss on her hand, leaving behind a fresh lipstick print. Her face flushes.

"Have fun tonight." Britt leans against the doorway.

"I wish you could come. But I will tell you all about it when we come back." I pull her in for a hug.

"You have enough blood?"

"My bottle is full." I toss a wink her way, and Gabby and I say our goodbyes as we head out the door to meet the guys and Megan downstairs. I double-check that the door is locked tight.

"She'll be okay," Gabby rubs my arm softly before I link our elbows and we head down to the car. When we get outside, I realize my mistake. I let them handle transportation. I thought they rented a car like normal people. No, they rented a limo.

"Get on in, ladies, it's Josie's big night!" Michael calls out, waving a hand dramatically. He has us slide in the open door before climbing in himself.

"Really, a limo?" My brow arches up.

"Yup, your first exhibition in *decades* is a big deal. We are taking the damn limo." Michael says. Christopher elbows him, and he draws in a sharp hiss.

"What my lovely boyfriend *means* to say is that we are proud of you. Both for your photographs *and* coming out tonight, so we want to make it special." Christopher says.

"What they said. Side note, how many people do you think have got it on back here?" Megan just makes a suggestive expression at the group.

"Gross. Megan, chill out. It is a formal event, not a *kink* one." Gabby chastises her friend, who shrugs and laughs to herself. Michael is barely containing his own laughter.

"You're both children." Christopher sinks his head into his hands and rubs his temples.

"Yes daddy." They say in unison, and Christopher sighs. I wonder how long he has dealt with their shenanigans today.

"Just behave at the event, I beg you." His head is still in his lap, he sounds at his wits' end.

"We will behave, darling." Michael kisses his cheek and nuzzles up to him.

The rest of the ride is filled with laughter and jokes. Christopher often seems like his partners will be the death of him. Gabby stays linked on my arm, looking like the most beautiful thing in the world. Even her masterpieces can't compare to her. I can't stop turning to peek at my girlfriend. Her tanned leg poking out from the slit of the gown is distracting on its own. But her face? That is truly a work of art.

"We have arrived, thank god," Christopher says as he lightly pushes Michael to the door, now opened for the group. Person by person, we file out, adjusting our dresses and suits.

"Are you ready?" I feel Gabby's lips tracing the shell of my ear as she whispers in it, the soothing scent of her perfume calming my nerves just a bit.

"Not at all. Let's do it anyway." I squeeze her hand three times as our group walks into the exhibition. It opened when the sun was still out, so we walk in while it is in full swing. I grip her hand firmly as the lights overwhelm me, the talking is loud, music flows through the room, and heels are clicking and echoing across it. I take a quick swig from my bottle to help lower the sensations. That, paired with a deep breath, and I think I am ready to move through the room, with a tight grip on her hand. We take in each piece, talking about our stories from taking them.

"Christopher, remember this one?" I point at the photograph, which features a sheer but form-fitting dress and stilettos with the bright city lights behind it. He went with me that night, and I was taking pictures of both of us under the sparkling streetlamps. Besides, I needed the moral support to strip on the sidewalk.

"People gawked at her. Women blushed and looked away, men ogled her. She was out there, nips on full display, and nude underwear being the only thing that prevented *everything* from being out in the open. I swear she almost caused an accident because a car stopped there." Christopher says.

"That's because my girlfriend is *hot*," Gabby adds in. Our chatter fills up the room, making me forget how big the night really is. Until an unwelcome guest arrives.

“Gabby, get behind me.” I jerk her behind my back, Christopher and Michael do the same with Megan, as De Medici, flanked by Theo, walks over.

“What an exhibition. It is very...unique.” Her face displays her disgust.

“It is being received well.”

“Yes, I’m sure it entertains the humans.” Her smile doesn’t reach her eyes; it is menacing.” Where is your niece?”

“I don’t know.” I keep my expression steeled even though my heart is racing.

“Don’t lie to me, Josephine Beauchamp. I can *hear* your heart give you away.” She pushes one of her pointed nails right on my chest, the sharp tip pressing into my skin.

“She is away.”

“Now that I believe. You should know. Every. Single. One of the Council chapters is looking for her, and we *will* find her.” De Medici doesn’t blink; she just stares deep into my eyes, trying to make me spill. Theo leans against a wall, picking a piece of lint off his suit and looking altogether bored with the situation. "Don't think I won't find her and *break* her until she confesses." She hisses out her words, keeping them too low for the humans to hear. But enough that the hairs on the back of my neck stand on end in fear.

"You won't."

"You'd better hope that you're right. Until next time. Same for you, blood bags." De Medici glares over my shoulder at the girls behind me and the guys, before turning around and leaving the exhibition. Theo turns and follows her out without another word. Once she is far enough away that she can't see me anymore, I take a large drink from my bottle before pulling Gabby to me. Even having De Medici nearby is a threat against her, I need to keep her safe. To keep her close. Views of her dying plague my brain; my heart is basically breaking from the worry. I *need* her in my life. I can't handle her dying.

"I want to go home," I say, just holding her to me. The others agree, and we head outside and pile into the limo, the atmosphere feeling far less jovial than before. I pull Gabby into me and hold her tightly. I need her close, to know she is okay. The guys are the same with Megan.

Just making sure the humans we are with are safe in our arms after the encounter.

"Josie, can we stay? Your place is more secure than ours."

"Of course. Are you finally letting me put vampire-safe locks on your door?"

"Yes," Christopher says as his face is nuzzles into Megan's shoulder. Much like my own, I have Gabby on my lap, arms around her, and her shoulder is the best place to curl up into.

"I know you don't like going at vamp speed, but can I please carry you upstairs?"

"I think going upstairs will be just fine." She kisses my forehead and I keep her pressed against me. "I love you, my muse."

"I love you, too, little owl." The rest of the ride is silent, each of us gripping our girlfriend's tightly. Once the door to the limo is open, we all run up to the top of the building and tumble inside before locking the door securely. I set Gabby on the sofa and go to brew her some herbal tea for her nausea. “How are you feeling?”

“Only a little woozy. The longer you run like that, the worse it is. So I’m okay.” Her fingers brush my own as she grabs the mug from me and takes a long drink. The guys are tending to Megan, who seems absolutely fine but is lapping up their attention. I sit next to Gabby, wrapping my arm behind her back, and I take out my phone to make a call to one of the vampire metal workers. He answers with a gruff tone. “Hi, when would you be able to install vamp-proof locks on an apartment?”

“Tomorrow evening.”

“Great. I’ll text you the address, just send me a request for the amount once you’ve finished.” I hang up the phone and fill the guys in. “Tomorrow evening, I’m taking Gabby on a date. Don’t unlock the doors while you are here because of Britt. I had some groceries delivered and loaded into the pantry so you can eat, Megan.”

“Thanks.” She says with a smile as she leans back into the guys.

The rest of the night is tense. We talk a little but the lighthearted feelings from earlier are gone. Now it is just processing yet another threat. Britt came out to hear what happened; the fear on her face broke my heart. It is person after person looking worried about what is coming up. All we can really do is keep her locked away and out of sight. Otherwise, who knows what will happen to her.

For now, it will be enough. For now, she is safe. And I intend for her to stay that way.

62

Eternity

Gabby

"What are we doing?" I ask Josephine as we climb up onto the outlook from one of our earlier dates. She has bags of food from my favorite Chinese restaurant, her largest purse slung over her shoulder, and a blanket tucked under her arm.

"Going on a date." She says, humor steeped into her tone

"You can't tell me *anything* else?"

"No. I can't. That's the point of a surprise." She keeps walking ahead, and I hurry to keep pace with her up the hill; little rocks tumble down as I step.

"You could always have the same kind of surprise as Christopher's party next weekend?"

"Then it wouldn't be one. *I'm* actually *good* at them. Besides, we are almost there."

"Hmph." I make a grumpy face that she can't even see as we climb up just a bit more. Once we round the corner, we come up to the overlook. It is a big grassy area that lets you view the entire city. The lights sparkle down below us, the hill extending further behind us with a short rock wall and more sloping above it. The sound of a rushing waterfall in the background fills the silence. She leads us down closer to the edge of the overlook, still far enough away from it to keep it safe. She lays out the flannel, checkered blanket. I sit down on it with her, looking at how she wrings her hands between tasks, a trait she only displays when she is nervous. She carefully lays out each container of food, the candle she made during another date, and pulls out the bottle of wine we enjoyed together on my first time at her apartment. She pours the wine into glasses she retrieves from her purse.

"Cheers," She lifts her glass towards me, and I meet hers with a clink.

"To us."

"To us," Her smile is breathtaking, her eyes have a light behind them that just seems *more* than usual, with little traces of nerves hiding behind the glow. We lift the glasses to our lips, taking a long draw of the Chianti. "Oh, I almost forgot!" Her face looks like she is genuinely panicked, like this one detail could make an already amazing start to the night better. When she hooks up her phone to a small speaker, I notice the song playing is from our aquarium date. Maybe she was right; it did make it better. Little touches from our dates are scattered around us. Tokens of us and our story. It is beautiful. *She* is beautiful. We dive into our food, making easy conversation to the backdrop of song after song from our first date. Warmth spreads through my whole body, and I can't blame the wine. It is just *her*. I didn't even realize I could feel this much love in any given moment. I didn't realize someone could love me this much to remember so many things.

After we eat for a while, even her, for what I assume is nostalgia's sake, she stands up and reaches her hand in my direction. "Would you like to dance?" My smile grows, and I clasp my hand into hers before standing. Her arms move to being placed around my neck, my own around her waist. I could stare into her dark chocolate eyes all night. We don't have to say a word. Looking at each other is enough. After the dance, she backs up a few steps, worrying her lip with her teeth, and with one more wring of her hands, she gazes up at me.

"Is everything okay?" I ask her.

"Yes. Just needed the courage to ask you the biggest question of my life." She shoots me an uneasy smile and clears her throat. "Gabriella Marie Young, ever since I met you, my life has been turned upside down. I went from hiding from the world, terrified to ever open myself up again, to being deeply and madly in love with you. I'm out frequently, eating human food, and I'm not afraid to love you. That feels like the most insane thing of all. I *know* that I need you in my life forever. I love you beyond what any words can convey." My mouth is gaping, hand over my lips as she is talking. The feeling of anticipation is rising in me. "I have known for a while that you were the love of my life, that I would want you by my side as long as your human life allowed. Then you opened my mind, convinced me it didn't have to be temporary, that I could truly have eternity with you. And I'm ready for that to begin." She drops to one knee, pulling out a black ring box. As she opens it, her gaze never drifts from my own. The ring is gold with green and pink gems in a botanical-looking design. It is *stunning*. "Gabriella Marie Young, will you marry me?"

"YES!" I end up shouting my response when I *tried* to talk calmly. Clearly, that did *not* happen. She still looks as overjoyed as I feel. I drop to the ground next to her, holding out a hand shaky with excitement as she puts the ring on my finger. "It is beautiful. But not as beautiful as my *fiancée*." I lean in and kiss her softly.

"I figured after the wedding I could turn you...I want you to be able to have wedding pictures. You'll be the most incredible, stunning bride, my little owl." The blush that had already been creeping up my face only grows stronger.

“I wish you could have yours taken, too.” I trace my fingers along her jaw, meaning every word I say.

“Maybe for our vow renewal.” She winks at me. “We can get married as many times as we want. I’ll never want to stop celebrating my love for you. We have forever ahead of us.

“I love you, Josephine.”

“I love you too, for eternity.” She places a kiss on my hand, and we stare out into the city lights, thoughts of our future play through my head, making me smile again and again. This is everything I have ever wanted and more.

Epilogue One

Josephine

Two months later

The wedding was everything I had dreamed of and more. Gabby looked stunning in her flowing, beachy gown. Gold jewelry decorating her hair, with a simple pendant around her neck, and a plain veil hanging over her curls. My own gown was basic by my standard, a rouched silk mermaid, with similar gold accessories and a more over-the-top veil. Each look was simply *us*. I don't think I stopped crying from the moment I saw her until we left, so I could take her picture. She was just so beautiful. And now she is mine. Mrs. Gabby Beauchamp. My wife. The thought makes me smile again, my cheeks aching from a night of happiness.

Earlier in the evening, she surprised me with something. She hired a wedding painter so we could have a picture from that night *together*. It will be us dancing, our friends surrounding us. I burst into tears when she told me, I didn't think there was a chance to see my wedding dress on me. Not from the day itself, anyway.

The Council had even laid off of Britt, so she was able to come for the night. The guys took her back to their place so my bride and I can enjoy some *quality* time together. I am preparing our bed for changing her once she comes in. She wanted to watch the sunrise outside one last time, something I would *never* deny her. The sky shifts from its dark black sky to the bright blue of day as I lay down some plush blankets and get lots of blood set aside for when she wakes up hungry. The lights are dimmed low, I have soft music playing, and some of her favorite flowers, peonies, scattered about the room. It is perfect. Then she peeks her head in. She looks so mind-blowingly beautiful. I don't think I'll ever be able to comprehend how I am lucky enough to have her in my life.

"Are you ready?" I wring my hands and look up at her, wedding dress still on, the veil long gone. My *wife*.

My nerves are electric. We spent hours talking after we got engaged about what it all means to turn. That she will be under the Council's rules, but also their protection from the outside world. That her senses will change, she told me that she would be able to paint me even better than before. I told her about her need to stay calm, and she said that having me by her side would make all the difference. We even talked about death. She reminded me that we have each other to lean on. She took every piece of information in stride until I felt like I *could* do this without her hating me for it. Without me being the villain in her story.

"Yes. Let's spend eternity together." She leans in to kiss me, and I hold her so tight she might as well have become a part of me. "What should I do?" She asks once I give her a moment for air.

"Let me undress you, then you're going to lie down and let me make you feel good." I press my lips to hers once more before turning her around and undoing the zipper behind her back, letting the gown fall to the ground, the intricate lace pooling on our floor. I help her out of her jewelry, leaving the ones in her hair and our wedding band. My lips brush against her shoulders and down her back as I help remove the cheeky panties in white lace that matched her wedding dress. I already have mine off in favor of a white silk robe, which I untie and let fall to the floor. "Lay down love." I grab a toy from my bedside table and turn it on, the vibrator filling the room with a low buzz.

"I love you. I trust you. I want this." She reminds me, keeping her gaze locked on my eyes. I kiss her softly.

"I love you too. You have to drink a sip of my blood." I rip my veins on my wrist open with my teeth and place the bloody wrist against her mouth. She licks it all and swallows the blood down. "Good girl," I tell her in a low tone. I begin kissing her neck, and I move the toy to circle at the apex of her thighs. Swirling the tip around her clit until she gets wet. I push the toy inside of her, and she gasps between the wanton moans. I mutter praise in her ear, kissing and nipping at her slender neck, making her whimper. I push in and out, letting the bunny ears on the toy hit her sensitive bud. She grabs onto my shoulders, scratching down my skin as I leave hickies along her neck.

As she gets closer, I know it's time. I want it to feel good when she turns. I want her to have the happy, pleasurable experience with it that I never could. "Are you ready?"

"Yes," her moan comes out breathless. "Please, more."

"Of course, love." I hold the toy down, letting the vibration center on her clit as I sink my teeth into her neck. The taste of her sunshine and warmth coats my tongue as I drink deeply. Taking every last drop I can as I bring her to the edge. As she falls apart against me, coating my hand in her own release, I keep drinking. Feeling her pulse grow weaker brings its own mix of emotions. The need to keep her safe conflicts with the primal need to consume and my own desire to have her with me forever. I push aside the part that clings to the hope of life and feed from her until she is completely drained of her blood, her aftershocks continuing through the end.

I pull my fangs from her neck and place a kiss on the wound, then on her lips, and lastly on her forehead. Then I wait.

A few hours later, she begins to stir, her eyes pop open, and I hand her a blood bag. She gulps it down ravenously.

“Welcome to eternity.”

Epilogue Two

Britt

The wedding was incredible. The mix of roses and peonies covered every table, rich and delicious food had every human full, and the vampires even took little bites. I got to dance and be free for a night. Auntie finally felt like it was *safe* for me. I excuse myself from the guys, making a pit stop at the bathroom before I stay with them for a few weeks while the newlyweds have their honeymoon. The hall is still covered in flowers, the bridal party plans on taking them down the next evening, and the lights paint it in a warm glow.

As I exit the bathroom, something feels off. The hairs rise on the back of my neck, and I pause. I feel like I'm being watched.

Suddenly something, or *someone* rams into me, and my back slams against the wall. The breath is knocked out of me. Looking up, I see a man in a mask that covers his face, pure black with small holes for his eyes and to breathe from. It is unfortunately hot and terrifying. I can't tell which is making my pulse race more, but either way, it is pounding so loudly I can *hear* it.

"I've been trying to get you for *months,* Brittany. The Council has been awaiting your stay." Then the masked man steals me from the hall before my brain clears enough to think. Before I can even try to scream.

Recipies

Recipe Card

Name Of Dish: Christopher's Blood Milkshakes

Time: 5 minutes Serves 2

Ingradients:

- 2 cups of vanilla ice cream
- 0.5-.75 cups of milk (adjust to preference)
- 0.25 cups of blood (grenadine/pomegranate syrup)

Instructions:

Combine ingredients in blender. Serve.

Recipe Card

Name Of Dish: *Josephine's Bloody Hot Chocolate*

Time: *20 Minutes* *Serves 2*

Ingradients:

- *1.5 cups of milk*
- *0.5 cups of heavy cream*
- *0.5 cups of blood (raspberry syrup)*
- *8oz of 70% [illegible]*
- *1 tsp of vanilla*

Instructions:

Combine milk, cream, and blood in saucepan on low to medium heat.

Once nearly boiling, turn off the heat and mix in the chocolate and vanilla until melted.

Let stand for 2 minutes. Stir and serve with optional whipped cream or marshmallows

If you would like a printable copy of the recipies send me an email at: r.m.vaneckova.books@gmail.com and I'll send you the files!

Acknowledgements

First and foremost, I want to thank you, the reader, for taking a chance on my book. I hope you loved reading it just as much as I loved writing it. I can't wait to get the second book, *Thrown Together*, in your hands.

I also want to thank my mom, you have been there for me every step of the way. Through the apprehension, excitement, editing drudgery, and absolute chaos moments. I love you, thank you for always supporting me.

Thanks to my brother, Cillian, for being the coolest kid ever. This may be the only part of the book you're ever allowed to read, but thank you for putting up with book stuff. Consider this an offer for a video game night.

A big thank you to my writing group. It has been so amazing finding community, especially ones that I can turn to when things go haywire. Thank you all so much.

A massive shout out to my friends. You guys are the best, thank you for the support through this journey and listening to my crazy ideas.

And a final thank you to my ARC readers, I was so excited to get this into your hands! It was a very personal story for me in a lot of ways. If you remove the vampires it is about a woman falling in love after loss, something that feels incredibly real. Thank you for taking a moment to read hints of my own story through Josephine and Gabby.

I want to end this on remembering someone who I would have loved to include in these acknowledgments: my Grandma. She passed in August of 2025 and I wish I could have seen her face when I handed her this book. She was one of my biggest supporters.

Thank you everyone for reading *Broad Strokes*.

Image from Taylor Hamerski Photography

Rosemary Vaneckova is a romance author from the middle of nowhere Wisconsin, i.e. farm fields galore. When she's not writing Rosemary loves to spend time with her pets and family, travel, and bake some delicious treats. She also can be found with her nose stuffed in a book...or crocheting some stuffed animal or another even though her yarn storage is begging her to stop. To keep up with Rosemary follow her at @r.m.vaneckova.books or visit her website www.rmvaneckova.com

www.ingramcontent.com/pod-product-compliance
Lightning Source LLC
Chambersburg PA
CBHW070300310726
48976CB00005B/1502

* 9 7 8 1 9 7 1 7 3 3 0 0 5 *